The Sword Lily Parables

THE ASSIGNMENT OF ANGELS

BOOK I

Anita S. Faherty

THE ASSIGNMENT OF ANGELS

The Sword Lily Parables -
The Assignment of Angels/ Anita S. Faherty -- 1st ed.
ISBN 978-1-7372131-0-9

Table of Contents

THE ASSIGNMENT OF ANGELS

PART 2
INTRODUCTION TO THE CRITTERS
St. Mary's-of-the-Future

PART 3
THE BISHOP, THE GREAT PÉRIGORD, AND THE PLAN

PART 4

DANGER ON THE OLD ROAD

St. Mary's-of-the-Future

The Meadow at
Castle Cliff
Uppity Bridg
Forest of Solomon's Cedars
The Dock at St. Ant
Lost and Found
The Median of The Old Road
Cell Fish Top Captain of Hell Headquarters
Peony Patch
TANKARD ON THE GRAY BAY
Crabby House
CRABBY HOUSE
MAYFLIES
Feara Phalin
BADAD VICE
QUICKSAND PIT
Murky River

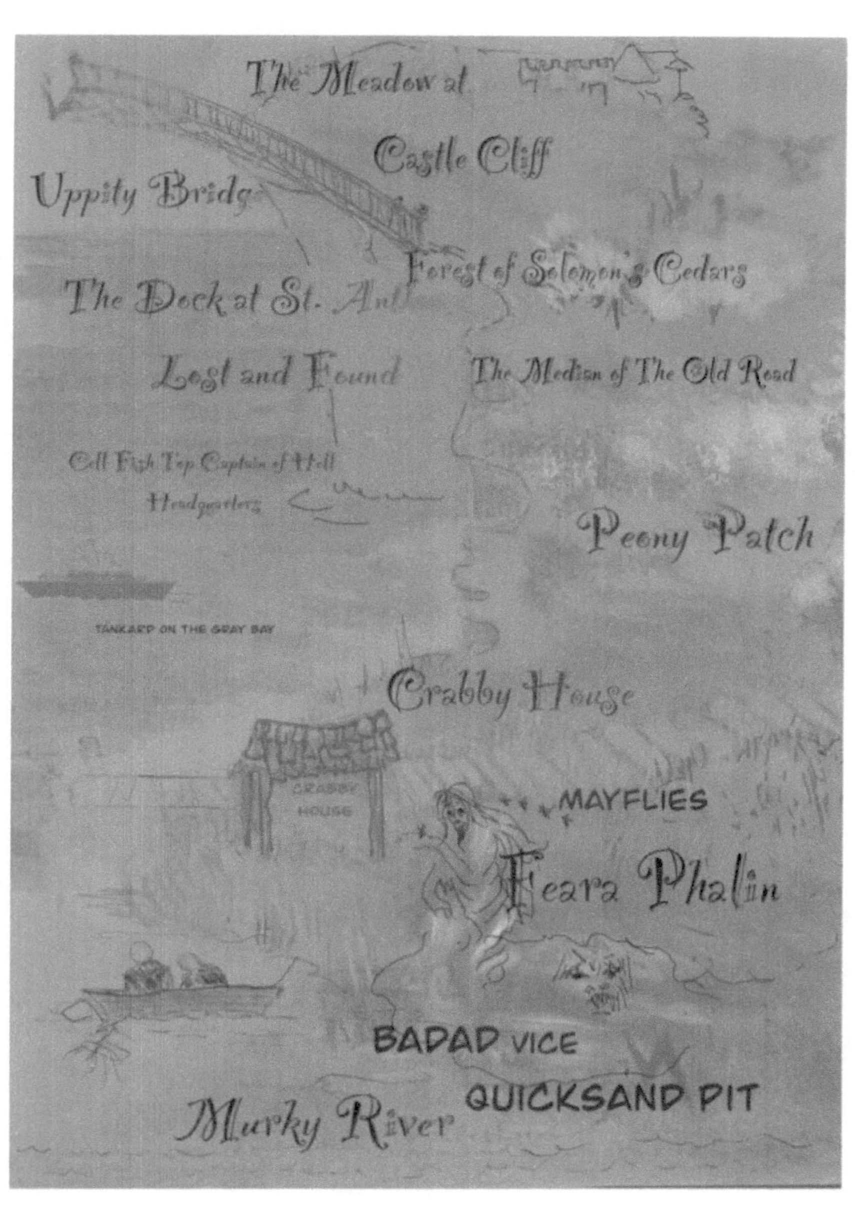

A MAP OF

THREE RIVERS

A LIST OF CHARACTERS

The Sword Lily Parables

The Assignment of Angels

BOOK I

Narration

Lucy Penn, the narrator of the story. She is a grown-up in 2001. Francie O'Malley's best friend at St. Mary's School for Girls in 1962 when Francie first encounters Beneficent Angel.

The Girls of St. Mary's, listening to Lucy tell Francie's stories of *The Sword Lily Parables*. September 11, 2001.

The O'Malley Family

Francie O'Malley, unlikely 12-year-old messenger chosen by Beneficent Angel to deliver an urgent warning to the world. 1962.

The Doctors Anne and Albert O'Malley, Francie's parents.

Diana O'Malley, Francie's beloved widowed grandmother, Mère.

Taffy O'Malley, Anne Taft O'Malley, 18, known as Taffy, Francie's favorite sister.

Megan O'Malley, 22, Francie's aloof, self-absorbed eldest sister.

Dr. Brian Cleveland, Francie's first love in 1962 and husband in 2001.

Lucy Penn's Family

Uncle Taurus, Lucy Penn's Uncle who inadvertently offersLucy some very bad advice. 1962.

Minnie Penn, Lucy Penn's mom, suffers from perpetual grief and depression. Lost her husband in the Korean War. 1962.

The Aunts, Mae and Maud, Taurus Penn's two busy-body sisters. 1962.

The Jerries Club Members

Apricot Davis, Francie and Lucy's know-it-all friend since kindergarten in 1962. She later becomes a nun, Sister Mary Angel in 2001.

Marguerite "Daisy" Escobar, Francie and Lucy's friend who fled Cuba during Operation Peter Pan. 1962.

Mary Louise "Cupcake" Carey, a friend whose mom bakes every day, much to the admiration of the Jerries. 1962.

The Heavenlies

The Powers That Be, Angelico, Wise Power, and Small Power, of the warrior choir of angels that must stop the Great Theft.

Blessed André, Heavenly Doorkeeper

Beneficent Angel, the angel assigned to notify the world of its perilous state. She chooses Francie as her messenger.

Marvelous Angel, the prestigious Angel of the Wind. With a slip of his wrist, he loses control of a wind called Fury and accidentally kills the Bishop of the Southerly Coast.

St. Rose of Lima, first Saint of the Americas. She is tracking souls.

The Critters

Scout, once a stone beaver at the feet of St. Francis of Assisi in Pastor's prayer garden. Now, alive, only to Francie. Scout is the "crackerjack support team" appointed by the Powers That Be to assist Beneficent with her assignment.

Deer, Scout's best friend, also a stone critter at the side of St. Francis in the prayer garden. Deer succumbs to despair and runs away from Scout and their home on the Murky River.

The Great Périgord, an oversized gander, beloved pet of the Bishop of the Southerly Coast. Périgord is commandeered by Beneficent Angel to impersonate his dead owner, the Bishop, in hopes of procuring a transfer for him to Midlantic.

Ant Emmitt, Father Brendan's guide through the forest of Solomon's Cedars. He is found working in Peony Patch opening the flowers.

A LIST OF CHARACTERS

continued

Caretakers

Garbo, Pastor's housekeeper in 1962. Garbo was a nanny to Francie as a toddler when Francie's mother, Dr. Annie, had emergencies at her clinic for the poor of the parish.

Gabe, Pastor's groundskeeper in 1962, and husband of Garbo.

Mr. Hubert, bus driver, and handyman at the parish. 1962.

Phyllis, New Pastor's housekeeper. 2001.

Widow Miller, a loving nearly blind neighbor of the parish of Our Lady's. does her best to watch over the Bambini.

St. Mary's-of-the-Future.

The Demons

Cell Fish, Top Captain of Hell, has captured Three Rivers and has eyes on all of Midlantic, and the world at large.

Swelly, an ambitious vicious imp of pride, trying to graduate to full demon, an extreme troublemaker.

Black Jack, a tempter of high rank, a real pro. He is an expert in the sporting life.

Dastard Diablo, the soul transporter to Hades.

Trickster, a thief, a stealer of souls.

The Helpers

Captain Rick-Eye, ferry boat captain. 1962.

Willy and Oz, flatboat runners to the mainland in the future.

Tom, custodian of the black valise in the future.

Pete the Fisherman, boatman and messenger. St. Mary's of the Future.

The Orphans

The Bambini, Philomena and Odelia D'Adelray, Siena, Mildred, and Ursula. These orphans can be found hiding in Pastor's prayer garden amidst the desecrated statues of angels and saints. They are ever watching the waters for a trawler bringing home their missing parents.

St. Mary's-of-the-Future.

A LIST OF CHARACTERS

continued

Some Nasty Characters

Wreckers on the rocks, were the first to succumb to Cell Fish.

Billy the Fish, tough character in Fishtown. 1962.

Marcus Nook, local drunk. Descendant of the wreckers on the rocks. 1962.

The Sisters of St. Mary's

Sister Angelina, a beloved nun, and teacher at St. Mary's School for Girls. 1962.

Sister Edna, 7th form homeroom teacher. She is tough on Francie and Lucy. 1962.

Sister Georgina, also a well-loved nun who worked in service. 1962.

Sister Rita Bernard, feared principal of St. Mary's School for Girls. 1962.

Sister Carmelisa, Widow Miller's old friend and next-door neighbor, a deceased Spirit of St. Mary's-of-the-Future.

The Clergy

Old Pastor, pastor of Our Lady of Perpetual Help. 1962.

New Pastor, pastor of Our Lady's at the time of the Terrible Day when Lucy narrates the story. 2001.

Father John, pastor of St. Mary's-of-the-Future.

Father Ed, Right Eye of the Realm. St. Mary's-of-the-Future.

Father Brendan, pastor of Inland, and Father John's good friend. St. Mary's-of-the-Future.

Bishop of the Southerly Coast, a well-loved prelate led astray by the demon, Black Jack, and tormented by Swelly. He meets with accidental death, caused by a slip of the wrist of Marvelous Angel. His sorry soul is in no shape to meet his Maker. St. Mary's of-the-Future.

The Church, Our Lady of Perpetual Help, also known as Our Lady's.

To the critters it is known as Olph's Dwelling-With-the-Bells, and Olph's Dwelling-Without-the-Bells. It is next door to St. Mary's School for Girls.

OCTOBER 13, 1884 ROME

"What a horrible picture I was permitted to see!"
A quote by Pope St. Leo XIII after a stunning revelation.

It is said that Pope Leo XIII overheard a conversation in which the devil said to God that he could destroy His Church if he were given enough time and power over those who would serve him.

Satan chose the 20th century

1

Sky of Ash

Day of Reckoning 2001

Francie was missing. Lucy pictured them back in 7th Form at St. Mary's School for Girls hiding behind the priest's garage. She could almost hear her snorting down a laugh. Like when Garbo caught them smoking, again, and afterward commented that she hadn't expected to find Moses in that burning bush, but the two of them, as usual. Francie O'Malley and Lucy Penn were best friends.

In a dark, Godless world, the river in front of her was murky with ash, just like Francie said it would be; the tales she once told as a child had come to life. Maybe God had been stolen, the Gifts and Fruits of the Spirit kidnapped by some mystical trapper. Sister Angelina drilled the merits of the Gifts and Fruits over and over in class, Lucy remembered that much, but the soundtrack was dead.

It all seemed rather prophetic now. Some angel—Beneficent Angel was her name—slipping masked glimpses of St. Mary's-of-the-Future into Francie's dreams day and night. Lucy didn't believe her at first. Now, today, she wanted to grasp those precious lessons, but they were out of reach.

She drummed her fingers against the window of her late mother's Victorian house, which is high on the hill this side of the river. Uncle Taurus, always mindful of a dollar, had talked her into chopping the house into apartments for income. Lucy kept the top floor for herself because of its spectacular view of the river and the city beyond. But today the view was smoke, laden with the dust of the dead. Were her friends among them?

Lucy grabbed her bike and pumped up the hill toward Little Capernaum, the section of Three Rivers where the parish church was situated. She crossed the Old Road and turned onto Miller Street. She parked her bike at the salmon-colored house with gingerbread trim and shuffled up the sidewalk hidden by the leggy impatiens she had planted there for Garbo last spring. The porch moaned under her footsteps, and the screen door rattled with her knock. She called through the dusty mesh.

"Garbo?"

"I'm in here."

Lucy let herself in.

Garbo looked frail in her big favorite chair. "It's awful, honey, ya know?"

"Just awful," Lucy sighed, taking a seat on the worn-out sofa. "The church looks like it's filling up."

"Yeah, they're gonna be mighty busy today, that's fer sure." Garbo was rummaging through her purse for a cigarette, grumbling to herself, "Doctor's orders, 'quit smokin' and quit dyin' yer hair.' I'll tell ya, it almost killed me to give up the glam."

"I remember," Lucy nodded, "you were 93."

"93, that's right."

Garbo took a long drag on her cigarette, watching the smoke for a while as it spiraled up to stain the ceiling above her.

She fussed with her straggly bun. Her hair was white now, except for the front, which was permanently tinted by the constant blow of nicotine that all but dripped from the crown moldings in the living room. She flashed Lucy a sober look, then back to the TV. Her electric blue eyes (she liked to say they once melted hearts) were not so vibrant anymore.

"So many dead," she sighed. Despite everyone saying Garbo was 100 years young, she had her spells, and this was one of them. She nodded to herself from a different place, not here, not present to Lucy. She was at the doorway to war, a war from the past. "Missing in action, that's what they said."

It was a haunting, she said. "I knew he was dead. I knew all along."

Lucy's eyebrows knit together. "Who was dead?"

"My husband, Gabe. Who d'ya think I'd be talkin' about, ya insolent girl!" Garbo blew a smoke ring and peered through it, into that other world.

"Smoking makes you nuts," Lucy laughed, "Gabe didn't die in the war, Garb. He died in his bed, upstairs, 25 years ago. He came home from the Great War, remember?"

Garbo waved Lucy's words away with the smoke. "It's the same. Don't matter. Missin' in action, same as dead. Brain-dead…soul-dead…it's all the same. War." Garbo held Gabe's gray hanky to her lips to hide the quivering. Lucy went over to her and rocked away the memory.

"He marched in the bicentennial parade, with the Veterans of Foreign Wars. He was proud as he could be. Don't you remember that?" Lucy challenged.

"'A course I do!" Garbo sniffed and rubbed her nose.

It surprised everyone that Garbo took Gabe's death so hard back then, being that his mental state had suffered. One might have thought that Garbo was only Gabe's caretaker, but that wasn't it at all. Pastor said no one could understand the dynamics of their marriage—or any marriage, for that matter. Sister Edna tried everything to put the spunk back in her dearest friend, but Garbo stuck with the grief. Until the day she stopped in the convent for coffee and Sister Ed cooked up the idea to serve a little plum brandy to the 'Widow of Miller Street.' Garbo got such a kick out of Sister Ed getting tipsy she laughed herself right out of her gloom.

Garbo put away Gabe's hanky and started in on how Lucy kept her going and how she was determined to hang in there until Lucy got herself settled. "Find a man. Or finish that stupid book, anything to get on with your life. Then, I'll be free to move to a nice plot of grass next to Gabe, down the hill at Happidale."

"I'll work on it," Lucy sighed.

"Ya shoulda given *one* of those fella's some consideration."

"Maybe so."

"Anyhow, when ya find a man loves ya as fierce and loyal as Gabe loved me, ya don't turn that away."

"I suppose you don't," Lucy smiled, recalling some of the bizarre candidates Francie sent her way over the years. Thankfully, Francie gave up the quest to find a man for Lucy when Francie and her husband, Dr. Brian Cleveland, moved to Haiti to open a children's clinic. Francie had fallen in love with Brian when the girls were only 12 years old. And having done a splendid job choosing her husband, she thought she would pick a winner for Lucy too. Lucy didn't want a husband chosen by Francie, but Garbo never stopped harping on her ingratitude.

Lucy moved to the window and pushed back the nylon sheers to watch the activity across the street at the church. Garbo's niggling faded to white noise, as Lucy's thoughts returned to Francie's visions. They were the very glue that bound them together all these years. She tried to write them down, put them in some sort of order, always falling short. Should she tell Garbo that Francie was missing?

"How's everybody doing over at Our Lady's?" she asked, swallowing her emotions. "Have you gotten any reports from the front?"

"What do ya think? 'Acourse I have!"

No one was wired into the parish like Garbo. She was well connected, having been housekeeper to the old Pastor until he passed away. Then she took credit for training up the new one. That was in her eighties. Old Pastor wouldn't fire her, and she wouldn't retire, so she trekked across the street almost every morning, returning home in the evening after supper. He said he had eaten her lousy chicken for so long his system wouldn't adjust to anything new. They were good, old friends.

Garbo came back to the present. "Poor, young Pastor, he's drowning in folks lookin' fer answers. Who's got answers to this? Kids are alone over there. I can see 'em standin' up on the rock, watchin' the river. As if they could see their folks comin' in on the ferry through all that smoke!"

Tears of helplessness clung to Lucy's cheeks. She tried to dab them away but finally gave in to the sorrow. She knelt on the floor and put her head in the lap of the old woman.

"What's all this?" Garbo asked.

How could she tell her Francie and Brian were missing? How? They were flying in to host their big fundraiser at the Sky-High restaurant in the city. It was all planned. They would make their presentation and would come home to Three Rivers for Garbo's 100th Birthday. It was going to be a big surprise. And now… "I—I need to pray," Lucy confessed. "I can't remember a single prayer Sister Angelina taught us."

"Ah, sure ya can, honey."

"I can't. It hurts too much to try."

Grief pounded at Lucy's heart. How could she bear another loss? First, the grim events of 1962 that had caused such suffering and took their beloved nun from them, then her mother's death. Her father, gone even before she was born, and now her best friend, Francie. Everyone she had ever loved seemed to leave her or die young.

Lucy's anguish touched Garbo deeply, stirring up the same memories in her mind.

"It'll come back to ya," Garbo assured her. "Think about today, for instance. All the people slobberin' in their beers, watchin' this disaster, don't ya bet they're tryin' to remember the Lord's Prayer! Go over to the church, honey, lend a hand."

"What could I possibly do?" Lucy sniffed, wiping her face.

"Well, let's see. This is the first time in 40 years the churches have been full. It might be 40 more 'afore it happens again. Go on now and help out."

Lucy got up and kissed Garbo's forehead. "I'll do what I can," she sighed.

"Atta a girl," Garbo nodded. "The Sisters'll put ya to work. You'll see."

2

Pastor's Prayer Garden

*For you cast me into the deep, into the heart of the sea, and the flood
enveloped me; all your breakers and your billows passed over me.
 Jonah 1:4*

Lucy crossed Miller Street to the winding path that dissected
the church lawn. The church doors were open, and people
were smoking and talking on the steps. It reminded her
of an Irish wake. Offering encouragements, shaking hands, and
kissing cheeks, she made her way through the bewildered and
suffering to enter the narthex of the church.

Inside, Pastor and the Sisters were progressing from group to
group, giving what comfort they could to the frightened and
bereaved. Lucy caught the eye of Sister Mary Angel, once known
as Apricot Davis—Francie and Lucy's worry-wart-know-it-all
friend since kindergarten.

She had decided to become a nun the very day Sister Angelina
died and took the name of 'Sister Mary Angel' to honor her.

7

The nun hurried to the back of the church and hugged Lucy fervidly. Apricot's encyclopedia of pertinent information could not supply words for this terrible day. Lucy watched as Apricot's eyes filled with tears at the sight of her friend.

"I'm glad you're here," Sister Mary Angel said, "you're just the one I need for a particular group. Come with me." Apricot wiped her red face and led Lucy by the hand outside to Pastor's prayer garden, where five young girls sat stricken with sadness. The nun began to giggle. "They remind me of us."

Lucy grinned back at her friend, conjuring up old memories of their preposterous mischief.

"These are our Confirmandi, candidates for Confirmation," Sister announced by way of introducing the girls to Lucy. "They're assembled here for religious instruction this morning, but the Sisters need to help those inside the church still waiting for news." Sister Mary Angel gave Lucy a pleading look and hugged two of the girls tenderly. "The family members of these girls are reported safe, but they'll be staying with us until someone can come for them late this evening. We don't want them to be alone."

"Hello girls," Lucy said, cautiously.

"Miss Penn attended St. Mary's School for Girls just like you," Sister Mary Angel explained. "And, I might add, she made her Confirmation here at Our Lady's, just like you will. Today, she will be telling you all about what the sacrament of Confirmation meant to her."

Lucy was trapped. "Ap, are you kidding?"

The nun gave her a quick wink and slipped back into the church. You could put Apricot Davis in a nun's habit, but she would never change. Resigned to her fate, Lucy took a seat on the rickety bench in the garden.

She noticed the girls' uniforms. A variety of sleeve lengths on their white oxford cloth shirts bespoke a conscious effort to affect a sense of individuality–rolled-up above the elbow, or tight at the cuff, topped by unbuttoned, navy wool vests. Their tidy collar pins dangled from open collars, completing their unanimous 7th Form statement of rebellion.

They stared at each other in uncomfortable silence. Awkwardly, Lucy pointed to their uniform kilts, "Black Watch," she offered, "… that's the Queen's Own Plaid, you know." She spoke of a time when she, Francie, Apricot, Daisy Escobar, and Cupcake Carey rolled up their kilts short, short, short, and ran down the hill to Tummy's Sweet Shop, on the dock in Fishtown. All else but the common thread between them melted away, sewing Lucy into the patch-work quilt that was St. Mary's School for Girls.

"How could something like this happen?" one of the girls asked, breaking their silence, and causing a torrent of questions to roll forth.

"Why did this have to happen in our lifetime?"

"We don't deserve such a big disaster."

A girl began to sob. "Do you think it's the end of the world?"

"I don't know the answers to your questions," Lucy said quietly. For a moment, Lucy wondered if she was sitting in a mist of Francie's saga – *The Sword Lily Parables*. Was today St. Mary's-of-the-Future, or would it be another day?

It didn't matter. The brave characters of Francie's endless tales—angels and saints, the critters, Widow Miller, and the priests—they had seen Francie and Lucy through the growing pains of their lives; even the threat of nuclear terror and the assassination of their young president. Francie's characters were alive to the two best friends. They taught them how to heal and how to grow. And today, Lucy would call on all of them again, in this mystical garden so chock full of their memory.

"The answers you're looking for might surprise you," Lucy offered, becoming unexpectedly playful. "They might even be prophetic, you know. In a way, they could be."

"What's that mean?"

"There are lots of prophecies—many are about terrible possibilities. For instance, have you girls ever heard of Pope Leo's Prophecy?"

The girls looked at each other, shaking their heads.

No, they hadn't.

"Why don't you come a little closer and I'll tell you about it."

They leaned in to listen.

"It took place at the Vatican, in Rome, on October 13, 1884. Pope Leo XIII said he overheard Satan challenge God, boasting that he could destroy His Church. God granted the devil 100 years, and the devil chose the 20th century to do it."

"Wait a minute. I was born in the 20th century."

"Me too."

"That's our century!"

"Mine too," Lucy said. Bile rose up in her throat as she looked at the sky. Obscured by black smoke, it struck her that maybe the devil thought he had won that bet. She knew better. She shook an angry finger rebuking the ominous cloud hovering over the river. "This is not the way the story ends," she said as she challenged Evil.

"Are you sure?" the girls asked.

"Oh, I'm quite sure."

"How can you be so sure?"

"It's a long story," Lucy said.

"Won't you tell us?"

"Well, I guess I could try. It began, for me when I was about your age, as a matter of fact."

"When you were twelve?" The girls settled themselves in the grass around the bench.

"Yes, when I—when we were twelve."

And that's how Lucy Penn came to tell the story of her best friend Francie O'Malley, the reluctant prophetess of 7th Form in 1962. A girl who saw visions of Three Rivers and the terrible desolation it would face if the children of the Parish refused to stand up with courage.

The girls were more than curious, "Stand up for what?"

"The Assignment of Angels, of course," Lucy replied, "if you're called on to do so, that is."

"How will we know if they call on us?"

"Oh, you'll know, believe me!" Lucy laughed and glanced at the stone statue of St. Michael the Archangel, looming large in the center of the prayer garden.

"Pope Leo's prayer is etched into the base of that statue right there. *St. Michael the Archangel, defend us in battle—*"

The girls got up and circled the stone statue. The fearful face of the devil under the sword of St. Michael startled them a bit. They read the description of the event etched onto a bronze plaque attached to the pedestal.

"Look here! It says, 'Pope Leo XIII.'"

"Garbo used to tell us about it," Lucy said, glancing across Miller Street at the salmon-colored house. "Do you girls know Garbo?"

Yes, of course, they did. Everybody knew Garbo; she was a famous actress, she liked to say.

Lucy laughed, "I'm not so sure about that, but I am sure that Garbo was the housekeeper in the rectory when I was a girl, and she was a great weaver of tales. Every week, Garbo would bake something delicious, we could smell it cooking in the oven from the playground, and that would be our sign to come to the rectory. Then, we'd drag the chairs around the kitchen table to make room for the long bench from Pastor's dining room, and we would fight each other for the best seats. When we were all ready, she would tell us a story. According to Garbo's rendition of Pope Leo's prophecy, Satan took up his challenge right away, wreaking havoc across the globe, and he was having great success until the day he sent Cell Fish, his top Captain of Hell, here, to Three Rivers."

"Three Rivers! Our town?"

Lucy nodded gravely. "Yes, Cell Fish came out of the deep and entered the world just off our coastline. Garbo says he might have taken a wrong turn, wanting to pop up in the Mediterranean, a little closer to Rome, but he wound up at Evil Sands."

The girls were full of excitement. "The beach across the bay?"

"The very same," Lucy answered.

"My grandpa heard stories about that place."

"It's still abandoned, too. And it's haunted!"

"But that's our beach! Why did the devil pick our beach?"

"I suppose it's because the peninsula sticks out a little farther than the rest of the coastland," Lucy reckoned, "and he accidentally created a perfect entry there for himself."

"How did he do that?"

"Quite by accident, I'm sure," Lucy said. "When he came up through the sea from way, way, way below, he caused terrible disturbances in the waters, which capsized the fishing boat of the good Bishop Périgord.

"Who's he?"

"He was the last Bishop of Midlantic, an extremely holy man, sought after by those in need of healing and counsel."

"What did the devil want with him?" the girls asked.

"What did he want?" Lucy repeated. "He wanted nothing less than Saint Peter's keys to the kingdom. The devil thought they could be the keys to the world, and, in his opinion, the world was his domain, and he wanted it back. If he could destroy the Church, he was sure the rest of the world would fall and knocking off a Bishop was a great start.

"Garbo says this Bishop Périgord enjoyed spending the summer months in Three Rivers. It was his favorite coastal parish in all Midlantic. On that fateful day, when he fell overboard into the swirling current, he drowned, leaving an open gash in the spiritual protection of our diocese. Cell Fish saw his opportunity, and he slipped right through that gash, finding a pathway into the land of the free and the home of the brave.

"If anyone could have seen it, and my friend Francie swears she did, they might have said it looked like a dragon or something, coming out of the sea. But, whether it was seen or unseen, the fact remained that a diabolical presence, an evil Captain of Hell, came ashore that day and set out to establish a foothold at the tip of the peninsula, near the jetty where the Bishop's body washed ashore.

"After the death of Bishop Périgord, the realm was left without a leader. No suitable candidate would come forth to replace him because a spirit of false modesty had taken over. No good cleric felt worthy of filling his shoes, and no bad one wanted to pale in comparison to the holy Bishop. Thus, began the division of Midlantic's parishes among the neighboring bishoprics, so that baptisms and marriages, and the like, were duly recorded. But, Midlantic yearned for its own Good Shepherd. The priests of the realm were but stepchildren on the fringe of the neighboring diocese, and they prayed for the day when the Pope in Rome would appoint one of their own to put Midlantic back together again.

"Without the leadership of a good Bishop, the realm became increasingly lax in spiritual practices, and the battle for its soul began. Good Bishop Périgord's spirit relentlessly patrolled the water's edge to protect his beloved domain, but all the while, Cell Fish still gained ground. Three Rivers became an easy target for one as clever as he."

The story startled the girls. "Is this a true story?"

"To the best of my knowledge," Lucy said. "As Garbo tells it, Cell Fish started right in on our shores with his reign of terror, not only stirring up the waters of the sea but the waters ofdiscontent as well. He sucked in the fisher-folk first until they became known as the "Wreckers on the Rocks."

But there was one thing that devil never took into consideration." Lucy paused, sitting back against the bench.

"What was that?" the girls asked.

"That maybe, God had a plan too."

...following the adventures of some improbable heroes who stepped up to the Assignment of Angels without even knowing it.

PART ONE

The Assignment of Angels

Lucy Tells Their Story…

3

The Jetty, the Rocks, and The Sea, The Wreckers and the Wash-A-Shores

When the disciples saw him walking on the sea, they were terrified. "It is a ghost," they said, and they cried out in fear... Matt.14:26-27

St. Mary's-of-the-Future

Many shipwrecks happened along those beaches, and a terrible laughter accompanied them. It hissed upon the wind, as the cargo and the bodies rolled in with the tide. And, if one heard that dreadful laughter, there was a chance one would spot the ghost of the good Bishop Périgord gliding along the edge of the seashore blessing the victims of the wrecks. All of this spooked the fisherfolk with awesome fear. And yet, some of their own sank very low, succumbing to the spell of Cell Fish.

"Garbo always told this part of the story with a good deal of flourish," Lucy laughed. "Being a theatrical person, she played each part herself."

" 'Tis the Gillis o' Maine."

"So, it seems."

"A right proper ship—worth the flirtation."

"Come now, ladies. Best get about our doin'."

They have a go of it every night, especially in the dark, with a storm a-brewin.'

Coo-cooing to the sailors, enticing them closer and closer to the jetty in the moonless, starless sky. If them sailors could see them hags, they would sail their ship clear off to Antarctica.

Sometime they bob up and down with their lanterns on sticks, holding them high to create the effect she's far out to sea instead of near into the rocks. That trick does in the Gillis o' Maine.

At first, them fishwives are as curious as the next clamdigger—worried sick, really—as to who's caught up in the tide. They never set out to cause such destruction. It come to them by circumstance, and desperate poverty is all.

"No survivors," fisherman sez.

"What ship were it?" clamdigger sez.

"Can't tell. Wrecked on the rocks in the darkness—fate of many a worthy rig," fisherman sez.

"Sad truth to that," clamdigger sez.

Daylight brings exhaustion from pullin' in the dead. Then, the trinkets come awashin' on the shore—beautiful things: pearls, gold chains, watches and rings, diamonds and things not seen before in the poor fish towns along that rocky coast.

"Could be pawned," one fishwife sez to another.

Clamdigger searches the pockets of the corpses bloated on the beach, which produces billfolds fulla cash.

"Who's to know the difference?"

"Ain't it a treacherous sea for sure?"

The crimes of the lure itself never cross their wretched minds. What hatches out of sympathy grows into apathy. Soon enough, they discard the disguise. Customers in the pawnshop step aside for the shameless business.

"It's a livin'," they admit. "No hard feelings—a livin', is all."

Death and destruction crash against that shore. Innocent cries for help ignored. It's possession of their goods they're after.

Guilt subsides. You might say it went out to sea with the tide. And if a righteous conscience awakens, them old crones hurdle their orders from their rocky perch all the louder, "How do yez think ya been eatin' these lean years? Git down the beaches and do yer part."

Them thugs and their unsuspectin' sons move in for the kill like they was told. Night after night, evil washes ashore, driving them into the chokehold of greed and murder. Their sins and offenses pile up on the coastland like the rocks themselves. It's no wonder future generations avoid that place, steeped as it werein death and sorrow.

That stretch of the beach come to be known as Evil Sands— most folks have forgotten why. But evil has a soundless voice— sometimes so shrill as to chill the bone.

The Great Bay, where the three rivers meet the sea and the marshy lands around it, were abandoned long ago—some say to the devil himself.

Garbo waved the smoke away from the sizzling butter to see what remained of the eggs she was cooking for Gabe. "That oughta scare the pants off 'em," she chuckled, having cooked up this week's story for her girls.

4

Doorkeeper

Heaven
An Unknowable Time in the Future

Blessed André did not get much business at the back door to Heaven. The post was a reward for his outstanding work attending the door of Notre-Dame in Montreal, in the country of Canada, on the North American Continent. And, of course, it can't be overlooked he had a great friend in Saint Joseph.

He didn't want to seem ungrateful, but he wasn't comfortable in such a sleepy job. On Earth, he had a gift for curing the sick, creating a steady stream of people in need filing up to the door of Notre-Dame. However, there weren't any sick in Heaven.

André did his job. He watched the steps to Heaven's back door. And that's what he did, without event, until the day Beneficent Angel went out on assignment.

She greeted Blessed André. "Good Always," she said, then asked him to unlock the gate.

"Good Always, bonjour" he sighed in a melancholy way,"nice to see a shining face from time to time."

The long brass keys clanged against the gate as André managed the unlocking.

"It's very quiet here, isn't it?"

Beneficent sensed his low spirits, "André, you don't seem well."

"Ah, oui, I haven't been myself," he admitted.

Beneficent rummaged through her gear bag and retrieved a jelly jar. It was full of tiny, effervescent bugs. She unscrewed the top, and out they flew. They had sparkles for eyes and four iridescent wings. Their buzzing was so endearing it aroused mirth in the orneriest of creatures.

"A good dose of the Joyfuls ought to cheer you up," she said.

They lit upon André, jiggling and fizzling, tweeting, and twiddling, until he was feeling refreshed. Without further fuss, they flew back into Beneficent's jar.

"It's important to stay alert," she scolded. "You are *the* Doorkeeper among all the Blessed of Heaven."

"I'm honored," said André, "really, I am."

"Yes, well—you should be. Some have seen incredible sights, right here. Why one past doorkeeper told me a frightful tale."

She looked both ways before speaking; most residents of Heaven weren't keen on the retelling of the awful story. "That doorkeeper said he heard the worst of sounds—a terrible grinding, crunching sound as if the scraping of gravel on sandpaper had been magnified a thousand times over—that was the sound. Then, there was the odor, a pestilent smell of iniquity permeating the air."

"Iniquity?"

"Yes, stinking evil. He said it preceded its owner in a film of oily smoke by two earthly hours."

This stunned André. He cautiously moved in front of the door as if to protect it from such a trespasser. Beneficent went on with her story. "The creature reached the gallery in unspeakable anguish.

'What do you want, you wicked thing?' the old doorkeeper said. 'You're not allowed beyond this gate!'

'I've got a proposal for your Christ,' said Satan."

"No!" said André.

"Yes," said Beneficent, "Satan growled, spewing venom from every pore.

'And what would my Lord have to do with you?' the doorkeeper asked him."

Andre's eyes were wide as saucers, as Beneficent Angel jumped from spot to spot, recreating the frightful conversation.

"Satan was fighting mad, 'Just get Him!' he said."

Beneficent became more serious and spoke with whispered reverence. "All of a sudden, Jesus Christ Almighty appeared at the back door to Heaven," she slapped the carved frame for effect, "this–very–door."

André looked around as if the Lord might pop up as they spoke.

"What did Jesus say?"

Beneficent shrugged matter-of-factly. "Jesus asked Satan what he wanted.

"Satan said, 'I can take your Church from you.'

'Is that so?' said Jesus.

'If I had enough time and power over those who would serve me,' said Satan.

'How long do you propose?' said Jesus.

'100 years,' said Satan."

Blessed André was astonished at the thought of Satan sashaying right up the backstairs of Heaven with his bold challenge.

Beneficent sprang off the threshold.

"Wait! Beneficent! What happened? Where are you going?"

The wings of the angel blew open like a parachute with a wind and a whoosh into the dazzling fullness of their glory. "Repairs. Blessed André, impossible business, repairs."

"Repairs?"

"Repairs! Repairs! Repairs!

The angel's voice faded into oblivion, "Good Alwaaaaays…"

"Good Always..." André said dumbfounded and locked the gate.

5

Three Rivers
A Parish on the Atlantic Coast

Spring 1962

The shrubs against the rectory wall were sculpted tight together, twenty bushes into one. Peeking out of the greens were two large soles affixed to a pair of gnarly boots, unconstrained by wet loose laces dangling in a puddle, and barely clinging to the feet of the groundskeeper, Gabe. He was struggling to attach an unruly hose to the outside spigot of the rectory wall.

Francie O'Malley handed Lucy Penn a cigarette, safe within their fortress of braided roses and honeysuckle, tree trunks and clapboard coming together in a single architectural element. Francie kept her eye on the winding cement path that separated them from the formal gardens of the rectory yard where Gabe was working below the kitchen window.

It was their favorite hiding place in the springtime, tucked between St. Mary's sagging property fence and the backside of the old estate barn, long since converted into the priest's garage. The barn also served as storage for a convoy of snow blowers, lawnmowers, and other custodial gear in varying stages of antiquity and disrepair. One could wonder how Gabe used some of the bent and rusted clippers, but despite the condition of his tools, the bushes remained the envy of the neighborhood and the pride of St. Mary's.

Getting to their fortress had its challenges. It was easy enough to sneak by Sister Serena, having a nod-off on her bench. The statues of angels and saints in the prayer garden supplied emergency cover should Sister Serena stir but slipping past the priest's back porch still entailed some risk of getting caught.

So, when Pastor crossed the yard to the church for the 12:10 Mass, and confident Garbo would be whipping up Gabe's lunch, they made their move. A quick step through the sword lilies, and they were home free. They could see out, but no one could see in—or so they thought.

Lucy took one last drag, inhaling long and deep, like a seasoned smoker. She choked on the smoke and dropped the cigarette to the ground. Francie tried to smother a laugh and wound up yelping out a few loud snorts instead. "Be quiet!" Lucy shushed, trying to stifle her coughs.

Garbo was drying dishes, looking out the window for Gabe. His omelet was getting cold, and that annoyed her no end. She watched the smoke rising from the lilac bush overhanging the garage. The bush emitted puff after puff as she stacked dish upon dish and cup upon saucer.

"Kids," she muttered as she brushed the curtain aside and scraped Gabe's eggs onto a plate.

The smoke signal reminded her to hide her pack of Pall Mall cigarettes before Pastor came back from Mass. He was constantly after her to quit. "…Always yakking about it being a vice and all. I gave up enough vices for one lifetime under yer spiritual direction, Buster, I'm keepin' the smokes!" She patted her contraband, safely deposited in the deep pocket of Gabe's moth-eaten sweater. Gabe put it in the Goodwill bag, and Garbo plucked it right back out again, rolled up the sleeves, and wore it under her apron nearly every day. She found it to be the perfect defense against the draftiness of the rectory.

"It's no wonder Pastor's off to some God-forsaken place on the equator," she complained, as usual, to no one in particular. "Who could get warm in a joint like this?"

She checked on the developing drama in the burning bush. Francie and Lucy had no idea she watched them out the window every day. She chuckled at how clever they thought they were, like they were the first kids in history to smoke behind the garage.

"I'll miss ya two scallywags—7th grade over already? Oh, my apologies, yer ladyship, ma'am," Garbo laughed to herself, giving a deep curtsy and a wave of her spatula to Sister Rita Bernard, principal of the school (who wasn't actually there) "I was meaning to say 7th Form, ya snobby old bird!"

It was hard to believe the girls were so grown up. Only one more year and her Francie would be gone. Thirty years Garbo cooked and cleaned for the priests, and that didn't include the two disastrous years she tried her hand at teaching drama.

"SHH!" Lucy hissed again, retrieving the evidence from the ground. She scraped her saddle shoe on the ashes and tossed the butt over her shoulder. The girls followed the arc as it soared against the sky toward Gabe's topiary bushes. A soft plunk, and it landed right next to him. They watched, breathlessly, as Gabe uncorked himself from the shrubs and noticed the dead butt littering his immaculate sidewalk. He picked it up and examined it carefully, then slowly followed the garden path until he came upon the rounded toes of four black and white saddle shoes. There would be no escape.

Gabe rose up like a giant. His big hand pushing aside a branch of lilacs to reveal Francie and Lucy smiling up at him meekly.

"Hiya, Gabe," Francie offered in a small voice, "fancy meeting you here."

"Just fancy that," Gabe said.

"We're having a stroll around the grounds, aren't we France," Lucy said, elbowing her friend. Francie earnestly nodded in agreement.

"I, uh, lost an earring. We've been looking all over for it. You haven't seen a pearl earring have you, Gabe?"

The two girls took the opportunity to slip out of their smoky fortress and comb the sidewalk for the imaginary stud.

Gabe produced the cigarette butt from behind his back and cleared his throat. "This what yer lookin' fer?"

Confronted with the evidence, Francie rolled her eyes. "Why me, Lord?" she moaned.

"And why's this the Lord's fault, Miss Francine? He don't even smoke." Gabe scratching his head. "And He don't cotton to fibbin' much, neither."

Smoking was a serious offense. Smoking in uniform was a more serious offense and smoking on church property was out of the question. They probably didn't have a punishment dreadful enough for smoking on church property. Expulsion comes to mind.

"Please don't tell on us, Gabe."

"It's just a dumb cigarette—don't turn us in," Lucy begged.

"They'll kick us off the class trip!"

Gabe was in a bind, "If Eagle Eye Edna seen ya with those eyes in the back of her head, I'll lose my job. You girls are a lotta trouble."

Things were too complicated. The rules were the rules. Gabe liked to stick to the rules, but then again, he loved these girls. Garbo said they reminded her of herself, when she was a girl, which was probably true.

"Why are ya always tryin' to get kicked outta this nice school?"

"School! This is NOT a school," Lucy protested. "THIS—is a prison!"

Gabe crossed his leathery arms on his chest. "Ah, prison, is it?" He seemed to turn on them, barely concealing his disdain.

"Yez ever been in a prison?"

The girls squirmed.

The bell rang. Little girls poured out of the playground, gathering in the cobblestone courtyard forming neat, straight lines.

Sisters also appeared from various places, two from the steps of the church, two from the playground, and another from the convent across the narrow Miller Street. While Sister Serena remained on her bench.

Sister Edna X-rayed the 7th Form line. Her eyes fixed on a gap. She scanned the property expertly, closing in on the missing students in moments. She called out sternly to the girls across the big lawn, "Francine, Lucille, stop bothering Gabriel. Come here and take your places in line."

"Yes, Sister," they called back, giving Gabe a last pleading look.

"Saved by the bell," he said, as they ran down the slope to the courtyard.

He put the butt in his pocket and went into the rectory for lunch.

6

The Sisters of St. Mary's: Sister Edna

Spring 1962

Sister Ed felt it was her duty to form the girls into young ladies in the fullest sense of the Saint Mary tradition. "Shenanigans," Sister Edna held, "are highly frowned upon at St. Mary's School for Girls." Sister Edna called every variety of misbehavior, 'Shenanigans.' Smoking behind the garage was overqualified.

Her detentions had been known to bore a sane, 8th Former to death. Death by detention was going to be the fate of Francine O'Malley and Lucille Penn before they ever reached 8th Form, but not today.

At the start of the school year, the Jerrys, the secret club of 7th Form, fancied themselves a thorn in the side of Sister Edna. But in Eagle Eye Edna, they had met their match.

Garbo preferred the antics of the girls to the sour dour frown of Sister Ed whenever Francie and Lucy crossed her—which was almost every day. Other than those heated moments, her dear friend, Sister Edna, was a dedicated teacher who genuinely loved St. Mary's and all it stood for. Garbo had seen life differently than this sheltered lady who became a nun at seventeen. Sister Edna went from St. Mary's, up the hill to the Mount, and entered the convent from there. You might say she had been in a St. Mary's School, in one form or another, her entire life. She was well-intentioned, but she dealt with children in the strictest manner.

And then there was her other side—

Over the years, Garbo had answered the door dozens of times greeting young women returning to St. Mary's to share milestones in their lives with their old homeroom teacher. Be it with a baby on their hip, or a diamond chip on their ring finger, the tall, sober creature, thin as a reed, so elegantly buttoned up in her nun's habit, would radiate joy and share in their happiness. It was hard to believe it was the same person.

They said it was Sister Edna's strict direction that had kept them on the straight and narrow. Sister Ed said she had taught them discernment—the key to staying on track. Garbo never had the privilege of anyone teaching her discernment. Well, not until Pastor, anyway. Her parents had traveled the circuit with a Vaudeville act. They left her in Little Capernaum with a gritty uncle from the old country. She never mentioned which old country, but Vlad the Impaler did creep into some of her stories. Her uncle spoke broken English, which made her feel ashamed. He beat her silly if she dared step out of line, which made her dare all the more. She swore he didn't scare her, but he did. Garbo was a beauty then, all fair and willowy, and was happy to leave Uncle behind when she ran off with Gabe and got married at sixteen. Gabe was drafted in the Great War in Europe soon after. She was so proud of him in his uniform.

Garbo had a habit of stopping in at the convent for a cup of tea almost every day, since it was next door to her house on Miller Street, across from the church. The nuns never seemed to tire of her stories, tall tale or true, no matter how often she repeated them

"He was as dashin' as anyone's fella," she said of Gabe. "It was Pastor got Gabe off the bottle, ya know. Married us proper in the Church, even had a little party for us with a cake. That was after the Great Depression. He put us both to work in the rectory, patchin' up our lives after years of strugglin'."

Today, when Garbo arrived, Sister Ed was alone at the kitchen table. She had the newspaper spread out and was devouring all the news about the upcoming events in Rome. The bishops of the world were preparing for the Second Vatican Council scheduled to begin the following October. Great events were in the works at St. Peter's Basilica for the opening ceremonies. It was to be led by Pope John XXIII, a big Italian teddy bear of a pope. Everybody adored him, and the whole convent wanted to go to Rome. But Sister Ed saw something different and shook her head with foreboding.

"The Church is changing. I can feel it in my bones like a furious storm brewing."

Garbo peered through her smoke rings teasing the exasperated nun. "I'm picturin' that right now. Fury whippin' through town. There it is, crossing the Old Road, blowin' down my fence and the roof right off Pastor's rectory.

"You cannot sway my opinion, Madam. The youngsters are changing, too. I don't want any of our girls blown off course when the winds of change come roaring by us. That's why I'm hard on the girls, Mrs. Busybody. They must know how to withstand Fury because I can see it coming."

Garbo tried not to laugh, waving her cigarette smoke out the convent window. "Ed, ya sound like the prophet of doom."

But Sister Edna held to her opinion that evil was lurking out there—somewhere—and you could rest assured that St. Mary's School for Girls would be ready for it.

Garbo pushed in her chair still chuckling. "Well, Sister, I gotta get Pastor's dinner on." She patted her old friend on the shoulder as she went to the sink and ran the hot water. "I'll just be washin' out my cup, and I'll see ya tomorrow."

Garbo crossed Miller Street, passing by her own house, and headed to the rectory. Gabe was on the back porch of the rectory, nailing up a loose piece of latticework. "Where ya been?"

"Across the street."

"Convent?"

"Yeah, Sister Ed's huntin' fer bear this time."

"Solvin' the problems of the world?"

"Sister Ed and her storm called Fury!" Garbo shook her head as she worked her way around Gabe's ladder and squeezed through the screen door.

"Nothin' more unforgivin' than a suspicious nun. I'm gonna have to warn Francie and Lucy, if they don't wise up this time, they're in fer it."

The racket of pots and pans clanging in the kitchen got Gabe agitated. "Why ya always puttin' yer dang favorite pan on the bottom? Ya use it every day."

"Cuz that's where it goes."

"Shouldn't."

Garbo went back to the screen door. "What if ya reported them two, about the cigarette, fer instance?" Garbo speculated.

"Who?"

"Francie and Lucy."

"Well, I didn't."

"Those kids don't know how lucky they are," Garbo muttered to herself, shaking her head. She retrieved a chicken from the fridge, stuck it, upside down in her favorite pan with the shake of a few spices and put it in the oven to roast.

$$7$$

Local Folklore

Spring 1962

As the 19th Century faded into the 20th, the Wreckers, too, faded into folklore. However, the tales of their awful deeds still stirred the pot down at the pier when someone reported a sighting of their disembodied spirits. The gruesome accounts of Wreckers and Wash-a-shores would crackle around the Crabby House all night, where the people gathered for some steamers and butter, or chowder and bread. Winter or summer, that old clam hut was crowded, just like it is today. You couldn't say it was the décor that attracted them. There was nothing but cement floors and old photos of locals, showing off their best catches. Some dated back to the turn of the century in need of a good dusting. When the whiskey got to flowing, folks examined the photos pointing out little white specks they suspected were poor souls cursed to wander the seashore. Much speculation arose as to the home base of those poor, trapped souls awaiting the Avenging Angel. Were they going to Heaven or going to Hell?

"If I see that smokin' bush one more time," Garbo warned Francie and Lucy, "I'm tellin' R.B. what you're up to." And she assured the girls that R.B. (Sister Rita Bernard, to those in the know) would think nothing of tossing them, bound and gagged, into an old boat and setting them adrift in the reeds of Evil Sands, just like Moses.

"Ya can fend fer yerselves out there among them tormented souls if yer not careful. I, fer one, won't give yez a second thought."

All the girls loved story day in the rectory kitchen, listening to Garbo's tales she claimed to be history. Garbo's theatrics curled the hair of little kids with her mysterious stories, but they didn't carry much of a wallop with the bigger girls anymore. She never thought they would, but threats and the like were an embellishment that added flare. Nobody believed the stories were true, chilling as they were. Who could really believe that evil, real evil, could be lurking about on their very own seashore right across the Great Bay? Certainly, no one above 5th Form. Nonetheless, even as Francie and Lucy prepared to leave 7th Form, they still enjoyed passing an otherwise dreary afternoon on the edge of their seats at her tellings. Nobody could tell a story like Garbo—absolutely nobody.

8

The Sisters of St. Mary's: Sister Rita Bernard

Spring 1962

Since 6th Form, the sole purpose of Francie and Lucy's secret club, The Jerrys, was to torment nuns. Well, not all of the nuns—Sister Angelina and Sister Georgina were the exceptions. There were a few lesser members of the misguided alliance, whose participation in the club was strictly a cheering section for the troublesome charter members, Francie and Lucy. They were Marguerite "Daisy" Escobar, Mary Louise Carey, commonly known as Cupcake Carey, and Apricot Davis, who had the nickname Apricot ever since she was born with peach fuzz for hair that grew into curls the color of apricots. One would have to find her baptismal certificate to know Apricot's Christian name. They modeled their antics on Tom and Jerry cartoons, thus the name, "The Jerrys."

Most teachers referred them to the principal's office, where Sister Rita Bernard handed down her assessment of the situation. And while their classmates signed out for Tummy's Sweet Shoppe, Francie and Lucy, more than the others, cleaned supply closets and changed the bulletin boards in the school corridors.

Sister Rita Bernard had once indiscreetly told Garbo that if it weren't for her mother, Doctor Annie, and the older O'Malley girls, she would have expelled Francie long ago. Just one more offense and the consequences would be dire for Miss O'Malley. As for Lucille Penn, well, what could one expect from white trash anyway? That's how Sister Rita Bernard sized it up.

Sister Rita Bernard came from a wealthy family on the North Shore and had a superiority complex. Garbo figured that was okay—she wanted to be Mother Superior, after all. She was an intellectual and a snob, better suited to an exclusive women's college, but that was not her assignment. Her assignment was St. Mary's School for Girls, a grammar school, for little girls. Garbo often commented on how it 'stuck in her craw,' so she ran the place like a college anyway. It was well known that she found children in 4th Form irritating when they had troublememorizing passages of *Paradise Lost* by Milton. She did, however, take some comfort in the fact that many of the girls were from good families, old money and new.

9

Pastor

Spring 1962

The school sits on a hill above a poor fishing village, known as Fishtown. Some of the daughters of the Fishtown families, such as Daisy Escobar, attended St. Mary's because of Pastor's miraculous knack for raising money. He engaged the whole parish in his plans. In addition to the annual fair, he had lobster races and dance contests in costume, out on the pier. Saturday nights in the summertime would often find Dorothy, the Lion, Tin Man, and flappers from the Roaring 20s, dancing under the stars with Elvis, Abe Lincoln, clowns, and Howdy Doody.

Everyone in town knew a St. Mary's girl when they saw one, and everyone was proud to have the school up on the hill. Francie and Lucy rarely lived up to the expected code of conduct, but, luckily for Pastor, they were usually in detention for unruly behavior and didn't make it to the townie scene often enough to disturb the school's good reputation.

Pastor never missed an opportunity to point out to the congregation the similarities between their section of town, lovingly known as Little Capernaum, and its namesake in the Bible, where Jesus often worked. In his sermon, Pastor sometimes embellished those similarities in the gospel stories to meet his needs.

"The Apostles St. Peter and St. Andrew were brothers and, like many of you, they were fishermen. They were partners with Zebedee and his sons, who became the Apostles St. James and St. John." All true.

Then, Pastor would eyeball some of his tougher parishioners with an accusing glance and say, "Jesus called them Sons of Thunder," reminding those guilty of last night's brawl that it was time to repent. Invariably, some self-righteous parishioner would have reported the brawl to him, after being rudely awakened by ear-splitting sounds of breaking glass and other such commotion, which teed up the perfect opportunity to drop his net on the guilty bunch and pass the basket. That was his big moment, and every so often, by this procedure, he squeaked out another year's tuition to put aside for some fortunate little girl from Fishtown.

Sister Rita Bernard had her doubts about the mingling of racial and social classes, but Pastor insisted. "If we don't educate the less fortunate, we will not break the cycle of poverty. Women will raise the next generation, Sister, as usual, and you will educate these girls to become good Catholic women."

As always, R.B. gave her sardonic response, "And the boys?"

"I think the girls will manage the boys nicely. Don't you? We shall address the education of young ladies." That was Pastor's opinion, and that was that.

Sister Rita Bernard had something more refined in mind. A proper school for girls with some of the hellcats he threw her way? Impossible! That is what Sister Rita Bernard thought, and that, too, was that.

Francie had no idea how far the repercussions of Sister Rita Bernard's wrath could extend. The Mount would rescind her acceptance if St. Mary's expelled her. Francie thought expulsion from the Mount was a great idea and instead go to the local high school with Lucy. At least there she could meet real boys and wear real clothes, instead of a frumpy uniform. Thus, regardless of parental pleas and periodic threats, Francie cared little about the future.

"What kid did?" was Garbo's conclusion.

The only thing the girls feared was missing the class trip to Washington, D.C. It was the highlight of the school year and a tradition at St. Mary's. The loss of it was a monumental threat. As far as Francie could see, it was the only risk on the radar. All year they planned for this trip; they could hardly wait. It was a rite of passage and would be the first time most of them would be away from their parents.

10

The Spirit of Evil Sands

For this reason, rejoice, you heavens and you who dwell in them. Woe to the earth and the sea because the devil has come down to you with great wrath, knowing that he has only a short time.
Rev.12: 12

Saturday, Mid-May 1962

The forecast for Saturday was 80 degrees, which was unusually hot for May. The Jerrys slept over at Lucy's Friday night and stayed up till dawn when they hatched the plan to sneak off to the beach.

Apricot insisted they be back at Lucy's house in time for Mrs. Davis to pick them up, which, by Apricot's later account, kept them from getting murdered. And although they did manage to escape threats unknown, they came awfully close to being left out of the class trip. Pastor wisely pointed out to their parents that, to his recollection, most of them had done exactly the same thing at the same age. Plus, he had already paid for the bus.

The girls never did tell anyone what really happened. They were in enough trouble for daring to cross the river to the beach, off-season, without permission.

Lucy left her Mom a note explaining that she and the girls had gone down the hill to Tummy's for breakfast. She left a note for her every morning. They rarely saw each other before dinnertime. Somehow, Minnie Penn couldn't quite get downstairs before her daughter had to leave for school.

She placed the note near her mother's coffee cup, then caught up with her girlfriends. They bought ice cream cones for their breakfast and enjoyed them outside on the dock, leaving the fishermen to have their coffee in peace.

The girls were giddy from lack of sleep. The sea air filled their lungs with exuberance, and the wind blew its freedom song through their hair. Francie pointed to the sky, blazing scarlet as the sun came up over the horizon. "Red sky at night, sailor's delight. Red sky at morning, sailors take warning."

"What's that even mean?" Daisy asked, working her ice cream into curlicues.

"I don't know," Francie admitted, "it's one of my Father's corny sayings."

"Let's go to the beach," Lucy interrupted.

"Don't forget, my mother is coming at two o'clock sharp," Apricot cautioned again.

Everyone rolled their eyes at Apricot as they walked the short distance to the ferry. Rick Eye was preparing to shove off. "Up early, girls?"

"We never went to sleep," Daisy exclaimed proudly.

"I see, yez all had a sleepover together, I'm guessin'."

Everybody liked Rick Eye. He was the perfect sea captain, all salty and scruffy with a heart of gold. He even wore a patch over his eye, having lost it in the war. Everyone called Rick Eye's boat, "the ferry." He used his old tug to earn extra money off-season, ferrying people back and forth across the area's waterways. He was the ferry captain no matter what the rig.

"When ya goin' across the river to the seashore, Mr. Rick?" Francie asked politely.

"On my way right now," he said. "I've a load of vegetables from your Pastor to deliver over to the Shanties. I suppose yez want me to drop yez at the beach on the way? Beach ain't open for the season yet."

The girls didn't answer, just stood there smiling. "Come on then," he said. "I'll stop at the Crabby House for some breakfast, do me a couple of Saturday runs, and I'll pick yez up down at the Pier House around 12:30."

"Can't you pick us up at 1:30?" Francie asked.

"Take it, or leave it, 12:30."

"We'll take it!"

The girls cheered as they hopped aboard ... all except Apricot. She was fearful of the gap from the dock to the side of the boat, which was about 8 inches.

"Don't be such a chicken, Ap, you're not gonna fall in," Lucy taunted.

Rick Eye finally put his thick, calloused hand around Apricot's upper arm and flung her into the ferry. Apricot was used to them laughing at her foibles and fears. Her curly bob bounced like springs as she landed. And now, feeling very accomplished, there she was, aboard ship.

Rick Eye dropped the girls across the river at a little cove below the entrance to No-Man's Landing at the south end of the shoreline. It was the least desirable location along the peninsula. The dirty untended beach and its tidal creek, thick with seagrass, separated the Pier House Beach with its boardwalks and bathhouses, from Evil Sands. Named for good reason, decades ago, folks thought of it as a barrier between the living and the dead.

"Ain't nobody patrollin' the shore," Rick Eye warned, "you girls be careful."

The girls crunched their way over the stony strip between the abandoned dock and the high dune on the riverside. They trudged up to the top of the dune, as Rick Eye's tugboat chugged away.

The day-trippers would be arriving in droves come Memorial

Day, ready to enjoy the pristine beaches of the north end, but for today, at dawn, there wasn't a soul around. The girls stood on the windswept dune like sentries on a wall.

"I can see for … forever," Francie announced wistfully.

"Maybe not forever, but pretty far!" Apricot agreed, with her usual clarification of the facts. "I need to sit down for a while, Lucy, I'm tired out from that climb. You never said it was so far up," she scolded.

Lucy laughed and tossed herself like a sack of potatoes onto the sandy side of the dune and slid down to the beach. The others followed. They decided to catch their breath for a few minutes, and, exhausted from staying up all night, they fell asleep on the sand.

When they woke up, the sun was high. Francie woke up first and ran to the water's edge. It was freezing. Apricot winced from a painful sunburn.

"Come on! We've wasted the whole morning," Francie shouted back to the others.

They frolicked and ran, screaming with delight as they teased the chilly waters, dutifully heading north up the beach to where Rick Eye would meet them.

Lucy looked behind at Evil Sands, eyeing the ominous rocks in the near distance. "You know that beach is even prettier than our beach. It's a shame no one visits there."

"No one goes because it is haunted," Daisy said.

"Why don't we go and explore then?" Francie teased Apricot.

"Don't be crazy!" Apricot barked.

"I'll race you to the jetty at Evil Sands," Lucy dared.

"Santa Maria!" Daisy gasped, babbling a prayer in Spanish familiar only to God and her family.

"You can't!" Apricot wheezed. "You can't!"

Francie looked down the beach to the jetty and up the beach toward the pier. "I'll do it if we all do it."

"We'll be late for the ferry!" Apricot whined, pulling Lucy by the arm.

Francie and Lucy looked at each other with a familiar glint of mischief, then bolted south into the creek.

"This is loco," Daisy objected, slogging through the reeds and the knee-high water.

The race was on. All the girls ran as fast as they could to the ocean, in and out with the waves, avoiding the bracing water. Francie was well ahead and winning the race, but she was out of breath, and it burned her lungs. Suddenly, she felt a strange shock of icy air. She continued to run, shuddering. Again, she felt the icy blast and something, someone, roughly brushing near her. She spun around, but nothing was there. Francie stood frozen in the sand. This left the others unnerved.

"What is it?" Lucy asked, catching up to her. "What's the matter?"

"I don't know," Francie said. "What was that? Why were you laughing at me?"

"What was what?" Lucy asked, confused.

"We're not laughing." The girls looked at each other, scared and puzzled.

"I heard you! I heard someone laughing," Francie insisted.

Apricot was terrified. "We've gotta go…let's go."

Lucy waved her back, frowning at her fear, and examined the stony expression on Francie's face.

"This is creepy," Daisy whispered to Apricot, who was hyperventilating. "It's haunted! I do think … it's really haunted."

"It is not," Lucy snapped.

"Is too!" Apricot cried.

"Haunted by what?" Daisy questioned with a gulp. "Good spirits or—bad spirits?"

Francie thought she felt a yank at her throat. She grasped her neck, a yelp of terror escaping as her sweet chain of golden hearts fell to the sand. A sudden wind whipped up a frosting of white caps on the waves. The ocean became choppy and fierce. The surf rolled in. It claimed her necklace and pulled it into the sea, leaving Francie panic-stricken. She splashed around in a frantic circle dropping to her knees in search of her lost treasure.

"Let's get out of here!" Apricot wailed.

Francie was like a frenzied dog digging for her necklace.

"Come on!" Lucy shouted.

But Francie would not stop.

Apricot and Daisy panicked and ran for their lives toward the ferry.

"It's an antique," Francie sobbed. "My sister gave it to me for Christmas. I have to find it!"

"Come on!" Lucy screeched. She ran back to Francie and reached out to grab her. Francie recoiled, shutting her eyes tight, her body tense. Lucy bent down to pull her up, but Francie wouldn't budge. In the bat of an eye, she saw something different—not Lucy at all—something dreadful.

"Francie! What's wrong with you?" Lucy cried. "Come on!" She yanked Francie out of the sand, Francie screaming.

"France, France," Lucy cooed, gently shaking her friend.

Francie reluctantly opened her eyes to the frightened face of her best friend, Lucy Penn. She staggered a few steps. The waves quickly washed away any impression of their footprints—as if they had never been there at all. Lucy held tightly to Francie, pulling her by the wrist. They ran in step as fast as they could, splashing through the reeds toward the safety of the public beach, never stopping for breath all the way to the pier. Nor did they look back to see Francie's necklace wash ashore, twinkling in the sunshine, caught in seaweed on the sand.

To their great relief, Rick Eye was waiting, waving them toward the tug impatiently. The first two girls rushed aboard—Apricot had no trepidations this time, she jumped onto the boat.

"You're late," Rick Eye growled. "I'm leavin'.

"No, Rick Eye, please. Don't leave them—my mother—" Apricot pleaded.

"They better be quick," he muttered.

"We're sorry, Captain Rick Eye," Daisy said, then shouted down to the beach, "Lucy! Hurry!"

Lucy and Francie flew up the dunes toward the steps of the pier. Rick Eye had been waiting half an hour, chastising himself for leaving them there in the first place. Now that he saw they were safe, part of him wanted to teach them a lesson and make them walk the long way back to the roundabout and take the bus.

He sounded the horn. Francie and Lucy scrambled up the top

steps and jumped aboard, bent over and panting for breath. Rick Eye maneuvered the tugboat away from the dock and pulled out across the river.

"I was of a mind to leave yez back there," Rick Eye muttered. "But Doctor Annie saved my kid last winter, and so's I owed her one." He glared at Francie with his one good eye. "Whatsa matter with yez, wanderin' around off-season? I told yez to walk up to the pier beach, where a soul could look out and see who's there. That sea is treacherous when it sets a mind to."

"I—I'm, we're sorry," Francie said softly.

And that was it. They didn't utter another word all the way home. Francie wouldn't say what happened, or what she saw— not even to Lucy. They were shivering and sun burnt. The sea wind didn't seem to stir up the same freedom song it had at dawn. It cruelly whipped their hair in every direction as they bounced across the choppy waters into the bay. Everybody just wanted to go home.

Lucy didn't think the adventure was worth it. Now, shewould have to spend the rest of the day, alone, in an empty house.

11

Francie's Father Takes Her to School

...and the Powers that are in Heaven shall be shaken.
Mark 13:25

May 1962
That Monday Morning

On Monday morning Francie's father, Dr. Albert O'Malley, drove Francie to school. The dark circles under her eyes stole the rose from her cheeks, turning her sprinkle of gingery freckles into gray-brown spots. She didn't wrinkle her nose at him in the way that melted his heart. Instead, Francie got out of the car with barely a word.

"Hey, where's my kiss?" he asked her concerned. "Oh, sorry, Pops," she said, and bussed his cheek.

"That's more like it," he called after her, but it wasn't more like it. He worried for his child as he watched her disappear from the cobblestone courtyard into the school.

Beneficent Angel was also worried. The Powers That Be called her to a hearing. The Powers are that choir of angels, who are charged with planning how, and by whom, appointed commands of their hierarchy were to be carried out. In this case, force Cell Fish, top Captain of Hell, to relinquish his grip on Three Rivers in order to save Midlantic. The hundred-year prophecy of the Great Theft had passed the halfway mark. Drastic steps had to be taken. The Powers appointed Beneficent Angel to issue a warning to humanity. And Beneficent was given substantial flexibility in how she was to get the job done.

"I'm not sure this plan of yours is working," Angelico, the esteemed Secretary of the Powers That Be, said quietly to Beneficent.

"But Angelico, you said yourself, the situation is dire," Beneficent defended.

Wise Power's vote held much sway. As one of the top three leaders in the august assembly. When he rat-tat-tatted on the table all was quiet. "You might have to re-think your plan," he said. "Of course, it's only a suggestion."

"Perhaps a glimpse of Cell Fish is too severe for a child of 12 years," Small Power added. Small, was well thought of, but extremely sensitive for a member of this warrior choir of angels.

"The message must be delivered if the parish is to mount a defense," Beneficent argued. "Cell Fish will still maintain control of those who will serve him for 40 more years!"

"Quite so," said Wise Power.

This agitated Beneficent. "I can't very well smite the wicked. If I do, there won't be anyone left to save!"

"That is true, also, but is it not it better to tailor the message to the age and understanding of your young messenger?" Angelico suggested.

"After all, you chose the messenger," Wise Power remarked, "a little girl, rather spoiled at that. What's her name again?"

"O'Malley, Wise Power, Francie O'Malley," Beneficent answered. "And how would *you* suggest I convey the abysmal prospects of St. Mary's-of-the-Future, if in fact, humanity does not change course?"

"Well, it will have to be conveyed without terrifying a child half out of her wits!"

Small Power sighed. "Yes, that would be better, Beneficent. Just look at the poor thing," Always tender, Small was almost weeping.

Through the clouds, Beneficent Angel and the panel of Powers observed the pensive Francie O'Malley as she entered her classroom. Francie was on edge and full of dread. That's when Beneficent examined Francie's surroundings. Wise and Small Powers were right. What could Beneficent do to make it easier for the girl? Suddenly, a kaleidoscope of brilliant perceptions, snapshots, histories, and sketches sped through her intelligence. Some were brilliant, some were grim. In moments, the frustrated angel began to radiate inspiration penetrating the very stone of the statues in Pastor's prayer garden. She had an idea that could work if she could just get Francie to look out the window…

Francie took her seat in front of Lucy, who poked at her shoulder. The promise of silly amusements was the order of the day, but Francie was uninterested in mischief.

"France, what's wrong?" Lucy asked surprised.

"Nothing. I want to study, that's all." She brushed her friend off like a fly.

"Study? For what? There's no test."

Lucy didn't understand the change in her best friend. Maybe Francie had a new preference. Lucy's cantankerous aunts always said Francie would dump her, sooner or later, for the rich girls from River Ridge, the fancier section of town, where the O'Malley's lived. Lucy never believed them, but the hurtful thought made her wonder. She wasn't from that side of town, but she didn't miss out on anything. Uncle Taurus always gave her money for stuff she wanted. They were best friends. They had always been best friends. But maybe her aunts were right, and the time of her abandonment had come.

Lucy had it wrong; it was fear. Fear kept Francie on guard, afraid to close her eyes, dreading the dark images that flashed before her. She stared out the window, exhausted. The familiar statues of angels and saints that dotted Pastor's prayer garden across the courtyard became watery and began to blur. Suddenly, they appeared to her in a whole new light, a great light. Each statue seemed spirited with a life of its own. Protectors sent from Heaven! Francie clung to Garbo's stories of heavenly helpers vigorously pitching in to do their job protecting the living. It was the very insulation she needed to keep herself safe from the memory of the evil thing on the beach.

Then came a smack of doubt. She needed some assurance. Would all be well? Francie's eyes flickered to the bench where Sister Serena sat with her prayer book and rosary beads. Who better to put her mind at ease than Sister Serena? A holy nun, the perfect antidote. Sister Serena was old as the hills, she would know for sure if the evil stories were true. Maybe she would even say it was her imagination, and that would be fine … super fine, in fact.

Francie could hardly wait for lunch. She traded her sandwich with Cupcake Carey for a pair of pink and white Hostess Sno Balls, then headed straight for Sister Serena's bench. She sat down and unwrapped the Sno Balls carefully and offered one to the old nun. Sister Serena smiled, graciously declining the sticky sweet.

Francie swallowed down a bite and licked out the filling, before approaching the conversation casually, as if they chatted together every day. "Sister, can I talk to you about something crazy?" Francie was serious, despite the pink marshmallow mustache sticking to her upper lip.

Sister Serena closed her prayer book, keeping an arthritic finger on the page to hold her place.

"Certainly, dear, I'm as crazy as they come. What seems to be your trouble?"

"Oh, I'm not in trouble. Really, I'm not."

"Good, good. Then is it physical? Are you ill? Smoke affecting your brain?"

Francie was surprised. She could barely look the nun in the eye. "You knew?"

"Of course, dear. Did you think I'd lost my sense of smell?"

"We thought you were asleep. Well, except for that time you stood up." Francie pointed a finger at the nun with a timid smile.

"Yes, and you dove behind our noble statue here of St. Michael the Archangel." The nun glanced toward the fierce figure just behind them. "A good choice, I might add, for a girl in distress."

Francie blushed. Sister Serena raised her face to Heaven. She closed her eyes, accepted a kiss from the sun, then directed a warm smile at Francie on her bench. "You see, dear, Sister Rita Bernard was conducting a tour of benefactors around the grounds, and they were heading our way. I was giving you a warning. I didn't want Mother Superior to catch you in a compromising situation. She would have had to act in the best interest of the school, you do understand?"

"Yes, Sister," Francie said, then paused, mystified. "Well…no, Sister, I kind of don't understand. Whose side are you on?"

The old nun laughed, "I am on God's side, child. At that moment, I felt that He saw me more as a guardian angel for you girls—rather than a police dog. I may be benched, but I'm an effective pray-er."

Francie swallowed the remains of her Sno Ball. She wished she had some milk to wash it down. Who knew they had a friend in Sister Serena? "I don't know what to say!"

"Let's leave it at this, Francine. God knows what would have happen to you if you were caught. The consequences would have been very harsh, and the resulting circumstances could have endangered your soul. I made a judgement, and that's the end of it."

"Thank you, Sister. You know, I think I'm going to tell Lucy you're all right… I mean, for a nun."

"Such a compliment, dear!"

"No, I mean it," Francie assured her.

Sister patted Francie's knee. "I'm sure you do, dear."

Francie licked the cream filling from her fingertips and upper lip, crumpled the Sno Ball wrapper, and put it in her pocket. As she slid the cellophane in, she remembered a note she had for Garbo, which was pressing against her fingers in the pocket. She pulled it out. "I gotta go," she said. Adjusting her uniform kilt, she offered a sloppy curtsy to the nun. For the first time, she noticed Sister Serena was wearing leg braces and had a pair of crutches resting between the bench and the bushes. Francie forgot all about the reason she wanted to talk to Sister Serena in the first place.

Francie gave her a wan smile, not knowing quite what to say. She tried not to stare at the crutches in the bushes but couldn't help herself.

"Garbo's gonna make us a casserole tonight. I have to give her this note." Francie held up the crumpled paper from her pocket. "My mother doesn't have time to cook."

"Garbo makes a wonderful casserole," the nun nodded thoughtfully, then returned to her prayer book.

Garbo was watching out the window. "What in the world is Francie doin' chattin' away with Sister Serena? I hope those silly Jerrys aren't up to somethin' mean. They should leave Sister Serena alone."

Francie entered the rectory from the back porch, and sat down at the kitchen table, very glum.

"And what's the matter with ya this fine day?" Garbo asked, waving her cigarette smoke around, and trying to act like she hadn't been spying.

"I didn't know Sister Serena was a … a cripple. Is that why she's always on the bench?"

"Did ya think she was lazy?" Garbo sighed impatiently. "Or did ya just not think at all?"

Francie shrugged with embarrassment.

"Ain't ya seen the other Sisters practically carry Sister Serena out to her bench each mornin' lately and collect her in theafternoon? She sits there with her beads and prayer book all day because she wants to be near you children. She says it keeps her young. She had an operation over Easter vacation. Doctor said she can't teach no more; she can barely get around. Clever girls, yer the tough ones—I've seen yez."

"We didn't know!"

" 'Course not," Garbo retorted, "but ya shoulda."

Francie knew what Garbo was getting at. Nobody knew her better than Garbo did. After all, Garbo had taken care of her since she was a baby while her mother worked.

Francie remembered when she was a toddler sitting on piles of wet newspaper spread out on the rectory floor. Garbo would dress her in Gabe's old shirt and roll up the sleeves. Then, armed with a jar of pink Gorham's silver polish and a handful of rags, the housekeeper would set before Francie mountains of church vessels in need of polishing. And, while Garbo stuffed Pastor's chicken, or roasted him up a leg of lamb, she shared with Francie all the secrets of her life. Every beef she had with Gabe, or the staff, or even Pastor, spilled out while the attentive toddler soaped up holy water fonts and candlesticks and everything else in sight. Little Francie knew instinctively that a nod of agreement reaped rewards. When the bell went off, the oven door would open, and the smell of fresh-baked oatmeal cookies would replace the smelly pink polish. Garbo would dry her off, sit her up on a chair, and the cookies, still gooey in the middle, would be hers. Her mother, Doctor Annie, didn't like her to have sweets, but Garbo said nonsense, oatmeal was good for you.

"I been watchin' yez," Garbo scolded. "The Jerrys tauntin' Sister Serena, to see if ya can get her to leave her bench."

"I didn't notice her leg braces before today," Francie fretted remorsefully, "I didn't."

Garbo washed her ashtray. "Ah, you're a kid, what could ya know? Stop yer moanin' now, or you'll wake the dead."

The common phrase sent Francie into a fit of tears. "Oh, the dead!" she cried, "I forgot to ask her about the dead—I mean the spirits."

"What dead?" Garbo gave Francie's chestnut ponytail a tender tug. "Come on now, I got the new Star magazine. Let's take a look at it."

"I don't want to look at magazines. I'm too upset about Sister Serena. How could I be so awful?"

Garbo sat down beside the disturbed child. Francie saw the tenderness in her hard, but still beautiful features. "Tell God you're sorry and be a nice girl from now on. You're not as awful as all that." Garbo smiled, dried her hands on her apron, and pressed her nicotine-stained thumbs on Francie's cheeks, swiping away her tears. She sensed there was more to this story. "What is it, kiddo? What's botherin' ya?"

"I don't know," Francie said reluctantly. "You're gonna laugh at me."

Garbo crossed her heart, "Scout's honor, I won't laugh." Francie looked straight at Garbo; trust was on the line.

It set Garbo off her stride. There was a sense of menacing conflict in Francie's doe-eyed appearance.

"So, what's this all about?" Garbo asked.

"*SO?* I saw—I saw—something."

"Why, ya look like ya seen a ghost."

"Well, I didn't," Francie retorted.

"Yeah, but if ya asked me, and if I didn't know better, I'd think you'da been to Evil Sands," Garbo snickered, pulling Francie's leg.

"No!" Francie protested, frozen with fear. How could Garbo know? She couldn't know.

Two can play at this game, Garbo thought. An outing to Evil Sands wasn't a real possibility, even for the Jerrys.

Garbo took Francie's chin in hand and studied her carefully, "You wouldn't be lying to me, Francine? Normal people don't walk around as pale as a specter with no reason."

"I didn't see anything, anywhere, okay?" Francie wailed and ran out of the rectory. "I didn't see any stupid ghost!"

Garbo's chair screeched across the floor as she jumped up to follow her. The wire on the screen door, pushed to its limit, smacked back against Garbo's hands. Francie was down the porch stairs in a flash and ran right into Gabe. He held her steady until she found her footing.

"There's somethin' eatin' you, Francie O'Malley, and the sooner ya get it off yer chest, the better it'll be for everybody." Garbo let the door slam.

Perplexed, Gabe inspected Francie's crumbling face before he let her go, then went into the rectory.

"What's wrong?" he asked Garbo as he straightened out the furniture.

"Nothin'," Garbo answered quietly. "Kids are kids, is all."

"You always say 'nothin'' when it's really somethin'."

Garbo wiped a few strands of hair off her forehead with the back of her hand. "Eat your lunch," she said, putting an extremely brown omelet on a plate in front of him. "Look, I fixed it real nice for ya."

12

Garbo Reflects

May 1962
Monday, After School about 3:00 o'clock

Francie dragged herself into the rectory kitchen. Pastor had seminarians coming to dinner, and Garbo was cooking up a storm. "So, yer back," she said. "Didn't think I'd be seein' ya this soon."

Francie was sullen.

"I've no time for wastin' now Francie."

"You're just like my mother—I'm never top priority." She took a lick of icing and left in a huff.

Garbo rolled her eyes, looking after Francie with a sigh.

"What's eatin' you girl?"

As Garbo repaired the cake, she thought about Francie's mom, Doctor Annie. A woman who gave her 'hundred percent' to the care of everyone else's children, especially the poor. After her middle daughter, Taffy, entered school, she threw herself into her work almost full-time. Her late-life baby, Francie, practically raised herself. For years Garbo kept an eye on her after school, especially when her mother had an emergency, which was almost daily. You couldn't say Francie was a wild kid, but Garbo did fear that her relentless pursuit of fun and daring would be her undoing. And she told her so often.

"Harmless enough now, little one," she would say, "but things ain't the same outside the walls of St. Mary's."

Garbo had a nose for real trouble. She could see it coming, much in the way Sister Ed saw Fury. There was a significant difference between trying to get a rise out of the nuns and being on Sister Rita Bernard's hit list. If she wasn't careful, Francine O'Malley could wind up at Ashtown High School, mingling with the toughest kids from the Bay area—a scene this sheltered child couldn't begin to fathom. They were arranged by a lottery, the luck of the draw. Six or seven small towns had only three high schools between them, and Ashtown High was the biggest. Nothing could be done about it. Living in River Ridge, where the O'Malley's had a beautiful home, made no difference.

Ashtown High School would undoubtedly be Lucy's fate. It was her aunts who sent Lucy to St. Mary's, hoping she could get a scholarship to the Mount and from there go on to college, but Lucy,though capable enough, was unfocused and lazy. Her father was dead, and her mother worked long hours in a dress shop six daysa week. Lucy applied herself to nothing but her jingles, and the Jerrys, her silly crowd of girlfriends who screamed laughter at her irreverent lyrics.

They were a pretty pair, Francie and Lucy that is. Two girls who couldn't have been lonelier—or more loved.

Garbo warned Lucy often: "It ain't good enough to be funny, Lucille. If somebody's gonna buy yer lyrics, ya need to spell the words right so's people can read 'em. People ain't mind-readers,

little lady, they're writin' readers. Learn your proper writin,' or you're gonna be cookin' for Pastor when I die!"

Francie had no idea how lucky she was, nor Lucy how unlucky. But Garbo did. She had witnessed years of heartbroken mothers and hard-drinking fathers, marching their ne'er-do-well offspring into the rectory. They called their daughters 'tramps' and tried to arrange quick marriages. They socked their sons right in front of Pastor, then begged him to find them legal counsel. Some even asked for help raising bail. Garbo witnessed a lot of tears over the years and cried most of them herself at onetime or another.

She married one of those toughs from Ashtown High School and, in her own short stay there, had tormented proper well-bred girls from St. Mary's. But, as fate would have it, 1917 came along, and the toughs became soldiers, and the soldiers became heroes. Gabe was one of them—although he was never quite the same again.

There was a real edge to him when he came home from the Great War. He was a bitter drunkard with a chip on his shoulder. Garbo ran away to make her fortune on Broadway. Since she was 'a real looker,' she was able to land a job in the Ziegfeld Follies. "A lotta glam," she told the nuns, burning their ears with tales of her escapades, like running off with one of the producers to the West Coast. The guy was going to make her a movie star. That didn't happen.

She kicked around Hollywood for years, sinking lower and lower down the food chain. Her looks turned hard. She became destitute.

Miraculously, Gabe went on a quest out West to find her. She had stopped writing to him, not wanting him to think his estranged wife wasn't every bit the bon vivant she pretended to be. Somehow, he knew and came after her, following one clue, and then another, until there she was, a counter waitress in a diner. Garbo poured him a cup of coffee without even looking up. In a monotonous circular motion, she wiped up a spill with a dingy terry-cloth rag. Gabe pushed a worn sepia photo of the two of them across the counter. When he left for the Great War, they had a snapshot taken at the train station by a friend. It took her a minute to even notice it. She couldn't believe her eyes.

Through a blur of tears, his tired simple smile broke through his day-old beard. And despite his raggedy suit and tie, she saw in him the possibility of a new beginning—her handsome hero, her husband. Right then, she decided they would stick together forever.

They had both traveled their separate roads to hell through a mirage of vices. Gabe confessed he had even done a short stint in jail for vagrancy and public drunkenness. He said he had tried to drown his memories of the war in alcohol and with them the desperate sea of death that followed him everywhere. Young, handsome faces, one after another, in their tin hats, bayonets fixed, questioning him night and day. Why was he still alive, and they were not? He wept as he spoke of that last horrific blast that set the sky on fire and blew his buddies' limbs in every direction. He could still feel the wetness of their blood and the rats running over him in the muddy trench. Garbo thought better of telling him too much about her time in Hollywood. It wouldn't change matters, and Gabe already hurt enough for one man. They never spoke of these things again but left them behind like so much baggage when they agreed to go home. They were both broke and broken, but happy enough to be together.

The Great Depression was cruel. They practically had to walk back to Little Capernaum, dreaming about the smell of the Atlantic and dancing under the stars out on the pier. They talked about fishing, the picnic grounds on Sunday afternoons, and just doing nothing watching the rivers meet the sea. Home, that's where they wanted to be. Garbo never understood why they rushed back to the town they abandoned long ago. But life had been simpler then, even with its hardships. So, they made it their goal, and it kept them going until they got to the Old Road one rainy night.

Lightning lit up the sky, thunder clapping, as the bus whooshed by the church. Through the raindrops, Garbo saw a statue of the Virgin Mary aglow on the lawn. The grey stone of the statue was gleaming white. It was a vision, she said. Surely it wasn't, Gabe

answered. "What would the Virgin Mary be doin' makin' a vision to you fer?"

"Well, I don't know, but we're gettin' off this bus right now to find out!" Then she barreled down the aisle, insisting the bus driver stop.

They made their way up the steep hill back to Our Lady of Perpetual Help Church.

Gabe planned to stay on the bus to the end of the line. Seeing they were half-starved, he planned to take Garbo to St. Anthony's Lost and Found, a place at the bottom of the mountain and a short walk under the bridge to the shelter. It was the last stop on the roundabout, not much farther down the Old Road. Gabe knew it well from his days after the Great War. They could get fed there at the soup kitchen. He was kicking himself for listening to Garbo about some twinkly statue as they shivered in the downpour—but he followed her anyway.

Gabe was a jittery wreck standing on the steps of the rectory porch. The statue of the Virgin Mary was plain grey stone, dripping wet, just like they were. They barked back and forth as the rain poured down.

"Land sakes, Garbo! Botherin' a priest in the middle of the night! You ain't got no respect for nothin'."

Gabe was too ashamed to ring the bell.

"Go on now, go ahead," Garbo hissed, pushing him at the door.

"No! Dang, you—you ring it."

"Be a man, you do it."

"It's your fault. You made us get off the bus. You do it."

Pastor opened the door without anybody ringing the bell. "Come in out of the rain," he said, "and stop bickering. You're ruining my supper."

13

Back to Sorrowful Francie O'Malley

May 1962
Monday, about 4:00 o'clock

It was late afternoon by now, Francie sat alone in the schoolyard and tried to do her homework, but her disappointment festered. "Happy thoughts," she told herself, that usually helped, but not today. No happy thoughts rose up on command. Today, her mother had promised to be on time. They were going to shop for her Confirmation dress. The girls of St. Mary's wore white academic gowns with red collars for Confirmation, but everyone got a new dress anyway.

Francie dragged herself to the children's swing set to wait. This was her 'lookout' whenever her mother had an emergency.

"No detention today?" Gabe asked as he walked by the swings on his way to the tool shed in the garage.

"Thanks for not ratting on us about the cigarette," Francie said.

"It's okay," he said softly, "saved by the bell, huh?"

"I guess."

"What ya lookin' so sad fer?"

"My mother has a patient, and I missed the bus."

"Sorry for your troubles," Gabe consoled.

"She promised to be on time today!" Francie whined, then glared at the kitchen window. "Even Garbo's too busy for me."

"Tough hand the Lord dealt ya, Miss Francie," Gabe said, raising an eyebrow in defense of his wife. "Hardly bearable, yer lot in life."

As he continued to the garage to put away his tools, he heard Sister Angelina teaching religious instruction through the rectory chapel window. Gabe stopped to peer in.

"Why don'tcha help Sister Angelina teach the catechism?" he called over to Francie. "She's got all them kids from the public school in there to prepare for Confirmation."

"I don't feel like it," Francie said.

Gabe moved back to the swings. "I thought you liked Sister Angelina."

"I do, I love her."

"Then why don'tcha help her out?"

"Because I don't feel like it," Francie snapped.

"Well, I can't feel sorry for a person who gets saved from detention by St. Mary herself but won't help out Sister Angelina. Seems mighty selfish to me."

Gabe left Francie pouting on the swing, but he stopped once more and leaned on his rake. "Ya know, Miss Francie, yer always misbehavin', or settin' up a story that don't have a happy endin'. Don't you like a story with a happy endin'?"

"Of course, I do! But I don't have a story like that. My mother doesn't care about me." Francie wallowed in her drama.

"Ah," Gabe scratched his whiskers. "I see. Is that it?"

"Yes! That *is* it! If I didn't get in trouble sometimes, she wouldn't even remember I got born."

"Yer Ma is a good woman and a good doctor. Ain't easy for a woman havin' a man's job and all. Ya oughta quit feelin' sorry for yerself."

Gabe gave up. Then he noticed some onion grass growing around the pipes of the swing set. He took his clipper from his overalls and went over to clip the weeds.

"Look down there, at the end of the driveway," he said, pointing down the hill with his clippers. "Do ya see Pastor loadin' upthe station wagon with food?"

Francie shrugged.

"That's fer folks who ain't got no groceries. Look at the kids who's helping him." He eyed Francie with a bit of disdain. "Ain't none a ya bright as a cricket, la-de-da girls helping him, just kids from Fishtown who got nothin'."

Francie looked away in defiance. She had set her toe in the quicksand of self-pity, and it sucked her in. Everything he said irritated her. She wanted her mother's attention, and nothing would substitute. Crossing her arms, she set her face in the fiercest pout.

Gabe went on, "They might not be as smart, or as rich as you girls, but look how they're laughin' and jokin' with Pastor. Ya see that?"

"Rich? I'm not rich!"

"Ya got so much, honey. Be happy." Gabe couldn't make her understand. "Hell, everybody's got troubles, but they're happy."

Francie looked down the hill and saw the flurry of activity. They were having a wonderful time.

"Why don'tcha notice somebody besides yourself for a change? Do ya even know any folks with real troubles?"

"That's not fair!" Francie protested, "My troubles are as real as anybody's."

"What if Pastor and Sister Angelina moped around all day like ya do. Didn't do nothin' nor help nobody. Then where'd we be? Worse yet, what if there weren't no Pastor?"

Gabe watched the man who had helped him turn his lifearound, then pulled the swing back and gave Francie a hard push into reality. She grabbed the chains as she set off into the air.

"Ya know, there wouldn't be no parish here at all if it weren't for him.

No school, neither."

Gabe pulled the swing back, surprising Francie. He jerked the swing chains and held them, so Francie faced the church. "This church was fallin' apart when Pastor came here. He works hard, so's everybody else can have a better life. And what thanks does he get?"

"I don't know," Francie whined.

"None. Ain't nobody thankin' him. Seems like ain't nobody even listenin' to him anymore. But he keeps on helpin' folks— with no complaints. And your Ma, she put herself through medical school. She never forgot the people of Fishtown, even after she moved to River Ridge. Dr. Annie don't deserve no bratty kid."

Gabe stopped. Doc's youngest child was almost crying. Her pretty little face was so unhappy.

"I don't feel like helping anybody, Gabe," Francie sniffed.

"There now, Miss Francie, I'm sorry." Gabe spoke in a gentler tone, "Garbo's always hollerin' at me about being so gruff."

He gave her a hug and headed, again, for the garage. "Try and see the bright side of things, little girl, be happy."

Francie was more miserable than ever until the awful sound of a broken muffler distracted her. Mr. Hubert, the school bus driver, was back from his daily round of delivering kids home from school. He switched vehicles and started up the engine of the parish station wagon, ready for his next mission: delivering food to the poor. As he drove away, Francie thought maybe Gabe was right. Maybe she should be more like the poor kids who were helping Pastor.

She walked down the cobblestone driveway to the place where the other kids had loaded the car. There were bushel baskets and vegetables all over the ground. Lettuce leaves, stringbeans, the odd potato, left by the kids who had gone into the rectory with Pastor for a treat before cleaning up. Francie wiped her face and started filling a basket.

As she plucked up tomatoes, resentment took hold of her. "I'll show everybody," Francie groused under her breath, "I'll take a basket to the most desperate place on earth—the Shanties. They'll tell Pastor on Sunday, 'Francie O'Malley, Doctor Annie's daughter, brought us the best basket of tomatoes.' Then everybody'll know I'm not selfish and spoiled. Nobody else was supposed to interfere today. No excuses. Just today, and she couldn't even do it once."

Francie tossed one last tomato on top so hard it split open. She threw the dripping tomato on the ground with a splat and headed downhill with her load.

Cutting across the lawn to the highway, she scanned the cars stopped at the red light on the Old Road. Still hoping to see her mother's car, she watched until the traffic light turned red, then green, then red again, three more times, but nobody came.

14

The Beautiful Pink Lady

May 1962
Monday, about 4:30 o'clock

Francie never thought about signing out to leave the campus of St. Mary's. Nor did she consider the possibility that her plan was not well-conceived. Her bushel basket grew heavier as she walked down the hill to Front Street, but she was determined to deliver the food to the Shanties and finish her good deed.

The fishing boats were crowded together. Paint faded and peeling, they bobbed and bumped between old tires tossed over the sides. Francie walked along the pier, as far as the Crabby House, looking for Rick Eye. A couple of old salts tipping back on wooden chairs were drinking beer on the Crabby House porch. A few others were gathering up and putting away their large casting nets.

"Excuse me, please, I'm looking for Rick Eye," she said to the men politely.

"He ain't here," one of the men said.

"Hey! Little St. Mary girl—where ya goin' with your basket?" Billy the Fish, a nasty piece of work, taunted her as he pushed through the screen door onto the wooden porch of the Crabby House.

"I'm going to the Shanties to take my tomatoes to the poor," Francie said.

"The poor don't want no tomatoes," he said.

"Well, of course they do! They're poor," Francie insisted, exasperated.

He skipped down the two creaky steps. "On second thought," he said, looking her over, "I'm from the Shanties. I'll take me a nice ripe tomato." The men on the porch slapped each other, laughing.

Francie stood her ground as Billy came too close to her and took hold of a tomato. The fishy smell of him finally forced her back a step.

"Where is Mr. Rick Eye? I need a ride to the Shanties," she insisted.

Billy stared at her as he sucked on the tomato. He bit out the stem with its green tendrils and spit it into the river. Seeds ran down his chin and he wiped them off with his arm.

"I'll take ya," A wiry little fisherman named Marcus Nook offered, chomping his near toothless gums together. He wore an odd assortment of gold chains, rabbits' feet, and dirty trinkets tied onto leather cords slung around his neck. But it was the sight of his grimy boat that made Francie gasp. It was exactly like the boat Garbo described a thousand times in her stories of Evil Sands.

Billy's eyes narrowed as he circled her eating his stolen tomato. He looked from Francie to Nook and back, then took another tomato and threw it. "Hey, Nook, catch."

"Tanks, don't mind if I do." Nook caught the tomato with a crackling snigger releasing a slight drool to trickle into his whiskers.

Francie glared at Billy nervously. "You should ask before you take something that doesn't belong to you."

"Is that so?" Billy said, surprised at her pluck.

"Yes," she said indignantly, "the tomatoes—they're supposed to be for the poor."

"And what do you think?" he snarled. "I'm rich like you?"

Francie stamped her foot, disgusted, and dropped the basket on the ground. "I AM NOT RICH!" she cried and burst into tears. She ran to Front Street as fast as she could. The awful hoot of the laughing men mingled with the cry of the seagulls as she ran all the way to Miller Street and trudged up the hill to school. Her eyes were stinging. She rubbed them with the heels of her hands, blisters formed on her fingers from the wire handles of the bushel basket.

The people of Fishtown thought of St. Mary girls as privileged, and many of them were, including Francie. But wealth is relative. In Francie's neighborhood, her house was rather modest against the palatial estates of River Ridge. In her mind, Daisy Escobar's house full of warmth and love was something to be envied. It was rich with an assortment of relatives, a brother and sister, aunt and uncle and cousins, music, dancing, and laughter. It was not the often-lonely place she called home since her sister Taffy went to college. She wondered why the poor always seemed to equate happy with being rich? She didn't weigh into the equation the burden of longing Daisy carried as she watched, day after day, for the arrival of her parents from Cuba. Nor did she grasp the idea that envy clouded judgment. In the same way that Francie envied Daisy's house full of love, Apricot envied Francie's house full of stuff—her own record player, Shetland sweaters in every color. Daisy envied Lucy's cleverness, and they all envied Cupcake Carey, who had a Mom that baked every single day. Even Garbo didn't do that.

The sun was going down now, and it was getting chilly. Francie untied her cable knit sweater from around her waist and slipped it on. Then she fixed her school collar pin to sit neatly just the way Sister Ed liked it, with the top button buttoned.

She waited for the light to change at the top of the hill. The sunset cast a rosy glow on the statue of the Virgin Mary, perched high on the brick pedestal overlooking the Old Road. There she was, Our Lady of Perpetual Help, Queen of Heaven, standing above her Mother's Day Garden in front of the rectory. Francie was relieved, even glad, to see the comforting image on the lawn across the street.

She retraced her steps up the hill and rested at the statue of Our Lady of Perpetual Help. She thought for a moment that Mary was smiling down at her through the warm pink light.'Our Lady welcomes everyone...' She could almost hear her father's words.

"At least you're always here when I need you," she said to the statue. "You're a better mother than my mother. Jesus was lucky to have you!" It was a bittersweet compliment for the Mother of God.

Her eyes drifted across Miller Street over to the convent. Sister Georgina was taking in the wash in the convent yard. Sister waved, and Francie waved back.

15

The Sisters of St. Mary's: Sister Angelina

May 1962
Monday, 6:00 o'clock

As the wind picked up, it became too difficult to watch the road any longer, so Francie went back to the prayer garden tucked behind the rectory. She sat on the wooden bench outside of the chapel and listened to Sister Angelina teaching Confirmation class. Francie and the rest of St. Mary's 7th Form received this same preparation during school hours as part of their daily religious curriculum. The children who did not attend Catholic school came to the rectory chapel once a week for instruction to prepare them for Confirmation.

"Today, we're going to learn about the gifts and fruits of the Holy Ghost. We want to be prepared when the bishop questions us, don't we?"

No answer.

"Don't we?" Sister Angelina repeated.

"Yes, Sister," the class answered in one sing-song voice.

Francie started laughing. Sister Angelina never failed to capture the hearts of her students, no matter how naughty the class nor dry the subject matter. Francie leaned toward the window to hear more. She pictured the happy nun whose smile could light up a Christmas tree.

"In order to become soldiers of Jesus Christ," Sister Angelina began, "we must receive the Sacrament of Confirmation. That is why you're here. For this purpose, we are learning about the seven gifts of the Holy Ghost. They are wisdom, understanding, counsel, fortitude, knowledge, piety, and fear of the Lord. And the fruits of these gifts are peace, patience, joy, love, kindness, goodness, generosity, gentleness, benignity, modesty, chastity, and self-control."

As Sister continued her introduction, Francie's thoughts drifted. She knew this lesson already. Well, except benignity. Nobody knew what that was. Best Francie could figure, it was a kind of special tolerance utilizing several of the other fruits.

"Jesus promised that God would send the Comforter, but what He meant was the Holy Ghost. It's in Scripture," Apricot had told her during class. Apricot even corrected Jesus.

Francie didn't dwell too much on whatever it meant to be a soldier of Jesus Christ and to receive the Holy Ghost. It was a complete mystery. She was far more interested in the party that her parents would host for her after the ceremony. It would be set up in a big tent in their backyard overlooking the river. Her sisters would be home, and best of all, she would be the center of attention for the entire day.

In this morning's class, Sister Angelina had asked the girls to act out the gifts and fruits of the Holy Ghost. Francie won a prize for acting out "Piety." She pretended piety was a princess and made a beautiful costume trimmed in violets to represent small little sacrifices one could easily do for others. Sister Angelina said it was a very thoughtful expression of what piety meant. Sister Angelina had a contest for everything and ingenious rhymes to help her students remember boring details. Once, she even had Lucy set her lesson to a jingle.

"Why don't we play the 'WHAT IF' game?" Sister Angelina asked the class in the chapel.

The class cheered.

"WHAT IF someone came along and stole God from us?" The timbre of Sister Angelina's voice astonished everyone, including Francie. "WHAT IF they took away His gifts and fruits? WHAT IF God left us to our own free will choices? WHAT IF…someone took away our religion?"

That sure was a different method of teaching catechism, Francie chortled and perked right up to listen more intently. She pulled the wooden bench directly under the open window, curious as to what this clever nun would say next.

There was silence in the classroom. Then, in the spirit of the game, one child spoke up: "We wouldn't have to go to church anymore." Children giggled nervously.

"No, you wouldn't, would you?" Sister Angelina said soberly.

These were big thoughts and provocative questions. As always, Sister Angelina had you thinking. What about the idea of God getting stolen? Francie's eyes scanned the stone statues of angels and saints in the prayer garden, her new friends silently offering their inspiration and protection. Goosebumps arose on her arms. She felt an icy chill. The faces of the angels and saints began to crumble, statues keeled over and shattered into pieces. She covered her eyes, then peeked through her two fingers. Everything seemed in order again. What was happening?

The large statue of St. Michael the Archangel loomed over her. Francie exhaled with relief and giggled, remembering a narrow escape the week before when Lucy flashed their secret signal with the broken mirror from her mother's old compact of face powder. Sister Serena had risen from her bench! Francie dove behind the statue and was nose to nose with Satan, who was under the sword of the furious archangel. It was no less chilling today, seeing the devil still run through with St. Michael's sword. She turned from the demon's tortured scowl to the short prayer engraved on the pedestal:

☙

THE ASSIGNMENT OF ANGELS

'St. Michael the Archangel defend us in battle,
Be our protection against the wickedness
and snares of the devil.'
Pope St. Leo XIII

She recalled her fervent plea: "St. Michael, please! Don't let us get caught."

But they were, by Garbo as usual, who was putting out the trash and tripped over Francie sprawled on the ground in a most unladylike way.

"Your skirt is rolled up too short, Francie," Garbo advised, "ya ought to fix that before the bell."

Garbo let the screen door fly. The slam jolted Francie back to the present and the soft murmuring of Sister Angelina's class, discussing the likelihood of God getting stolen. Francie watched the water gurgling in the small pool Gabe formed for Pastor's goldfish. It was circled by a slate border that served as a base for the statue of St. Joseph, foster-father of Jesus on earth, holding the baby Jesus in his one arm and a carpenter's tool and lily in his other, while the goldfish swam around below.

"How could there be no God?" Francie whispered, pondering Sister Angelina's challenge. Her whole life was set smack in the middle of God's kingdom—the school, the nuns, the Church, her guardian angel, and all the saints with their helpful patronage. Francie loved Garbo's stories about the saints and Sister Angelina's rhymes. She was constantly petitioning the Lord for every conceivable want. Things for herself and for everyone's sick grandmas, great uncles, broken legs, good grades, and the poor souls in purgatory. It was an impossible thought to have God stolen. It was especially impossible after her encounter on the beach, knowing now, how real evil was, God had to be there to protect her.

Her eyes went from statue to statue. "No baby Jesus! No St. Mary! No St. Anthony for the lost and found. It's not possible."

She looked farther afield at the tiny, gated pet cemetery, as old as the parish itself. There was a dog named St. Bernard who had served his Pastor in the Civil War. Even the dog had a little cross over his grave.

Francie gazed at the statue of St. Francis of Assisi. This was her favorite statue. A stone deer stood by his side with a weather-worn, blue-ribbon knotted tightly around its neck—remnant evidence of the Jerrys raid when the girls tied ribbons on all the statues in the garden. Gabe must have missed this one when he took his clippers to their prank.

She yanked at the ribbon and slipped into a puddle from Gabe's garden hose. "Gross," she groaned, examining the mud on her uniform. "Oh deer, look at my clothes," she muttered, glaring at the unsympathetic stone deer. To her surprise, Francie spotted a small stone beaver nuzzled up to the feet of St. Francis on his other side. "Gee, I've never noticed you before," she whispered and gave the beaver a pat on the head as if it were real. With that pat, and a little help from Beneficent Angel, the beaver and the deer took on a different quality, something like an animated film, and strangely enough, so did everything else in Pastor's prayer garden.

Francie ventured into a conversation with the stone critters: "Hypothetically speaking," she asked the statues, "what do you think of Sister Angelina's 'WHAT IF...' game? I mean, about God getting stolen."

She imagined the little beaver didn't quite know what to say. "Not sure? Shall I tell you what I think? I think nobody would be left! There'd be nothing in Pastor's prayer garden, but you and Deer and the rocks!"

Francie's head started to hurt. Stars and pinwheels of light alternated with black spots, zooming in, zooming out, now bright, now dark. She looked at her uniform covered in mud, then down the hillside to the Old Road, to the river, and Big City beyond. She felt ill and dizzy.

Francie O'Malley held her head. It pained her. She felt sad and forgotten and began to cry. "Where are you, Ma?"

"Things were changing in Francie's world," Lucy confessed to the girls in the garden. "She would never be the same again, and quite frankly, neither would I."

The girls settled into the world of Lucy's youth back in 1962, and the telling came easily to her. She asked them to picture the manicured garden where they sat, abandoned and overgrown, the buildings derelict and boarded up, the church, their school and the rectory all closed. And as they protested that it never could be, Lucy Penn began, for the first time, to tell her young audience *The Sword Lily Parables,* Francie O'Malley's amazing journey to the world of St. Mary's-of-the-Future.

PART TWO

Introduction to the Critters

St. Mary's-of-the-Future

A Story Within a Story

16

Along the Murky River

We will begin 'the story within our story' on the banks of the Murky River.

It would be nice to paint a beautiful scene here, one with weeping willow trees lazily dunking their fancy branches in the water. Where the birds chirping cheery melodies and a whiff of wildflowers and green grasses refresh us as we meander along the river's edge. It would be lovely to begin our story in this manner, but we can't.

Many things caused life along the river to change, not the least of which was the Picnic People. Oh my, the Picnic People, they did their share, it's true. Toss, throw, drop, plop, any which way they wanted, anywhere they chose.

The Picnic People disposed of their discarded wrappings in the fields and streams of the beautiful countryside without regard to the effects of such abandon, nor knowledge of the danger their carelessness caused to God's creatures and their environment.

You couldn't say, back then, it was entirely the fault of the Picnic People, not really. They just didn't know any better. The sad truth was, it went deeper than that.

17

How it Was

St. Mary's-of-the-Future

Most folks would say all the troubles began a long time ago when the holiest of men, Bishop Périgord, the Bishop of Midlantic, died, and no one could be found to replace him. It was during that transitional time, when the search for a promising candidate was underway, that the refinement and behavior of the peoples and critters of the mountain really fell off. One particular parish suffered the most—the Parish of Three Rivers.

A menacing spirit of mediocrity seeped into the ethers along the riverbanks, and everything began to change. One by one, the familiar scenes of peaceful fellowship faded away, and the temperament of man and beast became progressively more disagreeable. Friends who were friends became competitors, and then enemies. Kind salutations and comforting vocabulary turned sharp in the conversation of Talkers, and Talkers became Grumblers, and in time, the Grumblers became Yellers—oh, the racket! The Yellers, by some strange kind of spontaneous generation, spawned into Nasties. The Nasties morphed into Meanies and so forth. After that, you couldn't tell any of them apart, and life along the Murky River became an impossible place to be.

The Murky River was one of three rivers that flowed through the parish. It wasn't always known by that name; it used to be called the Mercy River.

In Little Capernaum, a section of Three Rivers, the church of Our Lady of Perpetual Help was situated. The critters knew it only as Olph's Dwelling-with-the-Bells. As if a lady called Olph lived there instead of the Lord.

Just above Our Lady's was St. Mary's School for Girls. At the bottom of the hill was Fishtown. It was situated on the docks of the Mercy River. Across the river was a peninsula, a spit of land with a sandy stretch of beach along the seashore. According to Garbo, the seashore had been a seasonal draw for 'day-trippers' since the Leni-Lenape tribes roamed those parts to hunt and fish.

Folks ferried in from Big City or took the bus to the roundabout, where the bus line ended and began. That was near the entrance to the Shanties, a desperate place for the poor, which was opposite the Great Bay Bridge, sometimes called the High Bridge, which leads back to Little Capernaum. It was all part of the Parish of Three Rivers, the largest parish in the Bishopric of Midlantic. The locals liked to say it was 'the entrance to the nation.'

Despite all the changes taking place, there was one family of critters along the riverbank that remained faithful to the old ways of nature and gentility. The critter couple was known as Mam and Pappy Beaver. They had many kits, and they raised them according to the natural order of things. They taught their kits how to build dams and lodges for themselves. They also taught them good manners and how to conform to the important set of rules that belonged to the folks of the mountain. The rules were etched, long ago, into great stones that served as the foundation for a notable rock that weighed nothing but stayed in place all the same. It was known as the Weightless Rock and was anchored in the grooves of those etched words.

On the morning they called the Lord's Day, the peoples of the mountain cleaned up their kits and gathered at the place of the Weightless Rock. The Beaver family, the Deer family, and others from the critter kingdom followed the peoples to. The entrance of Olph's Dwelling-With-the-Bells, where the critters assembled to listen for the singing. When the singing stopped, there would be shuffling of feet, the doors would open wide, and the bells would chime their glorious chorus. This stirred excitement in the critters outside because that was the sign the peoples would appear, and the critters would follow them to the picnic grounds for leisure time activities. This was a big event, and the critters could count on plenty of treats and treasures left behind when the peoples went home.

Some peoples encouraged the small critters to eat out of their hands. Others shooed them away. Funny enough, the shoo-away-peoples were the ones who left behind the most wrappers and containers. Some tossed them in the bushes; some left them right on the picnic tables. Mam Beaver could often be found working for her family, with teeth and claw, to pull free the remains of a thing the peoples called "candy." Everyone had wonderful afternoons at the picnic grounds on the Lord's Day.

Next door to Olph's Dwelling-with-the-Bells lived a man the peoples called Father John, a man of the cloth. He, and most like him, were especially good to all the creatures of the realm—peoples and critters alike. Father John and his black Labrador Retriever, a hefty dog often spotted with a red bandana around his neck, liked to hike down the Old Road to keep an eye on things. The road ran past the Forest of Solomon's Cedars, wound around Peony Patch, along the bluff, and down to the bay shore where the three rivers met the sea.

He was well-loved in these parts, and everyone nodded agreeably at Father John's wise words while the critters listened for the bells. His stories made the peoples laugh and sometimes made them cry. He never missed an opportunity to remind folks to look at life from God's point of view, especially on the day of the Lord.

These men of the cloth were ordained priests of the realm, and they were renowned for understanding and explanations. They knew what was right. They also knew what was wrong. And they knew what was in between, which was the hardest thing to sort out. Many considered Father John as something special among these men of the cloth. He was the pastor.

The rectory, where he lived, was not far from the Weightless Rock which was situated directly behind the church. It was strongly held that those who dwelt nearest the Weightless Rock were considered the luckiest of folks because the Weightless Rock contained the keys to eternal life.

Across Miller Street lived three small ladies. They wore veils and brown dresses that were tied in the middle with old rope. They were called Sisters, and Mam Beaver observed that this rope that each of them wore must have held them together, and, of course, in a way it did.

The Sisters frequented the picnic grounds too, but never before they watered the gardens. It was such an important task they extracted a promise from the Miller's wife, who lived next door, that in the event the Sisters went missing, she would continue to water the gardens just as they had done. Not forgetting the flowers in the Mother's Day garden, nor Pastor's prayer garden behind the rectory, nor the beds near the birdbath with the stone man dressed just like them, and most important of all, she was not to forget to water the Sword Lilies, the 12 Apostles, and the Ladders to Heaven. Those flowers needed to remain tall and strong. Especially the ones down the Old Road on the bluff overlooking the bay.

The Sisters often spoke of the days when the stone man in the prayer garden was a living man from ages past. His name was St. Francis and his spirit lived on and on, they said, because of his followers like themselves, who modeled their lives after his example.

St. Francis had the power to talk to animals. He made them understand the ways of all God's creatures. Nature, according to Francis, reflected a wee bit of the beauty of Heaven—and if this were so, Heaven was surely a grand place to live. Everyone was able to understand when Francis spoke, and all his followers tied their middles with old rope to hold themselves together and be like him, just like the Sisters did. And that old rope—it could stretch across centuries.

Also featured around the church grounds were a number of figures representing the critter kingdom. It was here in the habitat of the stone animals, in the vicinity of the Weightless Rock, that Mam Beaver came to know about human nature and the important rules that the peoples were directed to obey. The set of rules under the Weightless Rock affected all creatures, and everyone was obliged to abide by them without prejudice. For some it was too difficult, and in this, troubles festered.

"These ladies in the brown Francis robes are special," she observed, watching them carefully every day as they crossed the street, went into Olph's Dwelling, came out the other side, and into a lodge they called school. The Sisters taught the peoples' kits all about the rules that lay under the Weightless Rock. Mam Beaver learned to read and taught her kits the same, thinking it might prove useful someday with the peoples of the mountain.

In those days, Peace, Patience, Joy, Love, Kindness, Goodness, Gentleness, Generosity, Faithfulness, Modesty, Chastity, and Self-Control were honored guests. If invited in, they could change your life. They left you smiling, persevering, and content. Whatever you needed, they seemed to bring along. They lived near the Weightless Rock but were often seen fishing. The sightings were mostly by children, small critters, and a few older folks with special-seeing gifts. It was then that the waters sparkled with dancing stars, winking at the lucky ones who waded in to get a better look. It was imperceptible how the frequency of their appearances diminished, the river became grayer, and the sky became dull. It wasn't in a day, or a week, or any natural measure of time. Things just lost their luster, little by little, bit by bit, until the Mercy River became murky, and that's how it got its name: the Murky River.

After that, a few grouchy folks complained to the Magistrate that the bells of Olph's Dwelling were too noisy. The Angelus that once rang out at dawn, at noon, and quitting time every day eventually fell silent. The peoples became too busy to stop what they were doing to thank God for all they had, great or small. The custom of the bells and the prayers simply passed out of favor, and the bells rang out only on the Lord's Day until, after a time, they ceased altogether.

And then set in … *desolation.*

18

Desolation

St. Mary's-of-the-Future

F ew folks pay attention to what's really happening on the many planes of living realities. Many believe that dead is simply, dead. Some say there are no such things as pure spirits, like devils or angels; nothing could be further from the truth.

Everyone suffers the consequences when evil infects a being, or a place, whether they believe in it or not. It's the insignificant that suffer the most, the marginalized, the little ones, and the critters.

Terrible things happened here—too terrible to tell. But the story of how the earth shook and all goodness forsook the mountain, the riverbank, and almost the whole of the Midlantic Realm can best be understood by following the adventures of some improbable heroes who stepped up to the Assignment of Angels without even knowing it. Nor can it be appreciated without the story of how the youngest kit of Mam and Pappy Beaver escaped the fate of the others and earned a spot in Pastor's prayer garden, for all time, alongside her best friend Deer, at the feet of St. Francis of Assisi.

Their story began when Little Beaver wandered away from her lodge, even though her parents warned her to stay close. She didn't mean to be disobedient, but she had an eye for pretty things, and it was just such a thing that— well—caught her eye. Little Beaver noticed a slick of red fabric in the brush, and when she couldn't pull it free, she spent some time gnawing through a branch to bring the prize home to her Mam, branch, and all.

"If you bring these bits of fancy into our lodge, Littlest, they'll attract the hunters, or worse still, the trappers."

These words would haunt Little Beaver in the future, but at the time, Mam would succumb to the pleas of her youngest kit and tuck the prize into the walls of their lodge. Pappy often scolded Mam to leave the frivolous clutter left behind by the Picnic People alone. "Once our kits taste candy, they will not be satisfied with bark," he cautioned, "and mark my words, enchantment with the peoples' colorful paraphernalia will one day be our undoing."

On what became known as the Terrible Day, Little Beaver bundled together special twigs, tying them up with some string she had found. The bundle became so large she eventually resorted to seeking the aid of her best friend, Deer, as usual, to cart them home.

"Come on, Deerie, help me carry my stuff. I wraps 'em up so careful. I need to take all of it, please, Deerie Deer."

Deer was reluctant at first, for all too often, Little Beaver had persuaded him to join her in time-consuming projects, but eventually, he gave in.

Beaver expertly rigged up an intricate litter to cart her stuff home and attached it to Deer with a sky-blue sash ending in a bow at his neck. Still, it was not without complaint that Deer dragged the useless burden.

Nothing could impair Little Beaver's sense of fun. She ran beside him, making jokes, fluffing up the bow around his neck, reminding him often that this was a reward. She added every ornament they passed along the way to her treasure trove, never noticing the slight difference in the atmosphere, until Deer slowed to a stop. His sharp ears perked up as he stood motionless. "Beaver, be still as a stone," he whispered.

"What's wrong with you, Deerie?" Little Beaver asked in her playful way.

"It's not me," Deer said, on edge. "It's the riverbank."

"I don't hear nothing, Deer, I don't hear noth' at all."

"That's what I mean," he said, "I don't hear anything either."

They looked at each other uneasily, then ran as fast as they could over the hill to where Beaver's family lodge once sat skillfully built into the riverbank.

The vision before them was shattering. They remained at a standstill stunned by the sight. Beaver's heart thumped to a gallop, then crashed inside her.

"How's this happen, Deer? How's this ever happen?"

Her lodge was trampled to ruin. Her whole family was gone. Little Beaver's tears were too big for her eyes, but they wouldn't come out. She looked with her bleary vision for Deer. Through the watery blur, she saw him thrashing wildly, trying to free himself of the broken litter. He was running in circles, searching for his mother. Not there, no one was there, nary a bird, nor a bug was found, not a sound could be heard.

Stamped in the mud was a dreaded symbol of fear and destruction: the boot print of a hunter. Little Beaver ran to Deer, grabbing hold of the shredded blue ribbon. She wiped her eyes and pulled him to a halt, burying her face in the soft neck of her friend, then hurried to free him from the pile of trinkets attached to his back. Together they bravely approached the trampled lodge again. Little Beaver's childhood home was leveled, her Pappy's intricate work broken and twisted beyond recognition. The muddy waters lapped at its pitiful remains. Worse still was the hollow sound of the wind whistling through it.

"Mam, Pappy—where are you?" she cried. "Where they go, Deerie? Where's my fam?"

Deer sniffed around. There was no sign of life. He looked helplessly at the stricken kit. Little Beaver, immersed in the muddy mess, found the slick of red cotton, and held it up to Deer in horror.

Heartsick, he stood above Beaver nudging her with his nose, then knelt in the mud beside her. He spoke gently, trying to be strong and brave. "It's not your fault, Beaver, it's not. Don't blame yourself."

Little Beaver's tears burst forth. The two friends cried together for a long time. Darkness came, their families had scattered or worse, it was certain.

"Hunter found our lodge…my Mam…my cloth..."

"Don't!" said Deer. "They ran away, fearful for their lives, fearful they would lose their skins. That's all—they scattered—and they'll come back to the riverbank. We'll watch out for them. We'll wait for them here." Deer calmed himself. "I'll help you clean up."

Little Beaver looked at Deer with soulful but trusting eyes. Deer was resolute. "You'll see, our families will return when they think it's safe."

Little Beaver remained in the ruined lodge, too worried to run. She feared that her family might return and think her dead. So, confident in Deer's words, she waited.

Months went by, but their families didn't return. Deer stayed nearby and helped Little Beaver learn to take care of herself. They gathered twigs and bark for food and branches to rebuild her lodge. Some of the woods creatures returned to the riverbank, but fewer than before. Not even one had news of Deer and Little Beaver's missing relatives.

As time passed, the pair of friends took long journeys together in search of their lost families. They made countless inquiries along the riverbank and came to know every rock and reed, every flea and bee in the entire Parish of Three Rivers.

They also discovered where the enemy camped. They brought fearful stories of evil escapades back to the riverbank. They saw with their own eyes the threatening ship, remarkable in its size and darkness, now on the horizon, now on the river, and finally anchored permanently at the precise place where the three rivers

met the sea in the Great Bay—now called Gray Bay.

All the critters believed it was an abandoned vessel, a kind of ghost ship, but it wasn't. There was nothing empty about the boat on the Gray Bay.

It's sad to say that their searching proved fruitless. Never once in all their travels did anyone report a sighting of Mam or Pappy Beaver, their many kits, nor the Deer Family—not a clue remained after the Terrible Day.

19

Little Beaver and Deer Grow Up

St. Mary's-of-the-Future

As they grew up together along the Murky River, Little Beaver tried to remember the past. She tried to behave in the mannerly way Mam did. Little Beaver spoke no ill of another and settled many a squabble along the riverbank. Beaver wanted to cling to the days before her family and friends had fallen to the hunters. Or was it the trappers? Whoever it was, they left their menacing boot stamps in the mud along the riverbank where she once had a home.

Thanks to Pappy Beaver's diligent training, Little Beaver had good dam-building skills and rebuilt her family lodge in no time.

But, without Mam, she stopped going up to Olph's-Dwelling-with-the-Bells on the Lord's Day. And soon enough, Little Beaver got caught up in the pretensions that were seeping into everyday life along the riverbank. She reverted to her collections and perfected her lodge to such an extent she won the 'Best Looking Lodge' competition. This and similar honors were gratifying for a while, but sooner or later, the savory taste of success faded, leaving her wanting more, something else. She couldn't grasp what it was, so she started making a list of what it wasn't. The moment she lost interest in something, she put it on her *'List of What it Wasn't.'* Her list got exceptionally long. Deer accused her of being a malcontent and became cross whenever Little Beaver brought out her list.

"Hmmm, this isn't quite right, that isn't quite enough," she'd say.

"Why isn't it enough?" Deer would snap bitterly. "You're never satisfied! BE HAPPY!"

But Little Beaver wasn't happy. She wanted to remember her Mam and Pappy and what life was like before the disappearance of her family. It was all gray and fuzzy now. Try as she might, "happy" was too hard to remember. It was a leftover word. One of many such useless words Mam had taught her to sound out with Olph's alphabets. Deer didn't really know what "happy" meant at all. And poor Little Beaver couldn't recall.

20

An Introduction to Some Appalling Characters

One day, when the angels of God came to present themselves before the LORD, Satan also came among them. And the LORD said to Satan, "Whence do you come?" Then Satan answered the LORD and said, "From roaming the earth and patrolling it." Book of Job 1:6-7

St. Mary's-of-the Future

About the same time the Nasties morphed into Meanies and unpleasantness abounded, a horrid line of the Picnic People spawned, which caused a great threat to the critter kingdom. These descendants of the Picnic People terrorized the forest, the riverbank, everywhere. They were mean spirited and thoughtless, leaving fires burning in the forest, and trash without treasures. They screamed at each other and at their cubs during their leisure-time activities. Their screechy anger disturbed the earth, made the grass die, and the fires spread.

Bully Bargumo, a name that suited him well, was the leader of this horrid extraction, but Bully, you might say, was a 'prawn' to a much bigger fish, the captain of the dark vessel anchored in the Gray Bay—namely, Cell Fish.

Cell Fish was hell-bent on taking over the entire realm, and he knew just how to do it. He would take command of the Weightless Rock. Having obtained entry by knocking Bishop Périgord off his boat, he gained a solid foothold in Three Rivers. The rest seemed easy enough: control by patrol, that was the name of his game, and he appointed Bully Bargumo as the new Mayor of Three Rivers to help him.

Cell Fish assigned to Bully his number one official duty: evict the priests and confiscate the church property and all its wealth—little though it was in that particular neighborhood. Bully didn't get it, at first, that it was the Weightless Rock that Cell Fish was after.

To their utter surprise, the pastor refused to obey Bully's demands. This may have made Bully furious, and even nastier than usual, but it sent Cell Fish into an apoplectic seizure, which bollixed up his internal organs something fierce. This created enormous red boils all over his body that grew one out of another, until they burst, spewing green-grey venom into the Bay, eventually causing its awful discoloration. That's when the Great Bay became the Gray Bay.

The effects of these fits were disastrous. Chaos fell upon the natural order of things, causing many water creatures to die. Frightened critters left the riverbank in droves for fear of starvation. Under Bully's administration, Cell Fish produced so much thick green slime that it washed up on the shore like seaweed. Many peoples from the mountain mistakenly thought it would make good fertilizer and carried it up the mountain by the bucket full—even by the truck-load—and mixed it with the soil.

It crept over the mountain and the roads, until it finally reached the foundation of the Weightless Rock, causing the rock to be less secure. During a violent storm, the Weightless Rock shook away from its pinning, moving closer and closer to the edge of its foundation. And with one final rumbling of thunder, it tipped off the side and began to slide. The commotion of the Weightless Rock dislodging from its ancient foundation provoked the earth still further. It trembled, it split, and it quaked, causing great havoc the likes of which had never happened before. The Rock tumbled down the mountainside at breakneck speed, carving a gully behind it as it slid. It stopped a hair short of Quicksand Pit, at the edge of Fishtown, but it never fell in.

The parish grounds fell into a sad state of disrepair. Folks were scared, but it didn't cause anyone to volunteer to help Pastor. No one wanted to get involved in his troubles. And without the Weightless Rock, fewer and fewer peoples went up to Olph's Dwelling-with-the-Bells.

Some say the cracks in the mountain from that tumble were so severe they reached all the way down to Hell Itself, setting free all kinds of evil spirits to roam the earth seeking the ruin of souls. They manifested all over the Realm of Midlantic, but most significantly in Three Rivers where the event occurred.

Cell Fish constantly ranted and raved about controlling the Weightless Rock. And Bully was made acutely aware of the importance of that control by a particular beating he got from Cell Fish knocking him viciously about the head. Bully was seen for weeks after that beating still sporting big raw welts on his face.

Bully enacted the harshest of local laws, restrictions, and curfews. Even so, the citizens still resisted his authority. Most folks assumed his stepped-up cruelty was a byproduct of his discomfort, but it wasn't. He had learned a valuable lesson about power from that beating, and he was now after that power, for himself—with a vengeance. He was obsessed with the desire to unseat Pastor John *and* Cell Fish. "I will be the one who speaks in the name of the Weightless Rock," he told his buddies, "then the peoples of the mountain will do whatever I say."

You see, Bully had inadvertently learned from Cell Fish's furious rants (between wallops on his face) that control of the special properties of the Weightless Rock entitled the possessor to the keys of eternal life. The beating was a bargain price for such knowledge, and he aimed to have this prize. He pictured himself on the bridge deck of the dark tanker, with evil Cell Fish working for him. Revenge like that was worth a beating or two.

Bully planned to steal the Weightless Rock. He gathered a group of his bungling cronies, and in the dead of night, they inched their way down the gully to the place where the Weightless Rock had settled. Although it was weightless, try as they might, neither Bully Bargumo nor any of his lackeys could get the huge thing to budge. Bully's thugs couldn't lift it, nor could they push it up the hill, yet even with their clumsy efforts the Weightless Rock never tipped into Quicksand Pit.

The gang of them became so angry they cursed and stomped until they woke up Badad Vice from a 700 hundred year long nap! Bully was sure sorry that happened.

Badad's head rose out of the muck and mire of the boiling pit where he lived, shouting and roaring. "What's going on here?"

He was a creature of bestial appearance, matted and hairy. He had nubs of tusks and other features of a wild boar distorting any similarity to a human face. He also had aquatic features and abilities evolving from living so long beneath the earth in the steaming mud. No one knew the size of him. No one had ever seen the whole of him.

Bully was shaking. "Good evening, Badad, let me introduce myself. I'm the new Ma-Ma-Mayor of Three Rivers and—"

"Mayor? Mayor or not," the hideous fiend barked, "I don't like to be disturbed."

"Sorry, Badad, sorry, sorry, sorry—sorry to disturb you! You know it wasn't intentional. I-I've j-just come to take the Weightless Rock away and put it on its righteous foundation." Bully stuttered out his lame explanation while darting a nervous glance at his cronies (who went cross-eyed at that whopper of a lie).

Bully couldn't very well steal the Weightless Rock with Badad swimming around all riled up. He tried to calm the ogre down, but Badad Vice would have none of it.

"You're an incompetent Mayor, if you ask me, and you can't have the Weightless Rock. I'm taking custody of the Rock myself." Badad barked.

That's how he came to put his agent Feara Phalin in charge of guarding the Weightless Rock.

"And furthermore, to getsome sleep, I'm making a new edict:

No one can restore the Weightless Rock to its righteous foundation on the mountain except someone sent by the Powers That Be.

"And, from what Feara reports, thanks to you, Mayor, there's no one like that around these parts anymore." Then he hollered, "So, beat it! And leave my Weightless Rock alone!"

Badad churned in the bubbling mud, looking for his indentured slave. "Feara, get up here!" he bellowed. And with that blood-curdling order, a buzzing noise began, and Badad Vice sank back into the elements with a blubbery, blub, blub.

Up rose a swarm of mayflies giving form to a threatening creature that dripped a repugnant blackish liquid into Badad's steaming pit.

Bargumo and his bullies didn't stick around to formally meet Feara. Anybody indentured to Badad would be a reliably fierce guardian. Badad was the ancient son of Abaddon, who was such an evil character he even made Cell Fish gulp! No one found it necessary to challenge him or risk his wrath. They ran for their lives.

So, there sat the Weightless Rock, under the guard of Feara Phalin. Folks said the bubbles in the boiling pit were caused by Feara's eyes blinking, but if the truth be known, nobody ever got close enough to be absolutely certain. And nobody ever came to collect the Weightless Rock either. Nobody even tried to put it back where it belonged. There wasn't a single soul in all of Three Rivers who could claim to be sent by the Powers That Be.

21

The Right Eye of the Realm

St. Mary's-of-the-Future

Father Ed adjusted the patch over his left eye took the black valise and headed south. He was known as the Right Eye of the Realm. Only he could do the job of keeping an eye out for trouble on behalf of the Bishop.

The patch bore the coat of arms of the Realm, and Father Ed wore it with pride as a symbol of his position. He would look forward to a new assignment of another special job. He had always been in great demand.

Father Ed was sent into a parish in need of help. When a plague of lethargy preyed upon its liturgy, or any other malignancy whatsoever seeped into the fiber of a parish, Father Ed was sent in to assist. It was always the same, and it was always a difficult mission. His job was to remain there to keep its pulse and breathe its breath until the man of destiny for that particular place appeared. Sometimes these places were bleeding from the purse, sometimes from the heart, but regardless of the problem, Father Ed was sent there by Mystical Decree to watch over them and he often risked everything to ensure continued breathability.

According to Father Ed (and no one else could explain it better), parishes were not just places to be, or to pray, or to go to school. They were living, breathing communities in their own right. They had purpose, vitality, and personality, especially the old parishes established long ago by the great Bishop Périgord.

Sadly, since no one was able to fill Bishop Périgord's holy shoes, Father Ed's excellent services were needed all the more—technically speaking. Seeing his assignments came from the bishop, and with no bishop for all of Midlantic, the entire realm remained vulnerable to the ever-tightening grip of Cell Fish. And Cell Fish was making rapid progress unencumbered by the wise leadership of a holy man.

Under the circumstances, Father Ed did his best to do his job. Following this tip and that, he drifted from one place to another pumping breath into the lifeless carcasses of empty parishes that were harassed by Cell Fish.

Father Ed had just taken up residence at the Parish of Our Lady's on the Old Road at the invitation of Father John, who had recently noticed some alarming changes in his flock's behavior. Having no place to go, and no Bishop from whom to receive an assignment, Father Ed was happy to accept.

It was soon after he unpacked that the final devastation fell upon the parish. Bully Bargumo barreled up to the rectory and attached the bitterest seal on the door, *Eviction!*

Widow Miller, who lived across the street, heard the commotion and rushed to the church. Despite her dimming eyesight, she rummaged around the sacristy until she found the black valise. At the last moment, fearful that it would fall into the wrong hands, she thrust it into the arms of Father Ed, urging him to take the precious cargo of the Bread of Life with him, and of course, he did.

"Take it to Tom," she said, "at St. Anthony's Lost and Found. He'll bury it in a safe place until our own man of destiny comes to unearth it and return it to the center altar."

"I'll do it," Father Ed said and flew out the door.

"Tom will guard it with his life," she called after him, wishing him Godspeed. "I'm sure of that!"

Father Ed escaped with the black valise out the back door, just steps ahead of Bully Bargumo who came back with his hammer and nails to board up the place. When Bully saw that all the priests were already gone, he was full of fury. He had hoped to take one or two of them as prisoners.

He nailed up the rectory, then went into the church where he found the empty tabernacle on the altar—the door ajar. The school was empty too. Bully was so angry he took over the whole place and declared it confiscated for use as community property.

Father Ed headed down the Old Road and tried to return to peaceful thought by planning a route for his journey. He would cross the High Bridge, and once on the mainland, he would walk along the shoreline. The sea would be his companion, and he would attempt to forget all that he left behind in this dark place.

But before he left Three Rivers, Father Ed went to the dock of St. A's and searched for Tom. He transferred the black valise into his care, and Tom promised to guard it with his life, just as Widow Miller said he would.

"Well, I'll just be heading up to the High Bridge now, and continue on my way," Father Ed said, excusing himself.

"Where are you going?" Tom asked, cradling the black valise.

"To the mainland," Father Ed replied.

"It's called the Uppity Bridge now, Father," said Tom. "By order of Cell Fish, it's stuck in a permanent 'up' position to prevent any escape from Three Rivers. Can't take the Uppity Bridge to the mainland," he said, "but there is a way to cross."

And soon enough, two fellows in a flatboat glided toward them on the bay. These two young men, who were once captured and tortured by Cell Fish, but refused to serve him. Willy's hand was badly mangled and Bully, thinking him useless, tossed him out like so much refuse, and Oz too, his leg being severely infected. Willy found Oz unconscious in the forest, and they made their way to St. A's where they found a doctor down on his luck. Oz lost his leg,but the kind doctor fashioned a prosthesis for him. Oz was soagile by natural ability, it hardly held him back. The pair stucktogether and became fast friends. Having discovered they bothhad a sense of adventure; the two strapping boys built their boat.“This is Willy, and this is Oz,” Tom said. “They will ferry you over to the continuation of the Old Road. It's known as the

Coast Road on the mainland.”

“Hello, Father,” Oz said with a winning smile.

Willy, was a little shyer, but cordial enough to be sure. His disfigured hand did nothing to hinder his ability with a rope or an oar as he prepared the boat for their new client.

Oz was handsome, with sandy hair constantly falling in his eyes. He sprang from the boat to the dock with impressiveagility unimpaired by his peg-leg.

Father Ed climbed tentatively into the flatboat and settled in. Tom waved good-bye as Willy and Oz pushed off the dock for another dangerous trip across the Gray Bay.

Tom hiked halfway up the mountain, passed the forest of Solomon's Cedars to the open bluff overlooking the bay. It had once been a ballpark in better days, not a stone's throw from the old clam hut known as the Crabby House. There was a time when you could look beyond the fishing jetty and on out to sea, but not anymore. The atmosphere was gloomy now, and wet with mist and fog. Tom got to work, digging a deep resting place for the black valise. With loving care, he placed it there, buried it, said a blessing, and left.

PART THREE

The Bishop, The Great Périgord,
and
The Plan

The Future of the Southerly Coast

22

Francie's Fear

May 1962
Same Monday, 6:00 o'clock

The bells of St. Mary's were ringing. It was six o'clock, and the sound of the children shuffling around in the small chapel indicated class was finished. As the church bells rang, the shuffling stopped. The children stood quietly to recite the Angelus.

Sister Angelina led the prayer,

> *"The Angel of the Lord declared unto Mary."*

The class responded,

> *"And she conceived of the Holy Ghost."*

They still said the Angelus three times a day at St. Mary's, even if the rest of the world had stopped. Francie found herself reciting the familiar prayer to herself with the class.

"Hail Mary full of grace,
The Lord is with thee.
Blessed art thou amongst women,
and blessed is the fruit
of thy womb, Jesus.
Holy Mary Mother of God,
pray for us sinners,
now and at the hour of our death.
Amen."

Francie's reverie was abruptly interrupted by a car horn. Honk-honk, beep-beep!

Again, Sister Angelina,
"Behold the handmaid of the Lord,"

And the class,
"Be it done unto me according to Thy word."

Another Hail Mary,

"And the Word was made flesh and dwelt amongst us."

A third Hail Mary…

The jarring ring of the rectory telephone competed with the ringing church bells. Garbo picked up the phone. "Our Lady of Perpetual Help, can I help ya?"

Francie overheard Garbo carrying on through the kitchen window and detected annoyance in her voice. It had to be that irritating woman in the neighborhood who called about the bells. She called every night at 6:05 to complain. Garbo said you could set your watch by it. She knew it was time to go home when that call came.

"Yeah, I did tell him yer angry. No, Mrs. Ribaldi, he's not gonna stop ringin' the bells. It's St. Mary's month of May, don'tcha know, and this here parish will be ringin' the bells!"

Garbo got an earful from Mrs. Ribaldi but was not to be outdone.

" 'Course he's aware of yer connections. Should ya bring it up at the next town council? As far as I can tell, ain't nobody stoppin' ya. Good evenin', Mrs. Ribaldi!"

Garbo slammed the phone down with a scornful grumble. "Put a sock in it, ya old hag!"

Another beep from the car horn collided with the prayer bells and muffled Garbo's ranting on about Mrs. Ribaldi being an atheist. "She don't wanna listen to the Angelus ring. Imagine? The nerve—hatin' church bells."

Sister Angelina opened the door to the small chapel and pitched her last-ditch effort for the children's attention. "Tomorrow is rehearsal. We'll be processing in the church under the standard of our beloved parish. She held up a banner, on which a great white goose outlined in flight above a church on a hillside was depicted. Atop the church, in golden thread, was a cross, and beneath it were three wavy lines representing Three Rivers. These were the symbols of their Bishop and their Parish.

"And what does this mean?" She asked the class pointing to the embroidered gold letters, OLPH, on a sky-blue background. "Our Lady of Perpetual Help," the children cheered.

"Correct! Now let us make our sainted Bishop Périgord rejoice in heaven, as our Church blossoms with your zeal. This is who you are … this is the real meaning of life. Dear ones, you can do it! Be my brave and holy soldiers of Jesus Christ. Class dismissed."

Francie saw her mother waving from the car and began to collect her things. The class stampeded past Sister Angelina who was calling out encouragements to them to embrace the cross and live the faith. They almost trampled Francie sitting in the grass as they ran past her in their bolt for freedom.

"Children! Read between the lines as you study your assignment," Sister Angelina called after them. She glanced down and noticed a dazed Francie on the ground.

"I love my job," Sister chirped. The spirited nun raised her hands up, took a twirl, and let them fall with a slap at her sides. "This is my job! I energize each knight—but it's the angels that guide the soldiers of Christ!"

Francie knew these words well, curious as they were. After classes, you could hear Sister Angelina's voice ringing through the hallways of St. Mary's, joyfully proclaiming the good news of Jesus Christ. Today, she spoke to the children in the chapel, but Sister Angelina's love for God couldn't be contained in one tiny chapel. Francie knew it was meant for the entire universe.

The lovely nun raised Francie up from the soggy grass. She touched her finger to Francie's nose. "Always be a witness to your faith, Francine. That's how we crusade for Christ in modern times. You aren't hurt, are you, dear?"

"No, I'm okay, Sister," Francie replied, shaking off the mud.

"Why you've been crying," Sister Angelina said, surprised.

"Yeah, I just slipped and got kinda dirty. My mother's here now." Francie pointed toward the car.

Sister Angelina gave her a pinch on the cheek. "I'm so glad. Bonsoir, ma petite chère."

Sister Angelina was everyone's favorite. She was so dedicated to Jesus, she wanted everyone to love Him as much as she did. Poor Sister Angelina would never understand that absolutely nobody alive in the 1960s could love Jesus like she did. Well, at least nobody Francie knew, and she thought it was kind of adorable. She pictured Sister Angelina at the pearly gates with a dossier reporting all her holy deeds. She could become a famous saint, and Francie could say she knew a saint personally. According to Garbo, Sister Angelina was only about 30, so it wouldn't be for a long time.

"Please, God, don't let Sister Angelina down. I don't think she meant any disrespect by saying You might get stolen. I think she only meant for us to—you must know what she meant. You're still up there, aren't You? I mean, don't go anywhere. Amen."

Francie, happy with her prayer, and promising to be more respectful in the future, shoved the faded blue ribbon from the neck of the stone deer into her pocket and whispered an apology to St. Francis for desecrating his statue. What was happening? She really felt like she was talking to St. Francis! Whatever it was, whatever she had just witnessed, it was real. The critters were real, so very, very real, but how could that be?

The sound of the spring stretching on the screen door told her Garbo was leaving. In a second, it would slam, and Garbo would appear with a covered dish.

"Are ya deaf, child? Can't you hear yer mother beepin'?"

"I–I know, I'm getting my stuff."

Francie scrambled about, retrieving her books scattered on the grass.

Garbo was alarmed at the ethereal whiteness of her face. "Whatever on earth is the matter with ya, Francie? Yer lookin' real pale, like ya seen a ghost or somethin'!"

Francie sat back on her heels and looked up at Garbo wide-eyed. "Maybe I did, Garb. Maybe I saw the Holy Ghost."

"Don't blaspheme, Francine. It ain't becomin'."

Francie got up and held her books in both arms in expectation of Garbo plopping the hot casserole right on top, which she did. They started across the lawn together toward the car.

"Garbo ... do you think it's possible ... I mean, is there any chance that ..."

"What?" Garbo asked.

Francie had second thoughts. How could she explain what just happened? "Nothing. Never mind," she shrugged it off and tried to leave the desolate scene, or vision, or whatever it was behind her.

"Yer mystifyin', Kiddo, can't answer yer question unless ya ask it."

"It's nothing."

They made their way down the few steps to Miller Street. Francie's mom, Dr. Annie, as everyone called her, rolled down the car window in anticipation of the casserole handoff. She had an enchanting smile, so said her husband, but she didn't go in for makeup. A quick brush through her salt and pepper hair, which she wore tucked behind her ears, was about all the fuss she could muster. She wore a good tweed jacket and pearls and insisted the combination had her dressed for all occasions.

"How's my girl?" Dr. Annie asked, trying to hide her guilt. She took the warm dish and balanced it on her lap. She waved to Garbo, and Garbo waved back. Francie hopped in the car and took the casserole back. They were both quiet.

Dr. Annie broke the silence as she started up the motor, bracing herself for battle. "I'm sorry I'm so late, sweetie, I'll make it up to you."

Anne O'Malley constantly worried that she had abandoned her home before her child had fully grown. Facing Francie after a conflict arose at the clinic, which too often spoiled their plans, was difficult. Anne had constructed a resilient veneer over the years, but even so, she was aware of the chasm between them. As the practice of medicine infringed on their time together, her youngest daughter was growing up.

They barely spoke to each other without having a quarrel. Anne knew that Francie confided in Garbo more than she did in her own mother. She wasn't surprised, but she wasn't quite sure what to do about it. Garbo had looked after her youngest daughter since she was a tot. The arrangement had started out for medical emergencies only until almost every day had its emergency. On weekends, Francie's father, Bert, was home and delighted in the care and spoiling of his youngest daughter. And now, Francie was 12 years old and preferred the company of her friends. Dr. Annie missed out on her baby's childhood, and no one knew it better than Francie.

Her mother tiptoed into the waters of war. "There was no way out, Francie, there really wasn't."

"It's alright," Francie said quietly.

"So many sick children," Anne continued almost to herself. "Shall we run to the shop and see if Mrs. Penn can find us something pretty.

"It's closed, Ma. It's okay. We'll go another time."

"I know I promised you Francie, I'm—"

"Mommy, forget it. I don't care about the dress. I can go with Lucy after school. It's no big deal. I'll wear something I have—honest."

Anne did her best to keep her eyes on the road while she checked her daughter's pale cheeks and glazed eyes. There had to be a medical explanation for this uncharacteristically mellow behavior. She was braced for a fight but there was no fight in Francie. She resolved to take her daughter's temperature as soon as they got out of the car. She turned right onto the Old Road and headed south down the steep hill, past the church, across the bay to River Ridge, and their beautiful home on the water.

23

Francie's Fear Confronted

May 1962

Francie went upstairs to her large pretty bedroom. It was decorated when Francie was 8 years old. Their home was on the house tour that year to raise money for the hospital, and all the ladies in town raved it was the loveliest bedroom ever, even in the magazines. Tossed from a painted basket across the soft cream background of the wallpaper, tumbled sweet pastel flowers and wisps of blue ribbon. It matched seam for seam with the polished chintz fabric of her canopy bed. Francie thought it was too babyish for a pre-teen and wanted to redecorate, but her mom hadn't gotten around to it yet. Same old story, too busy.

She hugged her teddy bear, a staunch old friend that had sat upright on her bed ever since she was little. He was a good listener, like always, as she considered whether to tell Pastor what she had seen on the beach.

"Will he think I'm crazy, Bearie? What if Pastor decides I should be locked away forever in some attic like the poor lady we read about in Jane Eyre? I'd have to burn the place down to get out. I couldn't do that. Or, even worse, he would have me committed to an insane asylum, and Mom would have to sign the papers because she's the doctor! She probably would too."

She was afraid—afraid to close her eyes, afraid to tell anyone what she saw on the beach. Sitting at her vanity brushing her hair, Francie mentally dramatized her mother's concern for her into medical malpractice. "She's been looking at me really funny ever since I saw it," Francie whimpered to bear. "She couldn't know what I saw, nobody could know—unless it told them. What if it's following me? What if I brought it to St. Mary's, and now awful things are gonna happen?"

This was Francie's worst fear, and she needed relief, but how could she explain it? How could she describe the flashcards of evil that flipped before her 'inside eyes' in an instant? It seemed like a hundred years, but it was only a moment.

"I can still see it, plain as day, twined round with those heavy chains, and drippy seaweed, and covered with barnacles and mussel shells, and all kinds of rags and junk people toss overboard. Oh, Bearie, if it wasn't the devil, it came from the same place! I'm convinced of that much."

It rose out of the sea and dragged itself ashore. It smelled as if it were burning. And that wasn't all Francie smelled, she smelled death. Francie had never smelled death, but she was sure that's what she smelled. Another flash—a beautiful young bride, so pink and pretty and full of life—just then it washed up on the beach. Her veil wrapped around her like a burial cloth, and another grubby creature tugged her onto the shore. He ripped the rings off her finger and slashed through her veil with a knife to get her pearls. She saw the bride's face peaceful, as if in sleep, then decayed. That's when she felt the cold, then a push, and her necklace fell to the sand. She relived it a thousand times.

Ever since then, she was haunted by clips of desolation. People, like slaves, jammed into black tankers crossing the bay in darkness, children wandering around in the dampness without coats, or even sweaters, and no gloves. And sweet little critters struggling through a smutty greenish fog in an unknown wilderness that once was Three Rivers. Sometimes the fog was opaque, sometimes just a gray mist. It smothered the daytime and made the sunshine disappear. Everything turned to shadow. Then— FLASH—back to Evil Sands, where the tide was coming in, the water lapping over the bride. For a moment, Francie was heartened, she saw the bride move, but it was only a crab caught in her veil. And there were words too. Words crying out from far away in the future—or was it from the past? "Help me," the distant voice mourned, "You must try to help me!"

Sister Angelina taught them confession was the great Sacrament of Reconciliation, an outward sign instituted by Christ to give grace. Even the Pope had to go to confession from time to time to unburden his soul and be reconciled with the Lord. And so, in the end, Francie concluded the only way to get relief was to go to confession tomorrow and unburden her soul to Pastor, like the Pope did.

Because it was an official visit, the next day, Francie went the long way around to the rectory's front entrance. She circled the big side porch and Gabe's perfect bushes, then slowly climbed the wide stairs. Considering running away with every riser, she took baby steps to the stately front door. After much hesitation, she rang the bell. It was an eternity before anyone came to answer.

"Francie! What are ya doin', makin' me walk through this whole house to answer the front door?" Garbo snapped. "What's gotten into ya?"

That was exactly what Francie wanted to find out. Was she possessed? She couldn't tell. "It's official business, and you should feel sorry for me instead of getting mad."

"Whatever fer?" Garbo asked.

"Nothing," Francie said righteously. "I want to see Pastor. I want to go to confession."

"Well, he ain't here. You'll have to go to confession to me first, and I'll tell ya whether ya oughta bother him or not, or ya can wait till Saturday. Come on now, sit down and tell me what's on yer mind."

"You're not allowed to hear confession, Garb. Even if we tell you some secrets. Only a priest can hear confession." They both giggled at the housekeeper's proposal as Francie followed Garbo through the drafty foyer of the old rectory, past the QueenAnne banister, polished to a high shine, past the chapel, through the refectory, into the kitchen. She took a chair, scraping the floor as she pulled it away from the table, and sat down silently to gather her thoughts.

Francie quickly concluded getting Pastor involved had its drawbacks. What she wanted to confide in him didn't really count as a sin, except for the part about 'disobeying your parents', which he already heard about. They were in enough trouble for going to the beach off-season, nobody even knew the part about going to Evil Sands. She had to be extra careful, she couldn't risk getting her friends kicked off the class trip. Therefore, she decided it probably wasn't a bad idea to run the whole thing by Garbo. Garbo had definitely known some shady characters in her day and might not be as shocked as, say, Sister Serena.

"I've seen something terrible, Garb."

"Is that a fact?" Garbo said, waiting for a tall tale.

"I can't shake it out of my head, I can't. It's a fearful, terrible thing. And I mean—the bride, the poor little critters, the people on the black boats—they couldn't be real, could they? But they are real! I know it's true."

Garbo was baffled. She pushed her face back in a frown like a hen getting ready to peck. These kids were always pulling pranks, she was hesitant to get sucked in and have the joke be on her.

"They're probably haunting me cause of what I did."

"What could ya possibly've done to cause ya all this misery? Yer blessed with a vivid imagination, is all. That's what Sister Ed would say."

"I saw what it was like. I know what I saw," Francie insisted.

"Saw what? What 'what' was like, child? You've lost me," Garbo said exasperated.

"Without God," Francie whispered, "what the world would be like without God. Right here at Our Lady's. It was awful. The whole place was overgrown—all Pastor's statues in his prayer garden broken to pieces. It was deserted and gloomy."

"Saints preserve us!" Garbo said. "What kinda talk is this?"

"Am I going crazy?" Francie asked. "I don't want anything to happen to Saint Mary's. I love St. Mary's. I don't want to be crazy, Garbo!" Francie dissolved in tears, her head collapsing on her arms on the kitchen table. Garbo rolled her eyes and tried to comfort her, not having the foggiest idea what she was talking about.

"I saw these things. I really did. And I saw something even worse, but I can't tell you about that! I can't tell anyone."

"I think ya oughta see the nurse."

"My mother's a doctor. I don't need to see the nurse."

"Suit yerself then," Garbo said, pulling back.

"Do you think—is it possible—for God to get stolen?" Francie asked. Garbo was silent.

Maybe she had made a mistake trusting Garbo, but the visions of darkness overtaking her world filled her with apprehension. She was fearful that the evil thing from the beach had attached itself to her, or at least was following her around. What if she had brought it here, and it was planning to steal God right out of the church and take over the world? It would be all her fault for disregarding all the warnings not to go to Evil Sands, and in the end, everyone would know that she was the cause of the desolation of St. Mary's.

Francie begged the question, "It's impossible, right? I never really think about God except to ask Him for things. You know, for a boy to like me, or to take away my pimples if I get some, or to make my mother stop caring about everybody else's kids, but I know He's there." She looked up at Garbo filled with fear. "We pray to Him all the time in school. We pray for the poor souls in purgatory. We're always asking Him to watch over our science projects and the basketball team. Sister Georgina even asks God to dry the clothes on the clothesline before it rains."

Garbo zeroed in on Francie's tear-smeared face. "Well, except fer the part about your ma, which ain't so, so's God don't have to fix that one, He seems to hear yer prayers pretty good if ya ask me."

"Don't you know what I mean?" Francie sighed, "God is really Pastor's business, and the sisters'. Why am I seeing things? Why doesn't He pick somebody who could do something about it?"

"God don't make mistakes, little missy. If He picked ya, He meant to pick ya."

"But why ME?" Francie whined.

"He must think ya can do somethin' about it that nobody else can do," Garbo said with a firm nod of her head.

"Maybe it's my fault. I feel like everything is gonna change, and we won't always be happy together. Bad things can happen right here!" Francie warned.

Garbo put her hands on her knees and pushed herself up out of the chair.

"Ya poor kid, the worst thing ever happen to ya is Sister Ed's detention class. There's serious sufferin' in this world, Francie." Garbo stopped abruptly. "I gotta start Gabe's lunch." She opened the fridge and took out the eggs and butter, then nudged the white metal door closed with her hip. She looked intently at Francie. "I can't tell ya if what ya seen is true or not. And I can't tell ya what ya wanna hear neither. 'Cause 'a course it can happen. It has happened."

Francie's face went blank, her eyes wide with shock.

"What do ya think? Them Commies stole God from almost one-third of the entire world already, and they're still at it. They forbid the practice of religion. Ain't that stealin' God from a soul? Now they got their mitts on Cuba! A little too close to home, if ya ask me."

Garbo shook her head and her spatula at Francie. "And it was all in the prophecies at Fatima, besides. The Virgin Mary appeared to them little shepherd kids, told 'em all about it. Lousy Commies, they confiscated churches and silenced all the church bells."

"Is Mrs. Ribaldi a Communist?" Francie asked.

"Don't know," Garbo said. "Them Commies, they ship anybody don't agree with them off to Siberia—where it's 40 below in the sunshine. Russia, China, Hungary, Poland. It's the current situation in the world, honey. They've successfully stolen God from His people. Right under our noses."

"Why doesn't somebody stop them?"

"Like who?" Garbo asked with her hands on her hips. "Them that could do a thing about it, sit around fat and sassy not carin'. Poor wretched folks gotta have a revolution to get a piece of bread—no less a job, mind ya."

Francie ducked the shake of the spatula as the butter sizzled and smoked in the blackened frying pan.

Garbo had too many memories. "Tell me how yer gonna believe in God when the God-fearin' peoples don't lift a finger to help ya?"

Anger rose up in the housekeeper despite her effort to keep a lid on it. How could the world allow another diabolical evil to rise to power? She blew her top like a pressure cooker. More sons would die. That's what Garbo saw, more death. The Great War had set her husband's mind askew and WWII—more of the same. "Tell me how ya gonna believe in God then, huh?"

"I—I don't know," Francie stammered.

She didn't understand what this rage was all about, but her father could produce the same vehemence on the same subject.

"Them Commies come along, give ya bread and shelter. Yer gonna feed yer belly first, that's what folks'll do. And worry about God later. But then, ya see, it's too late. 'Cause they already locked the churches and took away yer freedoms. All in the name of helpin' mankind!"

"Well, who would be in charge of saving God from getting stolen? I mean, who can help us?" Francie asked.

"Now that's a good question," Garbo queried. "It's in the hands of the Powers That Be, I suppose."

Francie gasped, "That's what they said. 'Badad! Badad Vice!' That's what he said! He made a curse!"

Garbo looked out the window and saw Pastor getting out of his car. He crossed the yard toward the rectory. Quickly checking the countertops for cigarettes, she patted her pocket with relief.

The priest entered the kitchen. Francie was on her feet in a split second.

"Good afternoon, Pastor," she said with a respectful curtsy.

"Afternoon, Miss O'Malley, Garbo."

"Father," Garbo greeted the priest with a nod, both hands

being occupied. Then, winking at Francie, she tossed her head in the direction of the priest as he walked through the kitchen to his office.

She cracked an egg against the frying pan into the fire. "I guess the first line of defense to keep God from gettin' stolen would be him!"

Then, Garbo playfully called after Pastor, "Hey, Father, Miss Francine here was wantin' to see ya. Gotta minute?"

"Of course," he replied from the hallway.

"No, no, Father. It was nothing."

"Anytime, Francie," Pastor's voice muffled as he turned into his office. "I'm happy to help."

"How could you?" Francie hissed at Garbo.

"I thought that's what ya came fer?" Garbo chuckled.

"Well, I changed my mind," Francie retorted defensively. "I saw what I saw. If you won't believe me, nobody will."

Gabe came into the kitchen for his lunch.

"Gettin' smoky in here," he said, opening the window. He moved to the fridge. After serious examination of its contents lined up on metal racks, he cocked his head toward Francie.

"Want a soda?"

Francie lit up. "Yes, please!"

He opened her bottle with a church-key and did the same for himself. For the time being, Francie swallowed down her troubles. Taking her prize with a thank you to Gabe and a paper cup, she slipped out the back door.

Lucy was sitting on the church steps across the garden pathway. She was all alone and very glum. If truth be told, the chat with Garbo afforded Francie little relief. Her worries were now compounded by threatening stories of Communism on the march. She was happy to see Lucy, and she skipped down the wooden steps of the rectory.

"Hey, Lucy. I got a soda from Gabe. Want to split it?"

"Umm ... Yeah, I guess so."

Francie joined her best friend on the cement steps of the church. Carefully, she poured half the soda from the green bottle into the paper cup with 'Happy Easter' and bright yellow crosses printed on it.

They enjoyed their beverages in silence. Lucy took a flattened, brown paper bag out of her jacket pocket and produced a bologna sandwich she couldn't eat due to the acute ache of losing her best friend, Francie O'Malley.

It was there, while they shared their feast, that Francie told Lucy about the things she saw, the demon of Evil Sands, and the spell she suspected it cast on her. Lucy was awestruck.

"I saw it come ashore," Francie began, "and the shipwrecks too."

Lucy was captivated. "Go on," she gasped.

Francie recounted her visions, the souls that would be captured and made into slaves, the vivid array of characters that were destined to one day pepper the ruins of St. Mary's-of-the- Future. And saving the best for last, she told Lucy of the splendid critters who would try to save Three Rivers, Scout and Deer and Périgord, when the Commies come, with a mind to stealing God.

24

Marvelous

The Heavenlies

Marvelous Angel

The Opening Adventure

Marvelous Angel was assigned to hold back the wind. Self-satisfied with his important assignment, he allowed this tiny indulgence to puff himself up. This puffiness would be his undoing. Poor Marvelous had no idea that the ramifications of puffiness, that unexpected swelliness, would weaken him to such an extent—for an instant or two, in the very slightest way—as to provoke the most enormous disaster. Marvelous Angel lost control of the awesome wind called Fury.

Fury slipped from the angel's grasp and headed straight for the Southerly Coast to wreak havoc on the realm of a Bishop who, somewhere along the way, had misplaced his vigilance.

25

The Bishop

They were scattered because there was no shepherd, and they became food for all the wild beasts... My sheep were scattered over all the face of the earth, with none to search or seek them.Ezekiel 34:5-6

The Southerly Coast-in-the-Future

In the magnificent Villa-by-the-Sea lived a bishop, the revered ruler of the Southerly Coast. He was an effective shepherd with immense capabilities, dividing his time between visiting his parishes and studying documents useful in the ministry of his flock. This bishop had much knowledge and was sought after to instruct others. They came from all over the world to hear him preach or attend his seminars. He studied every question in the countless letters he received asking for his good counsel, carefully marking them with notes of clarity and wisdom as established in the Gospel and long upheld in the Church by the Vicar of Rome, His Holiness the Pope.

When he had inherited the realm, it was disorganized and unproductive. He persevered through those difficult times, demonstrating to his subjects, by good example, how to make a better life for themselves by making a better life for each other. He knew how to inspire his people. As a matter of fact, he was so accomplished at being a good bishop he eventually worked himself out of a job.

The Bishop took pride in the generosity of his flock. Everyone gave willingly to the poor until poverty was all but obliterated. The sick of the realm were cared for, and schools were established. The children were courteous and polite. The people knew they owed everything to their wonderful bishop. The Bishop gave credit for his good fortune to the Heavenly Father, for it was from Him that he had his authority, and he was grateful to be the recipient.

Prosperity abounded in this nearly perfect realm. The sun shone, and the palm trees swayed every day. Even hurricane season bypassed this fortunate realm. It had been ages since a devastating storm had hit the Southerly Coast. Life was perfect there. It was almost too good to be true, though it might be said in hindsight, "If it seems too good to be true, then it probably is."

And so, the people of the Southerly Coast began taking their good fortune for granted. The Bishop became content, and his flock became self-satisfied and self-righteous. They came to believe nothing could ever happen to them in their favored realm. They felt entitled to such prosperity because of their righteousness. That, of course, is a dangerous way of thinking, and their perfect world began to fray at the seams. It started with the Bishop himself, naturally, right at the top.

The first sign of this unraveling was the Bishop slipping from contentment to dissatisfaction. Even with all his activities, he found he was bored and restless. It occurred to the Bishop that the realm really ran itself. He felt his life was dull and uneventful. He was deluded into believing he had lots of leisure time and began indulging in several new pursuits, not all of which were beneficial to his realm. Some were quite unbecoming to a bishop, such as gambling for high stakes. Now, that started innocently enough at an annual charity event where he had a winning streak at the card table they called Twenty-One. It should be noted that there was a culprit at work here engineering this divisive slide. A representative from the dark side, a very slick character sometimes known as Black Jack.

The Bishop found the enticements of gaming so irresistible, he decided to branch out. He attended dog races and steeplechases and bought lottery tickets galore. Black Jack had a twisted way with pleasure imparting the same thrills to his victims, whether they won or lost. The Bishop's gambling gave him a rush of exhilaration that methodical realm-building never provided.

When his winnings went down, he ran up debts. There were sightings of suspicious characters appearing at the gates of the villa, inquiring after the whereabouts of His Excellency. Some members of the staff knew ruffians like these and were alarmed to see such shady characters in the vestibule. Still, they decided among themselves, the Bishop must be going out to the highways and hedges on the outskirts of the Southerly Coast to find poor souls to save, for there were no sinners left in their perfect realm.

The Bishop pilfered a few dollars from the poor box to pay his debts. To his great relief, no one noticed him swiping the money, which, unfortunately, only added to the temptation to continue this downward slide. All the while, he justified his actions by remembering the significant strides the realm had made under his talented direction. He even believed he should be compensated, like famous men in the corporate world who were rewarded with fortunes for far lesser accomplishments. Why not a bishop?

He looked in the mirror and smoothed his thin hair (which he now touched up with a bit of hair dye) and began to believe he was debonair.

He bought a pork pie hat with a grosgrain band and a narrow, rolled brim. A style favored by many a smart-looking man-about-town. It slightly missed the mark when paired with his new loud jacket, a bright lime green, his favorite royal blue shirt, and an extra-wide, polka-dot tie. That's what he wore when he attended the races. Well aware that it would be thought highly irregular for a bishop to be found in such sporting attire, he was compelled to sneak out of the Villa-by-the-Sea and cut across the cathedral grounds when off to a day of gaming.

"If the realm were a corporation," he often complained to the mirror, "I could dress as I chose. What difference does it make what a man should wear?" And then, incredibly, "It's what's in his soul that counts." It was striking that this notion never provoked the Bishop to consider the condition of his own soul, but that's the kind of thing that happens when Black Jack starts his masterful work on the good conscience of a righteous man. They become experts at justifying their actions and making exceptions to the rules—at least for themselves.

It was clear to the Powers of Evil that this bishop had slipped firmly into their grip. Black Jack's work was considered complete. Now, seasoned and cultivated in sinfulness, the Bishop was ready to be handed over to that trickiest of tricksters known as Swelliness—Swelly for short. He would be the Bishop's constant companion until his death. Satan had a soft spot for Swelly, but he was difficult to contain and was often a victim of his own pride. Nevertheless, he was the current darlingof the dark side despite his constantly stepping out of bounds to make a name for himself.

Swelly wasn't a full-fledged demon yet, more of an impish spirit. Once evil had captivated a righteous soul, it was Swelly's job to keep him there and gradually—without making waves— transform a candidate from a rascal into a scoundrel. It's really only a short stroll.

Because a person only misbehaves of their own free will. Swelly could only make suggestions using his trusty friends from Hell's Department of Messengers, Insinuations and Deceptions. But Insinuations and Deceptions are just the sort of characters that really get results. Envy and Pride being employed to do the rest, those two despicable word-meisters started whispering in the Bishop's ear: "You know, if your realm was a corporation, you'd be a wealthy man. You could afford to pick up a few markers in the sporting life. What's the harm?"

It was the perfect opening for Greed to enter the picture, then after that, a Spirit of Larceny—for ill measure—took over, sinking him down, down, down, with a hefty anchor.

And so, the Bishop helped himself to a few more dollars destined for the poor, who, because of his larking about, were starting to go hungry. As far as Black Jack could see these were dangerous prospects. Swelly pushed the Bishop to the brink of repentance. Swelly's behavior annoyed the sensibilities of a sophisticated pro like Black Jack. He preferred working with subtle smoothness, appealing to a man's vanity more than to his greed. He had masterfully ensnared the Bishop and wanted a more seasoned member of the Maintenance Department to take over. A demon who knew the value of keeping a victim lulled into believing his actions were justified, if not just. Such a demon would have been a better choice to accompany this bishop through life. It was essential, according to Black Jack, that a Vic never realize how deeply he is ensnared in the devil's yarn.

It was understood that the Bishop would have to die before Swelly's final promotion, but aside from a few extra pounds, he was a perfectly healthy man. It could be years before he kicked the bucket, and Swelly was reckless. This unglued Black Jack. He detested Swelly and hated losing control of such an important conquest, but Swelly moved steadily up the ranks and had the ear of the darkest Powers.

"Use the compulsive deceptions, these are the hallmarks of the sporting life," Black Jack advised Swelly. This irritated the imp, who had his own innovative plan to get the job done.

"Who knows when the Grim Reaper comes a-knocking? You don't. Things can be arranged," Swelly retorted, swishing past the steely professional with condescending scorn.

Black Jack glared at his impertinence. He squashed the imp with unbelievable force. His voice, like a razor, flayed Swelly fiercely. "Keep it mellow, do you understand me? For as long as it takes, then hand him off." Black Jack was growling by now. "If he seeks forgiveness, we will lose him!"

The handoff referred to the transference of a soul to Dastard Diablo, which happened at death. Dastard ran the escort service directly to Hell.

Swelly saw this Bishop as his ticket to full rank (no pun

intended). Black Jack did not intimidate him. Swelly knew it was a rare occurrence to snag a soul like this one, and this was his big chance. "Your tactics are old fashioned and a waste of time," Swelly sneered, "move off me, Black Jack!"

Now, a soul, to avoid entrapments, must be, at all times, on guard for Swelliness. That's why it's imperative to learn what's right and what's wrong—there is always the chance that Swelly is busy camouflaging the truth. Why, if he can trick a bishop, it's easy enough to imagine the confusion he can conjure in an ordinary soul.

None of the Heavenly Helpers assigned to watch over the Bishop of the Southerly Coast could rouse him out of his Swelliness stupor. The Bishop was defiant and determined to continue in his unseemly behavior, which started as just a bit of fun, but now entailed lies, deception, stealing, and a whole cadre of grave sins. The Heavenly Helpers had to increase their efforts. Corrections of this kind, by their very nature, aren't worked out as one might think.

Heavenly Helpers don't necessarily paint a pretty picture to redirect a party tangled up in Swelly's schemes. Often, when a simple prodding of the conscience and stirrings of guilt aren't successful, more drastic measures are needed. Some that might not be considered angelic in nature.

They decided to call on their own Department of Messengers and sent in Shame and Embarrassment. These hard workers can often do the trick to jar an otherwise good soul out of the clutches of peevish evil. They are often dependable enough to awake a quick flash of virtue and humility, and in that flash, the soul can be snatched back to safety.

And so, in due course, with heavenly orchestration, the Bishop began to run into people he knew under scandalous circumstances and in the company of the shadiest characters. He spent most afternoons at the racetrack and had several close calls darting behind grandstands and diving under tables to avoid being recognized by his admirers, not to mention his creditors. The whole business started giving him acute anxiety.

Then, one day around about Christmas time, while hiding under a horse blanket in a stable, trying to dodge a respected contributor to his annual Bishop's Fund, the Bishop heard a choir singing the Christmas carol *What Child is This?* The lyrics by William Chatterton Dix, written in 1865. And through the static of a radio in the barn, the lovely melody of *Greensleeves.*

Why lie He in such mean estate
Where ox and ass are feeding?
Good Christian, fear: for sinners here,
The silent Word is pleading.

This, this is Christ the King
Whom shepherds guard and angels sing.
Haste, haste to bring Him laud,
The Babe, the Son of Mary.

Right in front of him was an ass feeding hay out of a manger. The Heavenly Helpers thought it was a nice touch, filled with rich symbolism. It gave the Bishop the necessary prod.

Racked with guilt and remorse, the Bishop gave up gambling forever and the exciting endeavor of trying to beat the odds. He left his pork pie hat right there in the manger, along with his loud jacket and bright-colored shirt with the extra-wide, polka-dot tie. He walked the long way back to the Villa-by-the-Sea in his undershirt and thought about the Christ Child and his broken vows. His heart was heavy, and the sun was hot, but he felt relief—for a while anyway.

It seems an old stable hand found himself some dapper new clothes right there in the manger. As a matter of fact, he felt so blessed and full of wonder at having found such styling new clothes, on Christmas Day no less, he took the long bus ride to the big cathedral to thank the Baby Jesus personally for the miracle. He marched up to the first pew and took a seat directly in front of the pulpit, wherein the mortified Bishop recognized his sinfulness in the reflection of the happy stable hand.

But Swelly wasn't finished—not by a long shot. The Bishop retired to his library in his shame. And, having sworn off gambling forever, he sank into a terrible depression, and Swelly sang him a lullaby of self-pity.

26

The Bishop and Périgord
Become Friends

For the time will come when people will not tolerate sound doctrine,
but following their own desires and insatiable curiosity, will
accumulate teachers and will stop listening to truth and will be
diverted to myths. 2 Timothy 4:3-4

The Southerly Coast-of-the-Future

The Bishop's library looked out on a cobblestone courtyard
and a verdant lawn that rolled down to the seawall. There were
gardens everywhere improved with flourishing tropical plants.
This made no difference to the Bishop. He stayed inside with the
draperies drawn all day long. In a gloomy state of mind, he
reflected on his unseemly conduct. Surprisingly, it never occurred
to him to seek relief. Confessing one's sins is a rudimentary
teaching of the Church, any 8-year-old could have told him
that, not to mention the countless clerics at the Villa-by-the-Sea.

But he would not be consoled, nor did he much repent. He just felt sorry for himself. This was clever maneuvering on Swelly's part—employing just a pinch of Despair.

After a few months, the Bishop's secretary, concerned for his health, opened the heavy velvet draperies and the thin white sheers behind them. He insisted the Bishop go outside in the sunshine. The Bishop reluctantly agreed and took a stroll, alone, outdoors.

He dragged around his gardens, mentally reviewing his sinfulness, feeling sick and sorry for himself, but gradually the sunshine made him feel better. He noticed his perfect surroundings and his caring staff. Everything seemed to be running smoothly. He stopped thinking about what he had done wrong. Instead, he concentrated on what he had done right. He plucked fruit from his trees and enjoyed a snack while he meandered. He soon forgot his moments of humiliation and remorse and the manger in the stable. The Bishop of the Southerly Coast was suddenly extremely impressed with the splendor of his accomplishments.

Soon, he found his favorite bench between two potted orange trees and sat in the shade in front of the garden wall fragrant with a vine of white jasmine. The espalier of the tree of life climbed up the whitewashed bricks trained by his talented Mexican gardener, Raphael. In front of this shady spot was a pond, where on a black swan and a very large gander swam about. For years, the gander had followed the Bishop around the estate, listening to him practice his inspiring sermons. Gander especially enjoyed the Bishop's fine counsels, always offering encouraging words to his priests and sisters come for advice and blessing.

Gander tried to imitate the Bishop in all his mannerisms. He could walk like him, and even his squawks had a cadence like the Bishop's voice.

"It's nice to see you again," the Bishop said, striking up a conversation with the oversized gander. "My, how you've grown!" Gander squawked with delight at the Bishop's attention. The Bishop went on and on, to Gander and Swan commenting on the beauty of his gardens, manicured fruit trees, and symmetrical layout, congratulating himself on all his brilliant endeavors. Although the bishop didn't do anything. It was all the accomplishment of his talented gardener, Raphael.

Once again, the Bishop surrendered to Swelly's subtle twists of conscience. He began tossing out grandiose ideas to the oversized white gander, along with small corners of stale bread.

"Squawk, squawk!" (Gander always responded cheerfully.)

The Bishop treated Gander as an intimate confidant, someone with whom he could discuss all manner of important thoughts. He also had the added assurance that Gander would keep them secret. They became the best of friends. The black swan, on the other hand, kept to himself.

The Bishop walked in the garden every day. He sat on his bench by the pond and fed Gander full of interesting ideas and contemplations and a great deal of stale bread. Gander developed an insatiable appetite, growing hugely plump as a result of his friendship with the Bishop. So much so, that the black swan was forced to comment: "Gander, you are so fat that you will sink to the bottom of this pond if you're not careful." Then he swam away because he had broken his rule of keeping to himself.

Gander didn't care that he had grown fat. He adored his friend, the Bishop, and was highly flattered that his Excellency would share his significant thoughts and theories with him, an unimportant gander. He felt that it gave him new status around the estates. Everyone, including the Bishop's staff, acknowledged that they were the best of friends.

"I shall call you Périgord, after the late Bishop Périgord, who I had admired so much when I was a young priest. He was the wisest and holiest of men and ruled a realm up north of here in its glory days. I modeled my work after his, and I owe my success to that sainted man. He met with a gruesome accident, you know, poor chap, but I'm sure he's in Heaven by now. Yes, I'll call you Périgord. It's a perfect name for you," the Bishop laughed.

The big gander was positively thrilled to have such an honorable name. "Squawk! Périgord, Squawk!"

One day, after thinking about the saintly Bishop Périgord's example, and his youthful zeal for goodness, the Bishop approached Périgord. He began a speech that described at length how jaded he had become, a subject he feared he couldn't possibly discuss with another soul. It didn't seem to surprise the Bishop that Périgord's squawks sounded like words, or so he came to think, and he confided in him more and more.

"I can't seem to pray anymore, Périgord. Do you think that God has forgotten me? Or do you think that I have forgotten God?" Then he waxed on like a great philosopher in debate with himself, still never thinking to seek out another priest to whom he could confess his sins.

"You know, Périgord, my friend, I have accomplished tremendous things here in this Southerly Realm. Clerics come from far and wide to hear my sermons and see firsthand the fine results of my organizational skills. We're quite accomplished around here, quite accomplished. Just look at what I've been able to do with you!" He had already taught Périgord all the Psalms and many passages in the Bible, which Périgord knew (almost) by heart. The Bishop removed his pocket watch and sighed. He showed it to the great fat bird. "All of my official work is done, and as you can see, it's only 10:00 a.m., still quite early in the day. Sometimes I wish I weren't so efficient. Now I have nothing left to do."

But the Bishop had lost track of time entirely. He hadn't done a thing for his realm in several years. Nothing seemed to stimulate his prior zeal for the realm. He had become complacent in his duties and completely self-absorbed.

"You know, Périgord, with so extraordinarily little for me to do today, I feel I could devote some time to intellectual studies of my choosing. What do you say to that? I've often wondered what the appeal was to some of these far-fetched philosophies the Church has deemed dangerous and dark; let's see what they're all about."

"Squawk, squawk!" was Périgord's reply as he ate up some stalebread right from the Bishop's hand.

"So, you agree?" Bishop said, "It's worth a look-see." He got up from his bench and returned to his library.

After that, he immersed himself in diverse curiosities like Astronomy and Astrology and countless ancient philosophies. Many fancy ideas tickled his ears. And who do you suppose did the tickling? The answer was Swelly, of course. The most upright of men, even Bishops, can succumb to the seduction of myths and conspiracies from time to time if they are not careful, especially the unhealthy interest in dark arts and strange gods. Soon, Bishop stopped taking his dailystrolls as he became ever more engrossed in his new studies. He stayed inside and read all day, making elaborate charts of moons and planets. And as he tried to read the future with his many charts, his realm descended further and further into disarray. Many a devout soul fell away for lack of spiritual direction, and sadly many of his best clerics too. His now voracious appetite for curious knowledge distracted him from the truth. It is not that he embraced these false beliefs, but rather, the Bishop was obsessed with his scholarly pursuits as if studying what truth isn't somehow superseded his obligation to teach and preach what truth is.

After some time, Périgord grew hungry and wondered what ever happened to his best friend, the Bishop. Raphael was clipping the hedges as poor Périgord waddled by looking sad and lost. Sensing Périgord's distress, the kindly gardener pointed the way to the cobblestone courtyard in front of the green rolling lawn, in front of the garden, in front of the sea wall, in front of the sea. Périgord made his way across the manicured grounds and peered through the tall French doors with the sheer curtains. There sat the Bishop, in his red leather chair at his big mahogany desk, engrossed in his interesting studies.

Périgord stood outside the Bishop's library pecking relentlessly at the windows, seeking entry. The pecking was such a distraction that the Bishop motioned Périgord to come in. Périgord moseyed around the library. He checked out the bookshelves on either side of the fireplace and inspected the piles of suspicious volumes stacked everywhere. The subjects did not seem like the usual fare that had once occupied the Bishop's bookshelves, but the books were the Bishops business. Périgord was far more interested in the comfortable leather chair riveted around with brass nail heads across the room. It was a nice well-worn brown leather, and he settled on this for his nest. Eventually, he brought in a few of his favorite items from the cathedral pond. The library was soon a-fluff with feathers and down, becoming mighty untidy. The Bishop seemed satisfied with the arrangement and continued his interesting studies.

The servants brought copious amounts of food and wine to the library where the Bishop took his meals. He insisted on sharing everything with his guest and friend, Périgord. Well, not the wine—that he kept for himself, swilling glass after glass to wash down big crusts of bread soaked in thick brown gravy. He finally eliminated the glass altogether and drank right from the carafe until it was gone. He would then doze off in a boozy stupor, leaving Périgord to clean the plates. Périgord liked this sharing very much. The Bishop grew more corpulent than Périgord, who was thoroughly enjoying the food and service and was now the size of a small man.

As time went on, the Bishop stopped visiting his parishes altogether. The perfect Realm of the Southerly Coast began to decay from within. Everyone was following the Bishop's leadership (or lack thereof) and doing their own thing, drifting into all sorts of odd beliefs that Swelly sprinkled down like fairy dust. Off his flock strayed in every direction. The Bishop's neglect of his realm was destined to be a sorry tale, but no one could fathom just how sorry a tale it would be until the day his servant announced: "The skies indicate a terrible storm is on its way, your Excellency."

"What is it? What are you saying, man?"

"The people are leaving in droves. Please, Excellency, what shall I pack for you? We must evacuate with the others and help lead them to safety."

The frantic servant went to the huge French doors. With the edge of his sleeve, he tried to clean a windowpane.

"The ocean is frothing, Your Excellency, showing signs of the storm—look at the whitecaps!"

Bishop peered through his greasy spectacles with annoyance. He thumped the desk sternly with his fist, squishing some spaghetti. In imitation, Périgord stood on the desk—big as he was—and stomped one webbed foot, slipping on the spaghetti, and sending a teaspoon flying off the luncheon tray spilling hot tea on the other webbed foot. This caused Perigord to flutter with a painful squawk.

Bishop, ignoring the commotion beside him, looked out the window. "I don't see any gathering storm."

"But, Your Excellency," the servant pleaded, "the windows are fogged! Go outside and look for yourself. The people need direction where to go and what to do. Please, we've got to hurry."

"Nonsense!" said the Bishop. He released an uncomfortable belch as quietly as he could. "Go if you must, man, but leave me be. We haven't been affected by a storm in years, and I suspect we won't be this time either. I'm staying here. Tell me when the people return from this folly. I'll welcome them home and show them that all is well."

The servant was ashamed for not trusting the Bishop, but the sky and the sea didn't lie, and if the brewing storm were to come ashore, there would be certain devastation. "Are you sure, sir?" the servant inquired. "I must confess, I want to board up my house and leave with the others."

"I'll be fine. Go along now, there's a good fellow. We'll have a laugh about this when you return. My great gander and I will keep each other company. We're the best old pals, aren't we, Périgord?"

Bishop grabbed Périgord's neck and gave him a hearty shake. Perigord squawked out a raucous approval and swallowed a cream cheese sandwich and a lump of sugar.

"Squawk! Pals—Squawk! Périgord!"

The grateful servant left the room, and the Bishop applied his magnifier ever closer to his books.

Outside on the street, the people of the realm tried their best to help each other, as the rain began to pelt them, and the stiff wind began to blow. Some went one way, and some went another because there was no clear direction as to which way to go.

The die-hard Faithful detoured past the Bishop's villa, where they hoped their leader would appear. They wondered where their once beloved Shepherd might be, as they waited outside in the soaking rain, but he never came.

The last devoted subjects, weary and battered from the storm, finally left their fair realm of palm trees and sunshine. Despondent and disillusioned, they sought shelter and a new life elsewhere, for fear was in their hearts, and they knew not the course.

The Bishop stayed behind as Fury pounded the shore of the Southerly Coast. He never noticed that the streets of the villages were abandoned, and the stores boarded up. He was immersed in his interesting studies.

27

Beneficent

Heavenlies

The Demise of the Southerly Coast

Beneficent Angel set out, transporting the Big Book of Good News, and the Seal of the Living God. These would be essential tools for carrying out her nearly impossible assignment to take back Three Rivers and save Midlantic.

She entered the atmosphere just below the Realm of the Southerly Coast when suddenly, she was spun into a tumble by a violent wind.

Ordinarily, while passing over a place, the angel would shower it with munificence in a lovely rhythm, but instead of these blessings sprinkling down from her, they backfired and swirled up in a blizzard of benefits. Fury was pounding the shores of the Southerly Coast. Beneficent immediately sought out Marvelous Angel to inquire as to the unauthorized release of the winds.

The Southerly Coast was leveled. One slip of an angel's wrist had unleashed Fury, and it was the cause of irreparable harm.

Beneficent could see the tell-tale signs of Swelly. "What's happened here? What have you done, Marvelous?"

Marvelous was distraught.

"Oh, careless, Angel!" Beneficent scolded.

"How can I fix it?" Marvelous asked meekly.

"Fix it? You can't fix it! What's the matter with you? You're getting carried away with your own importance. You've wiped out an entire realm. How can you possibly fix that?"

Marvelous wouldn't hurt a fly. As strong and powerful as he was to merit such a job as holding back the wind, he was really the gentlest of spirits.

Beneficent was surprised at her own harshness. "I suppose it will re-blossom," she added in a kinder tone, "but the real problem is much bigger."

"I'm afraid to look."

"It's the Angel of Death, heading to the Villa-by-the-Sea."

Marvelous saw the real problem all too clearly.

"You've killed him! Oh careless, careless, Angel. Yet another realm without a bishop—another flock without a shepherd. My assignment to find a bishop for Midlantic is difficult enough, and now this mess of a place."

Marvelous, already fearing the prospects of his fate, looked down at the Bishop of the Southerly Coast, dead in his library, the walls of the villa reduced to rubble around him. Rippling waves calmly lapped against the bookcases, all that remained standing with the fireplace, in the library. The crystal chandelier lay shattered on the Bishop's desk, having fallen directly on his head.

Marvelous sighed with compassion for the dead bishop. "The poor soul. There's no one left in the entire villa to help him."

"Everyone seems to have read the sea and the sky and evacuated to safety—except that one great fat goose," Beneficent observed.

"What do you suppose the Bishop will do?" Marvelous whispered.

"I suppose, if he saw it coming, he would have done what he

should have done and prayed," Beneficent answered.

"What kind of prayer do you think?" Marvelous asked, uneasy.

"If I were to hazard a guess, I would say Help and Guidance, or perhaps Mercy."

"Oh, no! He mustn't pray—I mean he couldn't have; I mean he mustn't die. Do you think he did? Pray, I mean. Beneficent, you've got to help me. I'll fry if the Powers That Be are called in. I'll fry, Beneficent, do something. Please help me!"

Marvelous was understandably frantic. Beneficent Angel thought awfully hard about the uncomfortable realities of her own problems. She could foresee that she would be making constant excuses to the Powers That Be, as well. Representatives from every Choir of Angels had already done their best and failed. What made her think she could find a bishop to save Midlantic?

It was the policy of the Heavenly Court to be very persnickety about getting assignments filled, with just the right candidate, at just the right time. The Principalities, that Choir of Angels in charge of Realm Rulers, did not take well to realms left without rulers. In fact, they were fed up with Midlantic and were considering flooding it out altogether, but the Heavenly Father would not have that again. If one bishop was called to his eternal reward, another must be in the wings ready to fill the vacated seat. The Heavenly Father did not intend any flock to be left without a shepherd.

If truth be told—and this is a truthful story—no bishop, no cleric of any rank, no layperson of good character or quality, no member of the human race wanted the job that Beneficent was assigned to fill. She would be under considerable scrutiny. Even though the Powers That Be had assured her of their sympathy, they had very short memories when it came to this particular assignment. Now she had an idea. Perhaps a little unorthodox, but ...

"Interception," Beneficent said.

"What?"

"Interception is our only chance, Marvelous. It's a sort of fast-track form of intercession. We must intercede for the Bishop before the Bishop's last stream of prayers wafts their way up to Heaven seeking Help and Guidance for his soul. We can't afford this case to get caught up in the system. We will have to intercede for this Bishop first, beating Help and Guidance to the punch."

Beneficent was moved to pity for the distressed Marvelous Angel. After all, even Angels—from time to time—are subject to moments of weakness, like puffiness. He hadn't meant to kill a Bishop!

Beneficent's mind raced. "If he had an acceptable solution, then—well, it's always good to have a couple of high-ranking Angels on your side. Isn't it? We shall convince the Bishop to trust us."

"As well he should. But if we do not succeed?" Marvelous queried.

"Ah, it would be remarkably bad luck for you and eternal damnation for his poor soul!"

Beneficent cooked up her plan. She looked down at the miserable spirit of the Bishop and back at the troubled Marvelous Angel. "Don't fret so, we must help him," she said, "I have just the solution."

They set down on terra firma in a ball of blinding light. They were rehearsing together the ways of Advice and Assistance. These were attributes reserved primarily for Guardian Angels, but this was an emergency, and when souls are at stake, the Powers That Be expect all angels to do their absolute best, even if it entailed unfamiliar areas of expertise.

They appeared before the Bishop with much dazzle. The Bishop's lifeless body lay across his desk, with crystal prisms, from the crashed chandelier, twinkling in the sunlight all around him. One such prism had pierced his temple. A river of blood irrigated his ear, causing a steady red drip to soak his Roman collar.

Near the remains of the stately fireplace stood a repugnant-looking character, chuckling to himself as he picked among the books, tossing some in the fireplace and storing others on what was left of the bookshelves. He frowned, realizing there was no fire in the hearth. This he remedied easily enough with a snap and a flick of his claw-like fingers. A wet cloud of steam sizzled into a small ball of flame, bursting forth and hungrily devouring the books of devotion he had cast away with disdain. It was the devil known as Dastard Diablo.

The slick fellow read for all to hear the title of a hefty volume as he tossed it into the fire. *"The Complete Works of the Doctors of the Church,"* you won't be needing this volume anymore, eh, Bishy? No need for a doctor here!" Howling laughter shook the devil's jelly-like gut.

Périgord, unnerved by the intruder, was situated in his leather chair opposite the desk along with the spirit of the Bishop. "Squawk! Squawk! Who's that guy, Bishop, who's that guy? Squawk!"

Bishop stared at his bodily remains slumped over his desk. He continuously petted Périgord, who appeared to be sitting on his lap—if such a thing were possible. Périgord was aware of their close encounter and found it appealing that he and his great friend could communicate with a good deal more ease, an unforeseen benefit of the prelate's untimely death. This was the only perk the Bishop's soul might have found advantageous before departing the earth, though a poor consolation it was.

The dazzle of the Angels alarmed him. "What is this?" The Bishop asked, recovering from the glare. He battled to stand erect in the snap of Fury's tail, but he wasn't at all sure of his weightlessness, on account of being newly dead. His spirit passed directly through the gander, which made the bird flap with some alarm before settling back into his chair-nest. Marvelous was full of remorse as he scanned the devastation. He was ashamed to confess to the Bishop that it was a slip of his reckless wrist that had let loose such havoc.

"He's never been really easy to manage," Marvelous offered sheepishly, as the wind whirled the raggedy strips of what was left of the Bishop's black cassock trimmed in purple, the once distinguished long garb worn by bishops. His purple sash snapped and flapped around him. Fury boldly whooshed between the two spirits, demonstrating the worst contempt. Fed up with Fury's unruly behavior, Marvelous Angel was fortified with an exceptional surge of power and might. He took command.

"Excuse me for a moment, Your Excellency, I'll be back in a jiffy."

Marvelous flew out over the sea and bound up Fury. "I will squeeze every drop of rain out of you, every bit of fierceness and power. When I am finished, you will be nothing more than a summer breeze. You have embarrassed me. You have ruined me!" Then, Marvelous harnessed the wind, straightened his wings, and promptly returned to the ruins of the Bishop's palace, the devastated Villa-by-the-Sea. Beneficent gave Marvelous an approving nod as he set down. She then cleared her throat and addressed the Bishop's forlorn spirit. "I am the Beneficent Angel. I was coming up from the East when I—rather—we— noticed that you have had some trouble here. We felt we had best inquire after your safety."

This put the Bishop into quite a tizzy.

$$28$$

Negotiations with Dastard Diablo

The Southerly Coast-in-the-Future

My safety?" the Bishop asked, looking from one angel to the other. He was flabbergasted at Beneficent's choice of words. "My safety? I am dead, as you can see. It is trouble enough, that I have made no preparation for this moment. But look at my realm! The landscape has been obliterated, and the people were evacuated by the force of that— that furious wind of yours. I have nothing to show for my years of service," the Bishop wailed on and on.

Dastard Diablo inserted his overly large, disturbingly hairy jaw into the conversation.

"More's the pity, now isn't it?" He commented, flashing his green-toothed grin. Offering his insincere condolences to the Bishop, he strutted past the three spirits. He was slick as snake oil in his black cutaway, black ascot, red satin shirt, waistcoat, and red leggings. His hair was pulled back into a tight ponytail, parted in the middle, and cemented to his head with what smelled to the angels like rancid bear grease.

Giving the air a sniff, the angels also detected the intensely disagreeable smell of mildew coming from the large volume Dastard held in his arms. He cradled it close to himself, rocking back and forth. The title of the volume read: *The Occult A to Z.* They glared at the book.

"A real favorite of mine," Dastard said with a chortle, "many a great recipe for mayhem, eh, Bish?"

The angels gagged, and the Bishop moaned in agony. This sent Périgord running around, releasing frantic harsh cries of distress. "No Occult. No! Squawk! Squawk!"

"I especially enjoy the chapter on Black Magic. Didn't you, Bishy, dear? All those headless chickens and all, I know you did!" Dastard squealed with delight. Eyeing *Butler's Lives of theSaints* on the desk, he grabbed it and tossed it carelessly over his shoulder, toppling the coat rack whereon the Bishop's miter and vestments were hanging. Frantic Périgord careened into the coat rack as it teetered and fell over on top of him. He squawked with alarm and rose out of the pile, seeing stars, vested head to toe in the Bishop's churchly garments. The angels let escape a gasp of disbelief while Dastard foamed at the mouth, choking on his screechy laughter.

"I didn't practice the occult!" the Bishop moaned. "You're twisting things! That's not the truth. I was only studying—for intellectual purposes."

"You might've been safer reading your silly scriptures, poor dearie, but all the better for me. Ha! Ha! It certainly kept your mind off doing YOUR JOB!"

The Bishop ignored the demon's barbs and paced back and forth, bemoaning his dreadful circumstances. "I have no realm left at all," he heaved with grief. "No flock to shepherd. What will I do with myself? I am dead! How will I answer for this?"

"It's truly regrettable," the angels agreed.

"Not for me it isn't," Dastard argued. "I won you fair and square, so, stop complaining."

Beneficent slammed power onto the moldy book cradled in Dastard's arms and it dissolved in a putrid liquid splashing his red leggings. Out from the bubbly mess flew countless vermin that hissed into the moldy gases as they fled. All that remained were a few granules of sand that Marvelous blew away with a whistle of wind. Dastard was hopping mad.

"Angels ruin everything! Come on Bishy, we're leaving."

"You're the cruelest of demons," the Bishop lamented.

"Uh, I'd like to embrace that compliment, Bish, but you've been spending time with far worse than me. Let's review the facts here for a minute. You were not in the "state of grace" when you croaked, and you know the rules. The rules say you're mine. I don't make the rules—I just pick up the passengers. And I find you to be my next assignment. Yes, here it is, 'Pick up the Bishop of the Southerly Coast, as it is now defunct.' And so are you, I might add. I'll be taking you—with me—right now."

"No, please, I'm not ready. I have much to do."

"You might've thought about that, say, over the last few years while we tickled your ears with utter nonsense. But thanks to your angel friend here, you have *nothing* to do! You have no realm left at all. No one will miss you, and there's not a reason in the world for you to stay. Come along—no fuss." Dastard Diablo was relishing the moment. He could hardly stand this ironic twist of fate—a Bishop killed by an angel!

"Not so fast," Marvelous said. He stepped in front of the shivering spirit of the Bishop as if to protect him. "We're not going to let you take him just like that. It wasn't his assigned time. It was an accident and ... and what else, Beneficent? What are we going to do? You tell him. You tell this, this fry-guy we're going to save the Bishop."

Beneficent paced the length of the library, wading through the trickling sea as it washed in and out, making little waves over the antique carpet. Finally, she cleared her throat in anticipation of saying something important. Périgord looked up from a snack of sand crabs that were desperately trying to burrow into the patterns of the Persian rug.

"It just so happens, Your Excellency," Beneficent began "I'm in a position to offer you a replacement realm."

"You are?" the Bishop asked, quickly abandoning his gloom.

"You are?" repeated Marvelous, taken completely by surprise.

"Yes, I'm sorry I didn't mention it earlier. It's the perfect solution, one that suits everyone."

"Hey, it don't suit me," Dastard said. "You can't do this!"

Beneficent ignored him. "The place is in need of a bishop, a talented candidate—someone very like yourself."

"Oh?" The Bishop said, profoundly happy.

Beneficent beamed. "Yes, it's an, er…interesting spot up the coast, about halfway between bottom and top. The realm has needed a new ruler for quite a while, but we've been unable to fill the position."

Marvelous pulled Beneficent aside. "He can't take that position on account of me. How can you do this?"

"It's not for you—although you certainly might benefit. Losing the prestigious style of "Marvelous," I dare say, would be hard to bear," Beneficent cautioned.

"I don't care," said Marvelous.

"This is a chance to save the Bishop's soul, the whole Realm of Midlantic, and the children of Nowhere, poor little Bambini. It's a perfect solution. He's the right one for the job. It's my assignment, and I have complete discretion."

Beneficent was unwavering. This put Marvelous into a terrible quandary. The plan could save him and his title, and save the Bambini, the abandoned children wandering around the lost Parish of Three Rivers, but his guilt was still great. "No one wants to be ruler of that realm," Marvelous said. "Not even a dead bishop."

"The position simply has to be filled," Beneficent reasoned. "He could look at it—as—a challenge. God works in mysterious ways, you know."

They slowly began nodding in agreement. Marvelous was

coming around. "If he had the right outlook…"

"That would do it," Beneficent agreed.

"Maybe he could make a go of it."

The angels were satisfied with their justification. The realm needed a ruler, the Bishop needed a realm. Realm/ruler—ruler/realm—a definite fit. They needed a bishop for Midlantic, and no bishop, dead or alive, was going to take on the job when the Parish of Three Rivers had already fallen to the despicable Cell Fish, Captain of Hell.

They shook hands in agreement and quickly felt the hot stinking breath of Dastard Diablo curling their wings. "You're forgetting one simple fact, you two," the dark one said, tossing more holy books into the fireplace. "He's already dead, which makes him already mine."

Beneficent knew she had to address this issue—after all, she didn't come to have a top tier job for lack of capability. "We are not technically taking him out of your possession, Dastard. We just wanted to give him first right of refusal on an opening up North, where the Three Rivers Meet the Sea. You can accompany us. We'll stop for a short visit with your old friend Cell Fish. Wouldn't you love to show off your 'catch' to Cell Fish? It would make him awfully jealous. I mean, Satan has all eternity to deal with this Bishop. What's the difference? Hell, under the earth or Hell on earth, it's all Hell—it's all hot, is it not?"

Dastard mulled it over.

"This is too dangerous!" Marvelous hissed in Beneficent's ear.

"Nonsense, we'll get the Bishop some aid. I'll put in for helpers, cracker-jack helpers, I promise! Wait till you see, it will all work out." Then she addressed the devil, "What do you say, Dastard?"

The proposal was too delectable for Dastard to refuse. "It would be fun to see Cell Fish squirm. What's the harm? I'll be with you all the way, correct? You wouldn't dare pull a fast one on me?"

"Dastard! Us, dare? Of course not! You won him fair and square."

The Bishop's spirit sank in woeful abandonment. The gander couldn't make head nor tail of what they were up to, but he was saddened for his beloved friend.

"I'm still not sure about this," Marvelous cautioned Beneficent again. But in the end, Marvelous feared facing the just punishments of the Powers That Be. He had a lot at stake, so he finally gave in and agreed to the plan.

29

The Powers That Be

The Heavenlies

Beneficent and Marvelous put forward the following proposal:

To the Powers That Be,

Known to oversee the Powers That Are—the ones on earth. We are requesting that you, the Choir of Angels who must sign off on a bishop's capabilities, be pleased to transfer to the illustrious Realm of Midlantic, the Bishop of the Southerly Coast (as it is now defunct).

Please forward your approval to the Choir of Angels known as Principalities for appropriate paperwork, etc. and so forth.

Beneficent and Marvelous were hoping the Powers That Be wouldn't be too troubled by the technicality at the bottom of their proposal in the very smallest print:

Dead on Arrival

The great Gelico, Secretary of the Powers, reviewed the request. "He's dead already? You can't transfer a dead bishop. It's impossible."

An alarmed panel glanced over the report. "He's a glutton. That's a Capital Sin!"

There was no lack of dismay over the candidate Beneficent Angel was presenting for their consideration.

"And a gambler!"

"That wasn't his fault," Beneficent defended. "It was innocent enough."

"Black Jack's work, no doubt," Gelico remarked.

"But he's a bishop," another less forgiving angel argued.

"He should have known better. The object is to lead by example. Where was his leadership?"

"He was trying to raise funds for a good cause," Beneficent offered, "surely you can't find fault in that?"

"It was an act of charity—he didn't have his guard up," Marvelous added.

"A dabbler in the occult? He's in no condition to be admitted to Heaven."

"He never dabbled in the occult, he just read about it and wrote about it," Beneficent offered, she was not above begging. "You *must* look at his entire record, Gelico, please."

"I *am* looking at his record. That's the trouble. In the past several years, he has consistently ignored his responsibilities as the Lord's Shepherd. It must be noted his lack of judgment has been neither good for him, nor good for his flock. His record is abysmal. He is no candidate for transfer. Plus, he's DEAD!"

The Powers That Be huddled together and agreed on a statement.

"He has squandered his time on earth. Midlantic is a dangerous assignment, Beneficent. He is sure to fail and cause even worse havoc."

"With all due respect," Beneficent protested, "the situation in Midlantic can't get any worse."

"What makes you think this will work in Midlantic?" Gelico asked. "Nothing we've tried has dislodged Cell Fish. The peoples of the mountain seem to have made their choice. Cell Fish is ensconced in Three Rivers, and the realm is all but lost. It's too late."

"It's never too late!" Beneficent entreated. "Not until the last person takes their last breath. The realm can still be counted with the Militans if anyone puts up a fight for the rights of all.No man is an island—one body, One Head. I implore you, Angels of Power, this Bishop was once a very good bishop. Please let him put his skills to work. Secretary Gelico, give him another chance."

The Powers piled on. "Cell Fish is top rank."

"You are aware that all grace in this realm is captive?"

"This Bishop didn't attain salvation in his perfect realm. What do you expect in Midlantic? Beneficent, stop this foolishness."

"Gelico," Beneficent entreated, "the Bishop will be no worse off than his current circumstances, nor will Midlantic. Perhaps we can petition a little more time for him."

"Unlikely. Exceptions are difficult."

Beneficent stood her ground. The debate roiled on. They understood that the Bishop had succumbed to the snares of Black Jack and Swelly, and they might have overlooked the gambling perhaps—if it hadn't led to stealing from the poor! A bishop, they contended, was expected to seek forgiveness and repent, but there was no record of his doing so.

They were about to dismiss the case when Small Power reminded the Council of a complication. "Let us not forget the Queen of Revelation has called a Great Gathering of the Communion of Saints for the purpose of reassembling the Pink Skeleton. It is to be held in the meadow atop Castle Cliff in Midlantic, in fact, it is situated in the parish of Three Rivers. We, the Powers that Be, will be counted on to provide safe passage."

"It's true!" Wise Power gasped. "Representatives from the entire Cohort Ecclesia are required to attend—Militans, Penitens, and Triumphans. They'll never get through the thicket of obstacles that Cell Fish has managed to throw up into the atmosphere."

"It's a quagmire of evil."

"There is no light and no manner of travel. If we can't open the Old Road, there will be no gathering. We must send someone."

And so, it was decided. The Powers That Be would make an exception in the case of Beneficent's Bishop of the Southerly Coast (now defunct).

"I'll approve this," said the Secretary, "but only in a manner of speaking."

"A manner of speaking?" Beneficent repeated enthusiastically.

"Yes," Gelico said, pausing to indicate his acute discomfort with the plan.

"We will look to the devotion that had once marked the Bishop's character, on two conditions—a proxy must govern. I'm not fooling, Beneficent, no shenanigans! And the second, they *must* retake Three Rivers. It is impossible to send a dead Bishop—this cannot be done. But if you were to find a friend who is willing to stand in for the Bishop—a proxy, as it were, we will allow him a certain degree of latitude. That friend could execute the duties of the Bishopric on behalf of the Bishop, using his thoughts and ideas by the Power of Inspiration."

"Inspiration, are you willing?" Wise Power inquired.

"Why yes, of course. It is my honor to assist."

Beneficent and Marvelous were delighted. The rest of the powers added their own two cents one after another.

"Obviously, it would have to be a very good friend…"

"One that knows how this man thinks…"

"His best moral philosophy…"

"One who complements his management techniques…"

Finally, Gelico summed it up. "If you can find a friend like that, we will give him such a voice."

"It's agreed then?" asked Beneficent. "We can execute our plan?"

"Yes, reluctantly so," Gelico acquiesced, "if you find such a friend, you may proceed."

"Next," the bailiff roared. And they were gone.

30

The Plan

The Heavenlies

Implementation

Cell Fish derived his power from unleashing the despicable spirits of Pride, Jealousy, Greed, and Rage to do his bidding. They wheedled their way into communities with persuasions of false righteousness, things that had a ring of the greater good, but weren't really quite right. Peoples drifted further and further from the truth. *'From Trickery to Slavery,'* that was the Devil's motto—and it never failed. "Give 'em what they want 'til you drop the snare. Ah, yes, words to live by, simple enough to keep 'em there!" So, spoke Cell Fish, Captain of Hell.

Beneficent was still astonished at how easily humanity surrendered to the Father of Lies and, worse yet, preferred their entrapments to the efforts of escape. And now, the sweetest parish in the whole Realm of Midlantic, Three Rivers, was caught in his clutches.

The two angels would put their plan into action and hope for the best. But first things first, Beneficent and Marvelous agreed, they had to open the Old Road. That was a direct order from the Powers that Be.

Any memory of the Beatitudes, or Works of Mercy were also gone from the Parish of Three Rivers. Three Rivers happened to be the entry to the Realm of Midlantic, which happened to be the entry to the entire country. All of the gifts were missing: Wisdom, Understanding, Counsel, Fortitude, Knowledge, Piety, and Fear-of-the-Lord. And likewise, the fruits: no Love, no Joy, no Peace, no Patience, no Kindness, no Goodness, no Forbearance, no Faithfulness, no Gentleness, no Generosity, and of course, no Self-Restraint or Modesty of any kind remained in the parish. They were all gone.

Neither Marvelous nor Beneficent ever mentioned to the Bishop of the Southerly Coast these very elements of office—for example, Sanctifying Grace, and the Gifts and the Fruits of the Spirit—had vanished. And accordingly, all manners of education in the Gifts and Fruits of the Spirit had disappeared along with them. Without these riches, there wasn't much use for a ruler of the realm in the first place. There simply wasn't a way for anyone to recognize law and order. There was only memory. And the fullness of time had taken its toll on the memories that remained.

"There must be a few working memories left in the parish," Beneficent thought aloud.

"None too many," Marvelous said.

"Then we will stoke the embers of the few dim memories we can find."

"What we need to find is a willing friend of the Bishop,"

Marvelous advised.

Nothing would dampen Beneficent's optimism. "Should be easy enough, he was well-beloved in his day."

In seconds, Beneficent and Marvelous appeared before the Bishop of the Southerly Coast. The brilliance of the two angels startled Dastard Diablo and the Bishop. The angels explained their plan while trying to keep Dastard off balance.

"Just one willing friend, that's all we need," Beneficent encouraged.

"I don't have any friends," the Bishop said sadly as he regarded the countless letters sloshing around in the ankle-deep waters of his library and stacked on his credenza in sloppy wet piles. "In the recent past, I must admit, I didn't keep up with my correspondence."

The two angels looked at each other stunned. If angels could faint, Marvelous was teetering.

"Once I had a great following, you know," the Bishop said. "People came from far and wide to hear my counsel. Clerics, governors, socialites, I've had many influential friends. And other bishops too, but I stopped going to the conferences. As you can see, my entire flock has moved on to higher ground. Cook and Raphael, all my faithful servants have left me. I don't blame them. I was a fool. I can only count this gander here as my true friend. He knows my every thought, all my hopes for the realm. He knows most of the Good Book by heart, you know. He especially loves the Psalms, don't you, dear Périgord?"

"Squawk, Psalms, squawk!"

Beneficent was reinvigorated. "Would you say then, if he could speak, he would speak with your voice?"

"He would, I think. Yes, he would," Bishop said a little surprised at the thought.

"What do you say, Périgord? Will you act as Bishop's friend and stand-in? Are you game?"

"Game? Squawk! I'd say, game! I got game!"

Everyone laughed except Dastard Diablo, who wanted to get a move on with his illustrious prize. He couldn't fathom what the two angels were up to.

"I don't know why I waited for you," Dastard said with suspicion. The tufts and plugs of his hair were almost un-tamable; the angrier he got, the more they uncoiled. Cowlicks popped out of his ponytail—ping, ping, ping—plugs stuck straight up from his greasy do. His red, scaly head began twitching nervously. "What are you going to do with that goose?"

"Goose? Not a thing! Why do you ask?"

"I'll roast him up nice and crisp and force Bishy to dine with me," he snarled, regaining his swagger. "You'll see."

"Don't concern yourself, Bishop," Beneficent interrupted. "If you look at his middle, you will see Dastard is full of hot air."

"Am I?" Dastard asked, pinching the cheek of Périgord, and poking him in the belly. "I haven't seen a goose this ready for the spit since Périgord, France, in the Hundred Years' War. I set so many fires in that place, we ate roast goose for another hundred years—in Hell! Ha! We love French food, don't we, Bishy." Dastard grabbed the frightened goose, caressing his neck with his sharp nails. "No goose escapes my dinner plate, and this one won't either!"

Périgord gulped nervously. "No roast! Squawk!"

"Périgord?" Beneficent exclaimed with a laugh. "Oh, Dastard Diablo, you are a caution!"

This made the demon start to smoke. He hated being mocked, especially by an angel. "What's the joke?" he growled.

"Périgord! That's what we call him. He was named for the last Bishop of Midlantic, a great and holy man. A coincidence and funny that you should mention it."

"It must be a sign," Marvelous chimed in.

"Oh, yes! It's all coming together," Beneficent exclaimed. Then she whispered to gander, "Périgord, dear, will you try your best to save your friend and master, the Bishop, formerly of the Southerly Coast (now defunct) and soon to be—with your special assistance—uh, the new Spiritual 'Advisor' to the Realm of Midlantic?"

It is hard to know whether Périgord really understood the implications of his enthusiastic nod to the angels, but they were satisfied. They had a 'yes' from a friend of the Bishop and were ready to get on with their plan.

Dastard disregarded all vigilance. He relished the opportunity to show off his prize to Cell Fish—a Bishop of the Most-High Lord of Heaven. He could hardly believe his luck and was thoroughly convinced a few days stopover on their journey to Hell would do no harm. There was an entry to the Great Below not far from where Cell Fish anchored his tanker in the bay.

The angels worked out the details for travel. They were unable to assume custody of the Bishop. He would remain a prisoner and travel with Dastard.

The Bishop reluctantly agreed that the miter and robe, still draping Périgord from his run-in with the coat rack, might give the gander an air of authority, useful gear to affect the appearance of a real bishop.

And so, it was thus that an oversized gander oddly named The Great Périgord climbed onto the back of Marvelous Angel, in all his shredded bishop's finery, and off they flew to the captive Realm of Midlantic. They whisked up the coastland with the well-shackled wind, Fury, bumping along behind them.

Beneficent Angel held tightly to the seal of the living God as she cruised comfortably alongside Marvelous. Dastard tried to keep up, holding the Bishop securely tethered to himself with silver chains. He was a hefty burden. It was a terrible ride.

As they approached their destination, Marvelous Angel identified the parish of Three Rivers. The angels touched wings, igniting a firestorm of awesome colors. Beneficent headed heavenward and Marvelous, with Périgord on board, continued toward land. This time Beneficent Angel, up from the East, remembered to call out her warning:

"Do not damage the land or the sea or the trees until we put the seal on the foreheads of the servants of God!"

The thunder of the warning rang out throughout the world. The roar of her voice caused such shocking vibrations, the Great Périgord fell from his perch on the back of Marvelous. He plummeted through the air squawking wildly, flailing and whooshing, he would have to rely on his own wings. He strained and thrashed with terror as the art of flying came back to him. His wings plumped up, voluminous and snowy white. As they opened and fluttered, their full span was shot through with glory. Périgord took on a new demeanor—elegant, beautiful, and larger than life.

Unfortunately, as he tumbled through the atmosphere of Three Rivers, the Great Périgord's portly circumference got the better of him. He became unsteady and started to flail. A scrap of paper, having a bit of sparkle to it, floated aimlessly passed him in the sky. Down, down, down he fell, and with one nervous thrust forward, he caught the paper with his bill and landed in a swamp at the edge of the Murky River.

On the paper was scribbled a message. It was a homework assignment from Sister Angelina.

'I energize each Knight
but Angels guide the soldiers of Christ.
Crusade in a column under the standard of Our Lord.
Things will mushroom. Why you are—You can do it!

"Mushrooms? Squawk! I love mushrooms!"

PART FOUR

Danger on the Old Road

St. Mary's-of-the-Future

31

Confirmation Day

Pentecost
June 10, 1962

F rancie was full of excitement watching out her bedroom window. The caterers were carrying stacks of tablecloths and truckloads of flowers into the tent.

Aunts, uncles, cousins, and best of all, her sister Taffy were buzzing around outside, dividing up into cars.

"Francie, you're going to be late!"

Francie ran down the stairs, her white academic gown with the red collar flying behind her.

Her father beamed with pride at his little girl. "Are you ready for your Confirmation Day?"

"What if the Bishop calls on me, Pop? He could ask me a question."

"He won't," her mother said. "Get in the car. We'll be late."

The Bishop sat regally in the carved chair Gabe had dragged over from the rectory and placed on the altar. It was a dusty, tired throne, a gift to the rectory from some rich old soul moving on to her next life, but Gabe fixed it up, gluing it together in many a joint and topping it off with a fresh coat of shellac. After the entire congregation was quiet, the Bishop rose from his special seat of authority to commence the ceremonies. He leaned on his Crozier, a staff which symbolized his role as 'Shepherd of the Flock of God' and scanned the Confirmandi sitting nervously before him. To Francie's horror, his eyes stopped and engaged her own. She gulped, fearful of what was to come.

"Young lady, please stand and tell us your name."

Francie curtsied. "Francine O'Malley, your Excellency."

"Perhaps you can tell me, Miss O'Malley, what is the Sacrament of Confirmation?"

Her feet froze to the floor. A question!

Sister Angelina's heart was in her throat. She whispered in prayer the very words that, somehow, miraculously came forth from Francie's mouth.

"Confirmation is a sacrament in which the Holy Ghost is perfected in those already baptized, in order to make them strong and perfect Christians and soldiers of Jesus Christ."

The nun sighed with relief, and so did Francie. Sister Angelina watched with pride as her class processed in a perfect column up the stairs of the sanctuary to receive the Holy Ghost.

Francie approached the altar, and Taffy O'Malley rested her hand on her sister's shoulder, acting as her sponsor. An altar boy stood at the ready with chrism, the holy oil for the anointing. The Bishop dipped his thumb in the oil and pressed it against Francie's forehead. "I sign you with the sign of the cross, and I anoint you with the Chrism of Salvation." He tapped Francie's cheek as a symbol of the blow she might encounter for her Faith. "Congratulations, Miss O'Malley," the Bishop said to Francie. "Won't you introduce me to your sponsor?"

"Yes, of course, Your Excellency, this is my sister, Taffy," Francie said nervously. "O'Malley. I mean, her real name is Anne Taft O'Malley."

"Ah, yes, you are Albert O'Malley's granddaughters."

"Yes, Your Excellency, we are," Taffy said cheerfully.

"Did you know I went to school with your grandfather when we were boys?"

"He died and never told us," Francie said.

The Bishop laughed. "Very good then, God Bless you, and I will see the next candidate."

When the ceremony was over the doors flew open to the beautiful day, and the bells rang out the joy of the Church in Her newly Confirmed Soldiers of Jesus Christ. There was much gaiety as the cameras clicked and the congregation congratulated the newly confirmed on the steps of the Church of Our Lady's. It was time to celebrate.

Cars exited the church parking lot onto Miller Street in an orderly fashion. Families drove off to the many celebrations happening around the parish. Some went north on the Old Road a few blocks, then head down the hill to Pastor's party on the Pier. Francie's family headed south on the Old Road to the bridge and the festivities awaiting them in the elegant white tent set up on O'Malley's side lawn.

Over in River Ridge, the gravel crunched under tires in O'Malley's circular driveway, and car doors slammed one after another, beating out the sound of anticipated fun as guests arrived at Francie's party.

They say Dr. Albert O'Malley, Jr. was the best in his field until his eyesight went bad. When he couldn't operate anymore, he taught. He married one of his students, who he first met during rounds at the prestigious Warren Memorial Teaching Hospital.

There was a second encounter between them, when he made an unscheduled trip to the emergency room after an accident in the hospital parking lot, having walked into an ambulance door. He insisted the door had opened rather suddenly and had nothing to do with his reading in the Journal of Medicine while walking. Anne Taft was on duty that day and deftly sewed up the nasty cut on his forehead. The normal course of pleasantries revealed the two were neighbors, of a sort, being from the same parish, but on very different sides of the rivers. She was from a blue-collar neighborhood known as LittleCapernaum, and he from the tonier neighborhood of River Ridge. The Doctors Albert and Annie fell in love, despite the 15-year difference in age, and married not many months later. It was a triangulated relationship right from the start—Anne, Bert, and medicine.

Bert adored Anne and indulged her heart's desire, which, oddly enough, was tax-deductible, as he financed her free clinic for poor children in Fishtown.

Francie's parents would have been considered well-off. As a couple, they were well-liked and well-respected. The only difficulty was Bert's mother, Diana O'Malley, who resented everything about her daughter-in-law. Anne's story was much like her own—poor girl marries rich man. But, unlike Anne's story, Diana's unfolded in an almost comical panoply of self-indulgence. Her husband, Albert, Sr., had made a fortune in the stock market. Diana was his secretary and snagged the catch of the day. According to their son, she had put on silly airs ever since setting much store in money and the country club gossip of River Ridge.

Diana found Dr. Annie's relatives appalling, likely because they put her in mind of her own. She had happily abandoned her relatives in the outer boroughs of the big city when she married Bert's dad and moved to River Ridge. Her jealousy was tiresome, and her constant barbs annoyed her only son. Bert had resorted to telling his mother to keep her comments to herself or stay home, and a kind of peace prevailed.

Francie, on the other hand, loved all the relatives, and they loved her. At the party, Francie and Lucy demonstrated the latest dance craze to Francie's two burly uncles. Their wives joined in, crying with laughter at the wild gyrations of their husbands, both uncomfortably sausaged into ill-fitting suits long since outgrown from their own weddings. If it weren't for the sound of a waltz, they might have collapsed. Francie's father approached and took his baby daughter to the dance floor. Her light blue voile dress billowed around her as they twirled to the violins.

Lucy watched them dance for a minute, but her father was dead, and this kind of moment poked at that empty spot in her heart. She recovered quickly enough when the uncles asked her for another demonstration, wanting to practice for the next fast dance.

"It's your big day, Pumpkin," Bert said, kissing Francie's forehead. "You bring joy to everyone here."

"Except Meg," Francie added, scanning the tent for her missing eldest sister. "She didn't even bother to come."

"She'll be here."

"The party's almost over, Daddy."

Meg was the eldest of the three O'Malley girls. When Francie was born, Meg found a new baby to be an unwelcome intrusion in her otherwise perfectly happy life. Francie's arrival, according to Meg, was a definite drag on her burgeoning teenage independence, creating a rift between them from the start. Meg detested babysitting, which her parents often asked her to do when her mother was on call at the hospital. She became spiteful toward the child, so much so, that Anne felt compelled to seek advice from Pastor on the subject.

Pastor had a solution for everything. Francie took to her new baby-sitter, Garbo quite well, and peace returned to the O'Malley household. The arrangement eased Garbo and Gabe's financial burdens too. The rectory was never quite the same again, as it became the favored haunt of three-year-old Francie O'Malley. Most days, little Francie could be found riding her tricycle round and round the border of the rectory dining room's Persian rug. In return, Dr. Annie opened a children's clinic in Fishtown to care for Pastor's poor.

Diana eventually came to admire her daughter-in-law, Dr. Annie, although she continued to envy Anne's easy-going relationship with her son, something she had never had in her marriage. These days Diana didn't cause too much trouble in the family—except when vacation time rolled around. Since the death of her husband, she lived at the Palm Bay Club on the Southerly Coast. She constantly nagged her son to bring Francie down for visits. Francie adored her Grand-Mère, or just Mère, as she was instructed to call her, and Francie very often joined in o n Diana's secret schemes to affect such visits.

Grand- Mère, Diana O'Malley, was in her true element at a party. She created lots of fun with the college crowd, toasting them with champagne and regaling them with hilarious stories of her gadabout life. Her stories glossed over a few of the more vivid evenings with the late and great Albert Sr. when good times suddenly disintegrated into alcoholic stupors and terrible fights. Time eventually slowed them down, and her husband stopped drinking altogether, but it was too late for old Albert. He died, regrettably, of sclerosis of the liver. Francie had no knowledge of the strife between her grandparents, never knowing her grandfather. She found Mère to be thoroughly entertaining and wanted to be just like her when she grew u p. Her sister Taffy, on the other hand, observed her grandmother with greater caution and made a habit of remaining a guarded half-step away from Grand- Mère's antics.

Anne Taft O'Malley, 18, the namesake of her mother and lovingly known as Taffy, was a nursing student at Georgetown University, having inherited her parents' love of medicine. She had a studious look, parting her dark hair on one side and clipping it up in a barrette. She hid her soft brown eyes behind horn-rimmed glasses. Her father said her eyes were velvet brown; she liked that a lot.

Although Taffy wasn't quite able to erase how often Mére had taken pleasure in humiliating her mother in her early years, today, she would put all that aside and join in Mère's amusements determined to make this a happy occasion for her little sister, Francie.

Taffy stood in the breezy foyer and took in the lovely setting through the open front door. She breathed in the fragrance of the freshly mowed lawn, the perfect blue sky, and the ducks and geese quacking away on the twinkling river. It was a beautiful day. The party tent was a few yards away behind her on the other side of the patio. She retrieved the small box containing Francie's gift from her skirt pocket and perked up the satin ribbon tied around it. Dr. Annie and she had cooked up a plan at Christmas time when they found the special necklace and locket on a tray in the old pawn shop on Front Street. Dr. Annie speculated that it might well have been laying on that same tray of old junk since the turn of the century. It probably hadn't been polished since then either. Taffy bought the pieces and took them to Lucy's Uncle Taurus to fix the fastener and the filigree clasp of the locket. He was a welder by trade but did skilled metalwork of all kinds in his garage shop down by the dock. The necklace was Francie's Christmas gift, a string of intricately linked gold hearts. It was one of a kind, as sweet as could be. Francie loved it. Dr. Annie was touched by Taffy's thoughtfulness and promised to keep secret the locket, destined to become Francie's Confirmation gift. Today was the day.

Taffy placed the small box on the front hall table with the rest of Francie's gifts, then joined her friends in the tent festooned with yards of sherbet-colored silks and crisp white piqué of the girls' party dresses. In the center of it all, in a whirl of the spinning skirts of girls dancing with their gangly dates clad in navy blue blazars, was Francie, having a ball.

Taffy beckoned to her little sister, "Francie, come and meet my friends from school." Francie rushed over. Taffy's pals dutifully made a fuss over the beaming guest of honor as they were each introduced.

"Francie, this is Brian Cleveland," Taffy said, "he's in pre-med."

The music became awash of muffled sound, like diving under a wave. The handsome young man reached out and took Francie's hands in his. He stepped back gallantly and admired her dress.

His smiling green eyes sparkled with his compliments. Francie was lost in a forever place she had never known before. What would she say, where was her voice, where did it go? She mustered the nerve to look up at him. All she could hear were the rushing sounds of the forever-place-sea, and then the tiniest little "Hi" peeping out of her mouth. Brian turned from her, dropped one of her hands, and pulled his girlfriend closer. She was the daughter of a southern senator.

"Baby, let me introduce you to the belle of the ball."

Francie's head was swimming. Belle of the ball, he called me the belle of the ball. Brian's girlfriend looked past her and scanned the crowd for better fish to fry.

"Hello, Darlin'," she drawled, barely adding a disingenuous drawn out, *"congratulations."*

Francie was mortified. Her other hand, still in his, turned into a sweaty jellyfish. "I gotta go," she said, scanning the dance floor for Lucy. "Excuse me." She ran to her best friend, her ever-present port in a storm.

"She was so snobby," Francie sneered after filling Lucy in on her brief encounter with Brian and his girlfriend.

Francie and Lucy spent the rest of the party spying on the couple from a safe distance until their eyes followed them to a new crowd just arriving. The med-student, Brian Cleveland, and Southern Belle (that's what Francie named her) were lost in the shuffle of introductions at the entrance to the tent. It was Francie's eldest sister Meg, her boyfriend, and a gang of their friends just arriving from the city. Everyone was ooh-ing and ah-ing over something Francie couldn't see. And she also couldn't have cared less about anything to do with Meg O'Malley. Francie avoided her eldest sister as much as possible.

Meg had graduated from college the previous year and now worked for a fashion magazine. She fancied herself entirely too sophisticated for River Ridge anymore, much preferring 'Out East' to their prosaic little hometown.

"Well, sometimes in the summer when there's absolutely nothing else to do—if my father begs her—she might come home for the weekend." That's how Francie described Meg's family visits to Garbo.

While the musicians were taking a break, Francie and Lucy headed to the bar to refill their sodas. They analyzed Southern Belle as she gushed forth pleasantries with Meg and her sophisticated City friends. The girls begrudgingly had to admit she was beautiful. She did have the best dress, the best jewelry, the best hair, shining yellow white against her tan skin and pink lipstick, in the best shade; in a word, she was perfect. The handsome med-student, Brian Cleveland, joined his friends mingling with Meg's group after procuring some fruit punch for his girlfriend. His charm was engaging, and Francie had fallen forever in love with him. Brian slipped his arm around Southern Belle's waist, who accepted it with indifference.

"I hate her," Francie moaned, blowing bubbles in her soda.

"Look at that. She doesn't even like him!" Lucy observed, dutifully sympathetic.

Grand- Mère sauntered over for a fresh glass of champagne. She observed the girls' intense scrutiny with reserved humor. "Why so glum, sweeties?"

Francie bemoaned her handsome prince was smitten by a spell-casting interloper from the Southerly Realm.

Grand-Mère smiled, waving off Francie's unrequited love. "Oh my, cast your net again, Dolly. Lots of fish in that sea!"

Lucy's mother, Minnie Penn, had just arrived, and Lucy saw her across the garden with Dr. Annie.

"I gotta go," Lucy said and kissed Grand-Mère's cheek respectfully. "Bye, Mère. Bye, France, see ya Monday."

"Bye," said Francie, clinging to Mère. "See ya."

Mère hugged Francie tight as if to squeeze away her broken heart and danced her off in a twirl to the dessert carts to commiserate over chocolate mousse.

32

Confirmation Day Stolen

The Party
June 10, 1962

Lucy's Uncle Taurus was a bull of a man. Since the death of his brother in the Korean War, he saw himself as the protector of the family. Unmarried, he lived to work. He kept to himself, except for the occasional weekend suppers down at the Clam Hut, where he would take the family for steamers and chowder. He wasn't a warm sort of fellow. Pastor described him as an "upright man" and a good provider. "Taurus Penn oughta get a wife of his own to support, and keep his nose out of Minnie Penn's business. Poor woman! She's got so many people tellin' her what to do—it's a wonder she can think for herself at all." That was Garbo's opinion.

"He feels obligated to care for them," Pastor insisted.

"And I suppose that's that?" Garbo muttered, shuffling out of the room. It was an argument they had often. Garbo kept a running commentary on most parishioners.

Lucy's mother, Minnie Penn, was emotionally frail. In addition to the constant advice she received from her brother-in-law, her late husband's two sisters also pushed her around. The aunts, Mae, and Maud were teachers and schemed every which way they could to get Lucy a good education. It was a constant battle in their house—what a bad job Minnie Penn was doing raising "their" girl. What could they expect, they chided, Minnie was not an educated woman, and they wanted something better than the tough local high school for their dead brother's only child—in fact, the whole family's only child. It was simply a matter of too many adults stirring the soup—everybody had an opinion on what to do with Lucy. The formidable force of wills, time and again, ground Minnie Penn's will into dust.

Life had been a struggle for Minnie Penn ever since her husband was killed in action. Lucy never knew him, but she wanted to be the life of the party like he had been. She wanted to be everything he wasn't there to be to cheer Minnie's pensive moods. Lucy developed her funny personality partly to protect herself from her overbearing family and partly to make her mother laugh, which was everything to her. When her husband died, Minnie Penn too often forgot she had someone else to live for and sent her heart to the grave with him. Even on this important day, Minnie made excuses that she couldn't get time off from work and arranged for Lucy to go home with the O'Malleys after her Confirmation.

Dr. Annie embraced Minnie when she arrived to pick up Lucy. She tried to draw her into the party.

"No thanks, Doctor Annie," Minnie said. "The Aunts will be looking for us over at the picnic grounds. Pastor's got a nice party set up over there on the pier. It's for the whole parish. Of course, it's nothin' like this."

"I'm so sorry you won't stay," Dr. Annie said kindly.

Minnie looked around dreamily. She clutched at the neckline of her blouse, feeling woefully underdressed. "It's a beautiful tent. Everybody looks so nice."

"We're crazy about your Lucy, she's so full of spirit," Dr. Annie said, trying to make Minnie comfortable.

"Yeah, she's like her father that way," Minnie agreed, beaming a smile at her daughter coming toward her. Lucy rushed to hug her Mom. That special look was meant just for her. It was her greatest happiness. She didn't mind leaving Francie's party. The other girls and their families would be at the picnic grounds, and that would be fun too. Best of all, she would be with her Mom.

Francie moved from the dessert cart to the round table in the front hall piled high with gifts all for her. She inspected the boxes and cards, trying to guess their content. The glossy black front door with its lion's head brass door knocker, stood open to welcome any guests yet to arrive.

Taffy snuck up behind Francie in the foyer. "Want to open your present?" she quizzed with a tickle to her sister's side.

"Oh yes!" Francie squealed.

"Let's get Mom." Taffy took Francie by the hand and dragged her outside.

Doctor Annie saw them approaching and met them at the entrance to the house. "Is it time?" she asked Taffy knowingly. Doctor Annie motioned to her husband who was with Meg and her guests near the bandstand.

"We don't have to wait for everybody, Mom. It's just for us."

Taffy handed her sister the little box tied with red satin ribbon. Francie grinned from ear to ear and shook the box. She opened the card and read the note.

Taffy was just as excited as her little sister.

> *Dearest Francie,*
>
> > *To the best sister a girl could have. The first part of this gift was your Christmas present, now for the rest of it. Can you guess?*
> >
> > *Here's a clue: You are My Little Heart!*
> > > *Love Always,*
> > > *Taffy*

Francie made a curious face, kissed Taffy on the cheek, then opened the box with her eyes closed. She wasn't thinking about her Christmas gift, only the special gift she held in her hands. She carefully folded back the tissue to discover a black velvet box. In it was an exquisite gold locket. It was in the shape of a heart. On the front was etched a tiny cross with a diamond chip in the center. Inside was a picture of the two of them, and their initials engraved above the date. Francie's eyes filled with tears. She was distraught.

"It's a pendant for your heart necklace," Taffy said, not knowing what to make of Francie's reaction. Francie grabbed her neck. She hadn't mentioned to anyone that she had lost her necklace. Like the antique locket in her hands, the necklace was unique, irreplaceable, even more so in sentiment than treasure.

"France? Don't you like it? Let's put it on your necklace."

"Uh, I'll do it later," Francie said, slamming the velvet box closed with a snap. Taffy, on the verge of tears, tried to conceal her disappointment. Dr. Annie was surprised at Francie's behavior, but a drumroll interrupted as her husband stepped up to the microphone on the bandstand.

"Everyone, may I have your attention please." Spoons tinkled against glass, then silence.

"Dear friends and family, I want to thank you all for coming to our home on Francie's special day." Her father waved his arm, motioning to his family. "Francie, Taffy, and my beautiful wife, Anne—come on over here and join me for a minute."

The girls and their mother moved toward Bert, who was beaming with pride. Francie continued to choke back tears reaching for her neck. Megan and her boyfriend stood beside Bert. The crowd parted to let the family through to the bandstand. He helped them up and put his arm tenderly around Dr. Annie.

"On this great day, I have an extra surprise for everyone. I would like to announce that our eldest daughter, Meg, is engaged to be married." Meg kissed her fiancé and proudly raised her left hand and gave it a shake, her ring dazzling in the spotlight for all to see.

Francie was overcome. Her special day was stolen, snatched

away, just like her necklace. All attention was now squarely fixed on Meg—just like always.

"She barely even knows the guy," Francie scowled.

"Francine!" her mother shushed, shocked at her child's rude remark. "Be gracious, please!"

Francie smarted, the party was no longer hers, the talk of a wedding excited the crowd. Megan asked Taffy to be her maid of honor and her friends to be bridesmaids. She turned to Francie as if an afterthought, and said, "I guess you're too big to be a flower girl. You'll have to be a junior bridesmaid."

Francie reached her boiling point. She couldn't control her temper for another second. "You ruin everything. You always ruin everything!" She stormed into the house, running through the foyer, past her gifts, and out the front door, still clutching the velvet gift box from Taffy.

"What a brat!" Megan said to her mother. Dr. Annie was smiling to keep up appearances and was grateful for Grand-Mère's ostentatious exuberance, making a fuss over the ring and the groom and striking up the band. It was a great save.

"You should have given us more warning, dear," Anne said coldly to Meg.

Meg knew her mother was furious. "Daddy didn't have to announce it, but really, Mother, that kid shouldn't be allowed to act like a selfish little monster."

Anne O'Malley glared at her eldest daughter. "That 'kid' is your little sister, and I will thank you for keeping that in mind."

Francie ran across the circular driveway to the lawn that led to her favorite sanctuary down by the riverbank. She sat by the river at the edge of their property, weeping with the willows that dangled in the water. She watched the ducks and birds and all the activities going on in the world within her world. Wiping her eyes, she was too embarrassed to return to her party. Her pretty blue dress gave her no comfort. Her Mom had finally made the time to go shopping with her, and they had enjoyed their afternoon together, but that memory was washed away in her current misery. She was ashamed of her bad behavior to cover up for the lost necklace and hated herself for hurting Taffy and her mother.

Then anger welled up again against Meg, and she indulged herself in its bitter pill. "She really does ruin everything," Francie whimpered to some quick water creature skimming by in a hurry.

She opened the velvet box and removed the locket. As she held the locket close to her heart, the sting of embarrassment passed over her again and again. Francie's tears wet the locket as she kissed its cross. Taffy must know it meant so much to her.

Pastor parked way down the street and was cutting across O'Malley's lawn when he noticed Francie sitting by the river. He suspected poor Doctor Annie was having the same old troubles with her girls, Meg was probably home. He had left the parish party he was hosting over at the pier to stop in at O'Malley's party where the Bishop was in attendance, he, being an old friend of Francie's grandparents. Pastor was in a hurry to pick up the Bishop and take him back to the festivities at the pier, but he took the time to detour over to Francie. He leaned against the willow tree listening to her quiet whimpers.

"Look at that big goose over there," he said softly. "He's trying to get out of the water, isn't he?"

Francie was startled.

"He's so fat he can't seem to lift himself out of the mud."

She looked up at Pastor with a big sniff.

"Don't get stuck in the mud, Francie," Pastor said.

The priest's wisdom spoke of not succumbing to the demons of jealousy and pride, because now she was confirmed, a new soldier of Jesus Christ. She had enhanced graces and the Gifts and Fruits of the Holy Ghost to deal with these petty things and, whether they deserved it or not, hurting people was never the answer. He always seemed to say just the right thing. "Why don't you show me where the festivities are, Miss O'Malley," he said, making a slight bow offering his hand. And while they walked to the tent, he explained that a day of joy belonged to all. It was a day to share.

"You always want me to share, Pastor, but I'm tired of sharing."

"Don't get tired yet, Francie," he said. "Life requires sharing—your stuff, your gifts, your talents, even the people you love."

Francie was about to tell him about the necklace when they heard an announcement by the bandleader: "His Excellency, our visiting Bishop!"

"The Bishop is ready to speak," Pastor said to Francie with a grin. "Come on, we better hurry."

The sounds of splashing water sent the ducklings in the river in many directions. The great white gander fluttered his wings and, with a mighty painful squawk, he rose up and away and out of the mud.

Francie watched that gander from the sidelines of sleep that night. And as her mind reviewed her troubling day, she drifted back to her favorite spot under the willow tree by the river, then off, with the help of Beneficent Angel, to another world where that gander's troubles were far worse than her own.

In her dream, this different place was … Wait a minute, the place looked exceedingly familiar … It was Three Rivers!

33

The Book of Deuteronomy

St. Mary's-of-the-Future

The huge gander, Périgord, fell amidst the reeds by the riverbank. He pulled himself together and tried to get his bearings, but the sucking sludge nearly did him in. "Oh my, why did I agree to come here?" he fretted.

Freeing himself, he staggered along, calling out for his friend the Bishop, spouting the most absurd combination of skewed incantations.

"Bishop—Bishop, where are you? I assign you with the sign of the Cross. I anoint you with the prism of salvation." There was something familiar about the words, but the gander couldn't recall how they went together. They were like words to a favorite song ringing around in his head. "I don't know if that's quite right. What song have I sung? Or verse recited? Where are those words from? What am I quoting? Oh, Squawk! Squawk! What am I supposed to do? Squawk!"

"Calm yourself, gander. Don't squawk like a silly goose. To help your bishop, you must think like a bishop. You are the

Great Périgord! You must act with honor, not like a scared bird."

"Who is that? Who's whispering in my ear?" Périgord looked around nervously, but no one was there. "Oh, dear! I *am* a scared bird," he announced to the mist. Beneficent said no more.

Périgord had never left home before. He trudged through swampy pools of water and tufts of seagrass, but the colors of the sunshine were missing. Everything appeared gray, nothing like the colorful world he had left behind. There were no palm trees or fruit trees anywhere in sight. He wasn't even certain if this was part of the Bishop's new realm. Perhaps he was trespassing. "Oh, dread—forgive us our trespassing as we forgive trespassers!" Worrisome thoughts plagued him as he tried to unruffle his muddy feathers in this eerie and threatening environment.

With every step he took, he recited parts of prayers and scripture passages, but not well enough to place them in proper order so they might make sense. His dear friend, the Bishop of the Southerly Coast, was not on hand to refresh his memory, nor instruct him in the many important jobs a bishop must do to put things in good order. And try as he might, he couldn't remember.

Périgord scanned the landscape for signs of life. Maybe a kind soul would happen by who could tell him where he was. "I'm sure that from the least amount of information," he mused, "I can figure where I'm going. I've learned astronomy and astrology and geography and philosophy and lots of other phys from the Bishop—if only I had the smallest indicator." But now, he had only misery, and all he saw, in any direction, was swamp grass— tall, soggy-bottom, swamp grass.

Suddenly, an unusual sound caught Périgord's attention. It was a kind of glug-glug, not unlike a slurp-slurp. Beneficent Angel's golden seal was sinking in the mud. In a frantic dive to save the seal, Périgord slid through the slime and snatched it back from oblivion. With a sigh of relief, he collapsed on the shore.

After a time, he found a dry mound. Hmm, very good, he

thought, very good. He felt a chill, which he surmised was the effect of a huge rock casting a shadow over him. "If I'm in the shadow of this rock, then west must be that way."

He tried to fly to the top of the rock for a look-see, but his wing feathers were still stuck together with mud, and he could barely lift them.

Next, he noticed a road sign sticking out of the wet sand. It was sinking fast. He pulled and tugged at the disappearing marker, but the suction of the mud pulled it down, and him along with it. Exasperated and sapped of strength, he gave it one last yank. And with a pluck and a plop and a roly-poly backward, he landed in a ball. To his great satisfaction, he had pulled up the marker. He took it to a pool of water, not far from his dry mound, and rinsed it free of the sticky muck. The sign read:

BEWARE OF QUICKSAND PIT

"It's no use to anyone over there," Périgord squawked, "I will locate it in a better spot."

In this way, the Great Périgord performed his first act of reforming in the Bishop's new realm. He situated the sign on his mound for all to see. Regrettably, not a soul wandered by to benefit from its warning.

As the hours passed, Périgord became acutely anxious. He was used to being catered to and fussed over and, best of all, fed by the Bishop's staff. He missed Raphael, playing his guitar while he and Swan swam around their pond. What was he going to do in this vast waterway of three rivers and a bay? What a quandary—what an awful place to be. Where was his new cathedral pond and his new Villa-by-the-Sea? Who were his people? And what was his destiny? How was he going to find the imperiled children the angels had directed him to save? And after that, how was he going to save them? He pondered their dilemma, but most of all, he worried about his best friend, the Bishop. What could he have done to fall into the hands of Dastard Diablo? Would that awful character really cart him off to Hell, the place of fire, if he, the Great Périgord, was unsuccessful as the Bishop's proxy?

Périgord knew from the Bishop's many sermons that Hell was a place known to be much hotter than the sun, and Périgord could tell anyone from personal experience that the sun can make a place beastly hot, especially after Eastertide.

Beneficent and Marvelous left him without a portfolio. He brewed over being abandoned. "I have no programs the likes of which Bishop reviewed with me many-a-thousand times. There are no building plans or outlines to look over and nod my head and say, 'Hmmm.' Not a one. How could angels be so irresponsible as to dump me here with no means to advance? I think this is—Squawk! —too ambitious an expectation. I am only a goose."

It was just then that a soft breeze began to blow. Périgord heard the rustling of papers like pages in a book.

"Wind and paper, wind and paper, an unmistakable sound," he said.

There it was, on the riverbank, the big Book of Laws and Good News—Beneficent's own. She had dropped it there for him to find, but it was Marvelous Angel who sent the wind—just enough to rustle some pages.

And this is how it happened that the Great Périgord took up his position on the shore with the wondrous book and the golden seal to stand in for the Bishop in absentia, to take back Three Rivers and save Midlantic.

Périgord wiped the big book with his wing. He opened it up to a random page and found that he could read, not perfectly, of course, but well enough to grasp the thread of the scriptures. The Great Périgord nodded thoughtfully.

THE BOOK OF DEUTERONOMY, the big letters read. He pictured himself back home, cozy in his leather chair-nest, the French doors open to the sea, with the wispy sheer curtains blowing softly, and the Bishop's kind voice reading the words from "The Book of Deuteronomy."

"Ah, Blessed André, good always." Beneficent Angel said offering a greeting. They exchanged pleasantries at the back door to Heaven and strolled together to the veranda.

"And how goes it?" Blessed André inquired.

Beneficent filled André in on the current set of circumstances as they peered through the clouds to watch the story unfold.

"Isn't this an unusual way to fulfill your assignment?" Blessed André asked, observing Périgord far below.

"Quite so," Beneficent sighed. "A foolish man, this Bishop. If he had only stuck with it, his regular line of work that is. Instead, he imperiled his soul lost in his 'exotic studies', forgetting all about his job to shepherd the faithful. His people drifted off into every imaginable heresy."

"Does he have a chance for salvation?" André asked.

"Yes. 'A' chance…his only chance, this one farfetched plan of ours. I've done my best to petition for a crackerjack helper to assist the Bishop and the gander, Périgord, standing in for him. Only if needs be, naturally."

"Ah, bien, naturally. You can take comfort in that," Blessed André nodded. "Are you then relegated to the sidelines?"

"For the most part—but not entirely, I may yet have some input, with permission from the Powers That Be, of course."

"Ah, oui, of course."

Just then, Marvelous Angel touched down in a harried state and rushed to join Beneficent and Blessed André on the veranda.

"You don't think this is it, do you?" Marvelous quizzed, bewildered.

"What?" Beneficent asked.

"Is that the crackerjack helper you requested?"

"What do you mean?"

"Look closer! Look through the beam!"

The veranda of Heaven was equipped with numerous beams to provide the closest viewing of earthly goings on. Beneficent focused her special beam on the happenings of their case. Here they could follow the progress of Périgord and the soon-to-be helper they had requested for him.

"This cannot be right!" Marvelous said.

Beneficent was too stunned for words. Through the thicket of smog, the beam pointed clearly and without question to one little beaver, a runt, really, pouring over a long list entitled:

"My List of What Happy Isn't."

34

Father Brendan Finds
Father John at
St. Anthony's Lost & Found

St. Mary's-of-the-Future

Chatter on the dock as folks waited for transport to Big City had long since reduced to grousing.

"Oh, someone will work it out."

"I'm sure."

"I agree."

"It's difficult to get involved."

"Difficult enough to get to work. Where's the ferry?"

"Late again."

"Why doesn't anything run right in this community?"

Indifference was the order of the day. If they had only noticed the broken condition of the exhausted souls passing them by on the returning trawlers, maybe things would have been different, but by now it was too late. Offices were swept, and laws had been made. Cell Fish was in charge. Someone did work it out all right, but it was the wrong someone, and that created sorry times for Three Rivers.

The law now stated that 'Things of the Spirit' could never be put above 'Things Temporal.' And "never" meant especially on confiscated property. Father John, being a perpetrator of 'Things of the Spirit,' well, his very presence was considered a crime. This was the life of a priest under this chilling reign. He was outlawed by virtue of his vocation to save souls and build up the Church.

Cell Fish took swift action to obliterate every offending cleric. Father John and many others could attest to his noxious and cruel enforcement of the outrageous law, but the peoples of the mountain were indifferent, or at best uninformed—until after the fact.

Cell Fish had one agenda: To rid detestable Goodness from the mountain once and for all. Seemingly, Bully Bargumo, as the appointed mayor, had been working the devious plan at the behest of Cell Fish, but in truth, Bully was after satisfying his own craving for tip-topity-ness.

While news of Father John's banishment took a long time to reach the Parish of Inland, once known, Father Brendan, Pastor of Inland, lost no time in going to the aid of his friend.

Pete the Fisherman made his way down the Intracoastal to account for Father John's troubles. When Pete arrived, Father Brendan was having tea with a visiting Anglican prelate, the Right Reverend Archibald McCann.

"I can't believe it!" Father Brendan remarked with concern.

The briny messenger twisted his cap, eyeballing the purple stole of the confessional hanging on a hook. The fisherman never thought he'd wish for the comfort of the confessional box and the anonymity it provided, but he longed for it now. All of Three Rivers could use a sacramental cleansing and general absolution, he figured as he trashed his fellow citizens who made profits, not protest at the outrage. "Can't be helped, Father Brendan. Sighting a priest in that there district pays a lotta money."

Pete told of how Cell Fish had galvanized his power and taken control of Three Rivers, and the big plans that devil had to move down the coast and seize the entire Realm of Midlantic.

"From there, Father B, he plans to conquer the whole world," he added anxiously.

Father Brendan was disturbed to hear of the darkness that shrouded the confiscated parish of Three Rivers, the mountainside, and its lovely peninsula beaches.

"I say, isn't Inland part of the Realm of Midlantic, too?" Reverend McCann noted.

"Yes, making my parish vulnerable to the clutches of that vile demon." Father Brendan added.

"I'm rather scandalized to tell you the truth, old boy," Reverend McCann remarked.

"Scandal or no, sir, I come to relay the story," Pete said.

"Seems rather reminiscent of Paris in the Terror," Reverend McCann added sarcastically.

Pete was uncomfortable in front of the pompous British cleric dithering over his tea.

Pete's guilt by association was the driving force that had sent him the long way downriver to bring Father Brendan the bad news. The old fisherman had finally learned the meaning of "sins of omission"—the actions one could have taken for the good but didn't.

"It weren't my hand what collected bounty, Father."

"What was the price, 30 pieces of silver?" Reverend McCann sneered.

"Somethin' like that, sir."

"I say!"

Reverend McCann was an important force in the Anglican Church. He was an old friend of Father Brendan's. They had met at some conference or other many years earlier. Pete regretted not having asked to see Father Brendan alone. He was suspicious of the pale, fleshy-faced bishop of another faith in his strange collar and fine black suit. Pete's skin was the color and texture of leather. Even with the sun's rays gone foggy since the reign of Cell Fish, the windburn alone bespoke his trade.

"I be on my way," Pete said. "Thought you might wanna know 'bout Father John is all. You're the only man I know could help our Pastor, Father B."

"Yes. Pete, I understand," Father Brendan said, closing the door behind him.

Reverend McCann poured himself more tea. "My word, Brendan, I thought this was the land of the free. What in the world is going on here?"

"You'll have to excuse me, Archie, I best go and find out."

After having entrusted his Parish of Inland to the care of an associate priest and shipping the indignant Right Reverend Archibald McCann back to his episcopal see in England, Father Brendan hitched a singularly shabby boat to the back of his car and drove to the closest dock on the Intracoastal. If what Pete had said was true, he concluded, the river would be the fastest and safest way to travel up to Father John's parish. He would find him and bring him back to safety.

Father Brendan left before breakfast and sailed upriver to St. Anthony's Lost and Found, also known as St. A's, a do-gooder house established in the early 1920s to feed the hungry and shelter homeless soldiers after the Great War. It was a favored spot for tired fishermen to have some hot soup and rest on a cold night. All the news anybody needed to know could be found out at St. A's.

St. Anthony's was on the south end of Father John's parish at the bottom of the mountain, situated, with its own dock, under the bridge. Above it, the hilltop resembled a castle, thus its name, Castle Cliff, which stepped down to a vast meadow.

Sure enough, just as Pete had said, Father Brendan found Father John at St. A's. He was thin and tired, but despite his personal troubles, he was serving up soup to the needy of the wharf.

Father John was glad to see Father Brendan, and over a bowl of soup, he made vivid the terrible state of affairs in Three Rivers.

"Come back with me to Inland, Father John. I could use another priest, and you'll be safe there."

"Safe? Maybe or a time," Father John warned, "but if you are seen harboring one whom Cell Fish has designated a criminal, you could be in danger too."

Father Brendan dismissed his protest. "Dia dul le linn," he said in Gaelic.

"And what would you be saying?" Father John asked, smiling.

"I'm saying, *Then God go with us*," Father Brendan answered.

Father John smiled and agreed to leave. He said his goodbyes to the sad remnant of his flock, and the two priests left St. Anthony's Lost and Found for an adventure they would not soon forget.

They would have a time of it getting back to Inland, or even coming ashore. By a Cell Fish decree, Mayor Bully Bargumo had set water traps in many places, and his minions guarded access to the local docks. That thin soup would be the last food they would have for quite a while.

35

Little Beaver's New Name

*You still lack one thing. Sell everything you have and give to the poor,
and you will have treasure in Heaven. Then come follow me.
Luke 18:22*

St. Mary's-of-the-Future

No one could remember what life was like before the Gifts and Fruits disappeared because everything became smoggy. Folks changed; critters changed. Outwardly, everyone worked for entitlements that eluded them, hoping to show signs of superiority for the purpose of winning an advantage. Still, by the time they gained it, nobody could recall why it was significant in the first place. No one swept up their interior lodgings. No one thought they were ever wrong.

Unfortunately, that's the way things were in Three Rivers after Cell Fish arrived in his dark tanker and took charge on the Gray Bay.

Whatever the peoples angled for; Cell Fish obstructed. He pitted them against one another until jealousies soared and cooperation among neighbors and friends broke down completely. And that was in the beginning when the peoples still had a little fight in them. Once the Gifts and Fruits are missing from a place, all creatures suffer. They bicker, bite, and prey on each other.

The peoples became restless. Mothers left their kits and cubs to fend for themselves, and bullies stormed around at will, pushing everyone down, making rude and unkind remarks. Happiness became a memory that was exceedingly difficult to recall. Everyday life was lived without contentment in the cheerless parish and would be forevermore—or so it was thought.

This change especially affected Little Beaver and Deer. It became harder and harder for Beaver to remember what life was like before the Terrible Day. Then, as it happened, while fussing around her lodge one afternoon, she saw a boat out on the river. It had a motor. In the boat were two pastors, Father Brendan, and Father John. Brendan had a reputation for navigation, and he came upriver from time to time, to visit his good friend Father John. But his reputation as a navigator didn't help him much when the small craft got sucked into one of Bully's watery traps. At any spot, a trap could start its spin—round and round—like going down the drain. Then, conk! The motor would be ensnared. It was only a matter of time before Bully would come with his big net. He liked to call it "fishing for chumps." Then, howling with laughter, he arrested his catch for trespassing. He would likely send Father Brendan back to Inland without any supper. But Father John—he would make his life a misery.

The Little Beaver had heard of Bully meddling in the lives of Holy Men, and it didn't sit right with her, but what could she do? She observed the two from her lodge. It was a simple boat, kind of battered and shabby. The two priests took turns trying to start the motor—pulling, sputter, pulling, sputter. It was caught on something. Something was wrong; they knew that much. Their voices were kind and patient as they encouraged each other to try again. Father John said he was grateful for Father Brendan's assistance at this troubling time, and Father Brendan remarked that it was his pleasure to help.

Busy on the shore, Little Beaver heard all these things, but couldn't help noticing the priests weren't making any progress.

"It's only good manners to ignore someone else's troubles," she remarked to a caterpillar after gnawing off a branch she needed to repair a gap in her lodge.

"Who cares?" the bug snipped inching away uninterested.

"Hmm, maybe that's not quite right."

Something was confusing about that rule of good manners. It didn't remind her of Mam. It didn't have the right ring to it. Her Mam always helped everyone in distress. So, into the water Little Beaver flopped and swam over to the boat.

After investigating under the boat, she saw the problem right away: reeds—a tangle of greasy grasses tightly lashed around the motor.

Beaver considered helping. "But what if I get hurt? Those blades are mighty sharp," Beaver said to a consumptive trout, coughing and choking as he swam by. "If they pull the cord at the wrong time, my nose will be cut to pieces!"

"So—what's it to me?" the trout coughed.

"Hmm, that's not friendly," Beaver chided. She shrugged and swam away, unsure of her feelings. Then she remembered Mam's motto about helping others. It made her feel "Happy." It was worth a try. "At least I can puts it on my list, one way or the other."

Little Beaver popped up in front of the boat and tried to create a distraction. She had to get the priests away from the motor for at least a minute. Slapping her tail on the water, she performed a few good tricks. She decided to go for some drama and flailed around, pretendingto drown.

"Father Brendan," Father John called out, "throw me a rope. I think that little beaver is drowning."

"Beavers don't drown, Father John," Brendan remarked, looking over the side of the boat. "I do believe they're quite adept in the water, but yes, this one does seem to be in distress."

Father Brendan threw the rope to Father John as they watched with curiosity while Little Beaver increased her antics.

"What do you think it's doing?"

"Couldn't say," Father John acknowledged, throwing the rope. Beaver caught the rope with her teeth.

Then came the big dive under the boat. Chew, chew, chew. Gnaw, gnaw, gnaw. She hoped they would get the idea that she was trying to help.

A bunch of chewed up reeds rose to the surface of the water.

"It's free! The motor, John—it was the reeds!"

They had one piece of stale bread, and they threw it upon the water. "Many thanks, critter," they called out, and waved goodbye. The motor started right up, and they chugged away.

"So cheery those two, they must have 'Happy'." Little Beaver was convinced. (They were at least happy to be set free from Bully's trap!)

Beaver felt wonderful inside as she floated amidst the chewed-up reeds, eating her soggy bread. It was that same feeling, the one she had known when she was a small kit, when her family lived along a clean, sparkling riverbank. She remembered what it was to have 'Happy'. After keeping all those lists, she finally came upon what it was to be happy,instead of what it wasn't. Ever so pleased with herself, Beaver swam home. She could hardly wait to find Deer.

When she reached her lodge, a dizzying dread came upon her, and a lump rose up in her throat. Bully had gotten there first. Her prize-winning home was leveled. It was now one big tire track, with garbage strewn all around. Blood and duck feathers trailed from the back tail of a pick-up truck as it pulled away. The sound of Bargumo's foul snigger clashed with the terrified cries of the birds courageously trying to warn their friends.

Beaver was stricken, taking in the swath of destruction. The dreadful memories of the Terrible Day flooded over her. There were noises in the brush. She looked around frantically for a place to hide. It was Deer. Little Beaver sighed with relief, but Deer was full of rage.

"They're after more than ducks," he snarled. "Don't snivel about your stupid lodge—you can build another."

"No, Deerie! I'm not sniveling. I won't," Beaver choked.

"Be grateful you escaped with your fur. They were after your pelt to sell, not your twigs, and they were after me for the sport of it, and they'll be back. We must leave here. There's no reason to stay."

"But this is my home, Deerie. My friends are here. My life is here."

"What kind of life is this? Living in fear, scared all the time. Everyone else has already left. Be free of this. If it's not Bully, it will be the hunters or the trappers."

Deer rushed at Little Beaver, backing her into the muddy water. He meant it for her own good, there is no surviving where evil reigns. Beaver fell down in sorrow. Deer saw how much he hurt her and was horrified by his own actions. He knew he had become more discontent, even ill-tempered, but never with Beaver with whom he shared his happiest memories. He was ashamed of himself and walked away in despair.

Beaver slogged out of the water and sank in the tire tracks that were all that remained of her home. Dripping and shivering, she lifted her worthless award for 'Best Lodge on the Riverbank' out of the trampled ditch. Everything was ruined.

"Deerie," she called out, but thought better of it and let him go on his way. She wept bitterly for the death and destruction of all she held close to her heart. Deer did not return.

After some time had passed, Little Beaver half-heartedly began to gather up her soggy belongings. It's not in the nature of a beaver to sit around moping. She knew there was not enough time to prepare for winter. It was too late, but she remembered how wonderful she had felt just a while before when she had helped the Pastors with the kind voices. She could see them down the river, the shabby boat, and the two priests against a tent of blue sky. The sounds of their spirited fellowship carried on the water. It was the first she had noticed even a particle of blue sky in a long time.

"Perhaps Deer is right; maybe I should find a new home. But where'll I go? I haven't no one to look after, and no one to looks after me." Beaver salvaged the broken bits and pieces of her many collectables and tied them up with what was left of her favorite household accoutrements, her rags and tin foil. Soon it became a gigantic bundle.

Little Beaver looked for the boat on the river.

"Maybe I'll follow them," she said to a worm inching by, and

She began to give this idea more serious consideration. "I could catch up if I hurry. Somebody's gotta keep an eye on two pastors, there's always dangers on the Murky River."

Although she felt lonely, she didn't want to hear Deer's unpleasant voice anymore. Her special friend, who had once pranced and laughed with her in better days, her dearest Deerie, like everyone else, had become harsh, angry, and sour. She wanted to follow those voices that laughed in the face of hardship and worked together even though they weren't sure how to fix a thing. They kept trying, like her Mam and Pappy, they persevered. "Those two have knowing of what I knows but can't recall."

Wiping away her tears with muddy paws, she decided right then to follow the boat and started downriver carrying so much stuff she couldn't see one step ahead. "I thinks they could use a scout," she thought, tripping, and stumbling on her blinded pathway. Just then, Little Beaver heard the motor of the boat picking up speed. They were leaving! "No, no, no, not without me, NO!" she cried, trying to hurry, but hindered by her worthless belongings. If they got too far ahead, she would never find them again. She tried to run, but only managed a waddle, her pressing burden weighing her down.

Honk-honk, beep-beep, the small boat began to make its way. "Wait!" she cried.

The tail end of her list tumbled out of her bundle, and as she ran, she tripped, and as she tripped, it unraveled until she was entangled in the long scroll of 'What Happy Wasn't'.

Fearful, the priests would get away from her and take with them that tiny fragment of something or other—that one thing she could soundly count as "Happy"—Little Beaver's eyes scanned her scribbling, frantically choking on every line. She threw down her list and took a big breath, then stepped carefully toward the water, but a fretful pull sucked her back to her belongings. She needed her things to set up a new home, her awards, her buttons, and bits of fabric, her ball of aluminum foil, and her colored bottle collection. She threw herself, sobbing, on the pile of stuff. Then sadly pulled herself together and tied them up again into her pathetically cumbersome bundle. She rolled up her list, sniffling and sighing as she read each and every item again to the very last entry:

"Chew through reeds to help others—Happy."

Little Beaver grinned her grinniest grin, without a backward glance, she dove into the water with a big fat splash. She came up for air under a lily pad, to the great annoyance of Frog, who was sitting on top, croaking complaints to his companions.

"I will be their scout!" Little Beaver shouted, tossing her lily pad bonnet up in the air, unseating Frog and his friends. "I will be their scout!" she shouted out again, laughing and splashing with glee.

Having stepped up to the Assignment of Angels unaware, Mam and Pappy Beaver's youngest kit came to be known as Scout along the Murky River. And from this point on, the Powers That Be set upon Little Beaver significant challenges for her to overcome. The first test Scout passed with flying colors. She abandoned all she owned on the riverbank to follow the shabby boat. She was now unencumbered and free to be used as a formidable agent against the enemy in the all-out effort to save humanity from the Great Theft.

But try as she might, Beneficent Angel just couldn't see it. How was this little beaver going to help save Midlantic?

36

Scout Meets the Great Périgord

St. Mary's-of-the-Future

The journey along the Murky River would not be without its adventures. Scout was determined to follow the pastors wherever the river took them. Sometimes she could hardly keep up as they motored along. And sometimes she languished on the riverbank wishing they would get a move on. She was proud of her determination to be their scout; certain they didn't realize how dangerous the Murky River could be for two pastors alone in a simple boat.

"Mostly you can't see past your nose on the Murky River, but maybe that blue sky tent, provides them some visables." Even so, Scout thought it looked kind of conspicuous. She knew that Cell Fish or Bully could pop up any moment and capsize their boat. And so, she fancied, she must stay alert— like a soldier.

"Never was a scout as good as me. They'll make a stone critter of me, and I'll stand forever in the garden at Olph's Dwelling-with-the-Bells. What an honor for my species."

Scout's exalted thoughts of glory for her breed were abruptly interrupted by the call of duty. There was something ahead on the shore. It was someone reading a glittering book.

Half underwater, half on land, Scout beat a path through the marsh. She crept around the Weightless Rock at the edge of Quicksand Pit. Peering between the tall grasses to get a better look, Scout was breathless at the sight before her.

"I thinks it's a bishop! We ain't had no ruler of the realm since—can't remember when. He's looking contently. I wonder what he's doing sitting in the mud reading a sparkly book like that? He's precarelessly close to Quicksand Pit if you ask me. Where's his attendants?"

All these questions set Scout in a stew. She tried to recollect stories of a bishop far away in her memory. There was a legend along the Murky River of a Bishop Périgord, but he was only "a something" you heard about, maybe from her Mam, or Gram-mam who told those stories.

The very root of her quest for 'Happy' was anchored in her memory of the stories of life under the reign of a prudent bishop who had been so beloved by the peoples of the mountain. But prudent leadership and direction had long been forgotten. Now, only terror reigned in the guise of Cell Fish and Bully. Scout struggled with the details to get the story straight. "The Great Périgord came once a year," Gram-mam said, "when the trees were full of blossoms and the earth was warm. The peoples of the mountain always worked hard to make things special for Bishop's Day. Pastor and the Brown Dress Ladies drilled the kits in their lessons."

Scout struggled to remember all the details of Gram-mam's recollections. It was the day the children become soldiers of Jesus Christ and received Gifts and Fruits of the Holy Ghost. On that day, Gram-mam would take Mam to wait, along with the other critters, outside of Olph's-Dwelling-with-the-Bells to catch a glimpse of the new soldiers with their special Gifts and Fruits.

THE ASSIGNMENT OF ANGELS

In those days, Bishop Périgord said mysterious words:

"I sign you with the Sign of the Cross and I confirm you with the chrism of salvation. In the name of the Father, the Son, and the Holy Ghost."

And after that, the doors opened, and there was rejoicing all over the mountain.

This part was difficult to understand, just who they were— Jesus Christ and Holy Ghost, for they were One, along with Father God Creator. They were called the Trinity. Sometimes Pastor picked a clover in the grass to show the children how something could be three and one at the same time. He said it was a holy mystery. That sounded right.

Scout had many questions as she observed the curious creature sitting on the mound reading his book. A Great Périgord was a grand figure, he had fine clothes, and a tall hat called a miter, but this Great Périgord looked kind of rumpled, wrinkled, and torn. Scout couldn't help but think this one looked more like a big goose! That couldn't be right.

Although Scout loved the stories passed on to her, she didn't know why the Great Périgord was so great or why he was important to the realm. Who were the soldiers of Jesus Christ? Were they meant to guard the Gifts and Fruit and failed?

Some folks told her the reason the Gifts and Fruits went missing was because nobody bothered to remember them. They must have just left and gone elsewhere—maybe to a place where they might be useful. Others said there aren't any Gifts and Fruits at all, and never were, but Scout knew better. Mam told her, "Tain't nothin' lovely left on this mountain without the Gifts and Fruits. They've been stolen, and that's that."

Without the Great Bishop Périgord and his Soldiers of Jesus Christ, darkness had spread everywhere. Scout didn't know why, but she did feel that 'Happy' was tied to this mystery. She felt it in the bottom of her heart and kept it there, in the same place where she cherished the memory of her Mam and Fam, and all that missingness made her angry.

"Them soldiers of Jesus Christ got lazy and didn't guard the realm. That's how Cell Fish took over and put us in the darkness. If he catches a whispering about the light of olden days, he sends Bully. There's no mercy; even fireflies are afraid to light up the night. We could definully use some soldiers of Jesus Christ right abouts now, ones that ain't so lazy!"

The splendor of heroics raced through Scout's mind again, giving her the courage to approach the bishop on his mound in the swamp grass.

"This cannot be the helper I petitioned for," Beneficent gasped. "It's not possible!"

"All signs point to that little beaver," Marvelous said.

"I'm simply flabbergasted! I put in for a first-rate support team. The Powers That Be assured me that Périgord, as Bishop's proxy, would have everything he needed to accomplish the task." Marvelous and Beneficent were dumbfounded as they watched from Heaven's Veranda, Scout approach the mound where sat Perigord.

Scout came as close as she dared, and with great curiosity peered cautiously at Périgord through the reeds. She had no idea that the fate of her enslaved realm was tied to the wing span of this Great Périgord—imposter that he was. Nor did she know the exalted and important mission she was about to embark upon.

Scout looked back over the tall swamp grass in search of the shabby boat, then stretched to see the Great Périgord sitting on his mound. He was regal, a picture of serene patience engrossed in his sparkly book, but she couldn't deny he was messy, which didn't fit the description of a Great Périgord.

"Maybe this Great Périgord is in distress. Maybe he needs a scout to find his way. What a fine bit of rescue work this would be!" She could barely contain her excitement.

The gander held tightly to the golden seal as he propped up the huge mud-caked Book of Good News on his lap. It was drying nicely in the rays of the sun. That struck Scout as kind of odd. "You rarely see for sunbeams through these gloomy skies."

The Périgord knocked mud off the book in clumps with the tips of his wings, still solid hammers of mud themselves. The dried mud crumbled on impact, which pleased Périgord greatly and enabled him to turn the pages more easily. He never noticed Scout watching him with fascination, nor sneaking up to his side, not until she made a thump with her tail to get his attention.

Périgord jumped a mile, all ruffled in the feathers, squawking indiscreetly, "Squawk! Who are you?" He rummaged around in the secret pockets of his torn robe, which the Bishop had stuffed to the brim with invaluable tools for his new office. He pulled out a pair of spectacles, thinking they might make him look more convincing. He fumbled and mumbled, setting them on his beak, and peered down at Scout. Then, in his flummoxed state, clearing his throat and speaking in the most imperious voice he could muster, he said: "How can I help you?"

Scout was impressed with the resonance of his tone. He sounds like a prince. Oh, lovely, lovely. How fortunate for me to meet such a great one as this, how fortunate. Scout was atwitter with excitement. I can't wait to tell Deer! For a moment, she was pricked with a quick and severe sadness that swept in and out of her heart. Deer would not be there to hear about her adventure when she got home, nor did she have a home anymore. The imperious voice of the Great Périgord brought her back to the matters at hand. Scout put aside the disturbing image of her ravaged lodge.

Périgord studied the beaver. He decided it was now or never. He would have to act with all the dignity he could manage to imitate his master, the real Bishop.

Périgord came off rather stuffy, the real Bishop had a more casual demeanor in his lifetime, but Scout was duly impressed.

"I say there, who are you?" Périgord asked.

Scout introduced herself parading back and forth in front of him with a good deal of flourish, until she tripped on her tail and fell chin first in the mud. "I'm a non-significant critter in service of the realm, Your Excellent Highness, Sir."

"And do I look like someone who is in need of your services?" Périgord asked as he sat there elegantly. He acted as though he was neither lost, nor covered with mud, nor sitting in the Bishop's robes ripped and torn, nor in any distress whatsoever. There he sat, not to be challenged.

"Well, no, sir. Well, maybe, sir. Do *you* think you're in distress?"

The Great Périgord looked around. He was trying to act surprised that Scout might ask such a question, depending all too keenly on his vestments to disguise his gooseliness.

"You mights be finding yourself off course, Your Excellent," Scout suggested.

"Don't be silly. This is my new realm—at least I'm nearly certain it is. I have studied geography. I have studied the stars, philosophy, and topography." Secretly, Périgord wasn't at all sure where he was, but he gesticulated this way and that with his mud-encrusted wings for effect. "When I find a point of reference, I will utilize my voluminous worldly knowledge to chart my way," he announced, "to the Seat of my new realm, the Cathedral Pond. I don't mean that. I mean my property—as it were, to my new Villa-by-the-Sea."

"Oh, my goodliness!" said Scout, scratching her head in an effort to figure out how she could explain. She tried to assemble her response so as not to discourage him. It was times like this she longed for Deer's good thinks!

"Well, you see, Your Périgordness, 'As it were', Sir—just ain't where it was anymore. And 'the way it is', ain't at all the way it were anymore."

"What? Explain yourself, explain, explain!" Périgord's command with a hefty squawk.

"An explanation, please!" he insisted.

Perigord was getting the hang of being bossy.

Beneficent Angel, on the other hand, had some serious concerns about her charming animation of the critters in Pastor's prayer garden.

"Does it not strike you, Beneficent, that this little critter is taking on a life of its own—somewhat out of your control?"

"Hmmm, yes, I must say, it does seem so," Beneficent agreed, "And it also seems to be orchestrated by the Powers That Be. What do you make of that, Marvelous? Just what do you make of that!"

37

The Mission

St. Mary's-of-the-Future

Scout didn't want to risk angering a great ruler of realms, especially if he was going to be ruling this one, but she wanted him to grasp the convoluted situation in which he found himself. Her many experiences with the enemies at large made her realize just how indispensable her services might be to a lost Great Périgord.

"This ain't to imply, Sir, that your worldly studies of Geograph and Astrola…mology aren't useful. But I'm afraid to say that there's barely an inch of this realm that would match up to the terrain on any maps nowadays."

"Astrology," Périgord said indignantly. "Or astronomy, you know, stars."

"Well, there hasn't been a star sighted in these parts for quite some time. As a matter of facts, we haven't seen a star since it rained burning coals hurled down to earth…"

Scout had Périgord's full attention. He was utterly startled to recognize a brief quote from Scripture.

"Peals of thunder, rumblings, and flashes of lightning! Then, the earth was shaken…"

"Really?" said Périgord.

"Why yes, Sir. It shook so bad the Weightless Rock slipped off its foundation and slid all the way down our mountain."

"Is that a fact?" he asked.

Scout carefully approached the enormous boulder that cast a shadow in the rarefied presence of the Périgord's intermittent sunbeams.

"This is the Weightless Rock," she pointed out, running over as close as she dared. "And here it stopped, just 'afore Quicksand Pit."

Périgord took a step toward her.

"Beware there, Excellent! This is a terrible place. It's the very home of Badad Vice, an awful creature of loathsomeness. Do ya see those big boots?"

Scout got braver with every sentence and drew closer and closer to the pit. "Them boots been there since I can remember. Deer says if they ain't there… BEWARE! Because that would mean that Badad was out on the prowl. They say he's ten times more worser then Bully Bargummy ever was!"

Périgord sighed. "Worse is sufficient, there's no such thing as 'more worser'." He may not have grasped every nuance of learning, but Périgord did know his words and tenses. His Bishop was a stickler for proper English.

"Thank you for that correct, Sir. I always depends on my friend Deer for such things. My speaks are not perfect by any means."

"That is apparent, but never mind."

Périgord searched through the Bishop's torn vestment for his small book of Psalms.

"The boundaries of a Périgord's realm are called out quite clearly in Ezekiel," he informed Scout. He combed the well- worn book with golden edges. Scout was more interested in his secret pockets.

"Oh, dear, Ezekiel. Ezekiel is not in the Psalms," he said, frustrated, "Ezekiel is in Ezekiel."

The little beaver climbed up on a log and looked over Périgord's shoulder to see what he was studying so diligently. He rummaged through his secret pockets and retrieved a folded map and a magnifying glass, then spread the map out and smoothed it. He looked up and around, then down at the map with his special glass, while Scout climbed up and down, over, and around, trying to follow what Périgord was doing.

"Can't you see I'm busy?" Périgord said. "Stop being a pest and go home." He was surprised at himself, but annoyance kept creeping into his manners.

This stung Scout sorely. But to her credit, she bounced right back. "I don't have a home anymore, Sir Périgord. I've decided to be a scout—for my friends, the pastors. I follow them everywhere, just trying to keep their boat afloat. I'm a very good scout. I'm thinking of making it my business, you know, look after this one, look after that one. Maybe you need some looking after, Sir?" Scout made her pitch. She was thrilled at the prospect. "What a terrific honor, wait 'til Deer hears this...scouting for a Great Périgord."

"You don't even know the reason for my presence here," said Périgord, speaking about private things out of Scout's scope of knowledge. Poor Périgord was already weary of his burden and decided to explain a little about himself.

"I'm here on a mission," he began. "A mission about..."

Scout hung on his every word.

"I know from my appearance that I might look rather curious. It's just that—I seem to have been dropped here— uh—from above. I need to find the seat of my realm, my cathedral, my staff, and the children. I've come to save the children. And, er...uh...put things in proper order. That's it, in good order." He became serious, even urgent, in his tone. "I've come across this big book and this important golden seal. I'm just now about to peruse the big book to get some instructions. I'm sure they're in here someplace. I'm sure you mean well, but I don't think your qualifications are suitable to help me."

He patted Scout roughly on the head with one wing, while he brandished the golden seal with the other. Then, he turned his full attention to the big book, and simply dismissed her.

Scout could see that the Great Périgord did not want her help. She nodded good day. Deeply disappointed, she turned away. Périgord gave Scout a furtive glance and became apprehensive at the thought of being alone. He fell into a spell of confusion, whereupon it came to him: 'Do unto others, or they might do unto you?' Something about that wasn't right, and Périgord didn't recall anyone leaving his Bishop's company so dejected.

"Oh, bother, what's wrong here?" Perhaps the critter was of little use to him, but being alone in the foggy gray abyss was not so great either. The critter would at least be familiar with her surroundings and could lead him to a landmark that might help him chart a route to the seat of the realm, where he could find a leather chair, a gardener with a guitar, and a large supply of stale bread and gravy.

Then, something nice happened. "Ah, good, a little sunshine breaking through, fine, fine, fine. Good for us, some sunshine." Périgord spoke loudly, so Scout might hear. "I'm sure I can find my instructions. I had almost found them before you interrupted me."

He gave a raised eyebrow, but Scout continued her dejected trek past the Weightless Rock, careful to steer clear of Badad's cruddy boots.

"In the event that you know a worthy scout that might be familiar with this particular area, I might be interested in a guide—of very high character—only to find my bearings, mind you, just for that reason alone."

Scout couldn't believe her ears. She turned around, full of elation, and dashed back to Périgord's side, presenting herself before him at full attention.

"I'm just such a caricature, Your Excellent. I know where all the bears are," Scout said, flashing her toothiest grin.

"Squawk! Ignorant critter," he muttered under his breath. "Character," he said in an exacting way, "and bearings, meaning the direction of movement—like a compass. Oh, never mind, NOT BEARS!"

Scout took no offense, because she didn't know what ignorant meant.

The Périgord laid out his crumpled map again, and with the utmost gravity, he spoke to the beaver.

"My mission is to save the children, and there is another thing—well, I wish I could explain it to you, but I can't."

"I'm at your service, Sir Excellence. I can be a big help, now that I know the nature of your quest. You see, I know all about the children. Where they are."

"You do?"

"Sure, sure, I mean—it's not hard to know. You have to follow the Brown-Dress-Ladies-tied-in-the-middle, in one door of Olph's Dwelling-with-the-Bells and out the other side, to the lodge called School."

Scout didn't know the Brown Dress Ladies were long gone. It wasn't at all the same as when her Mam took her to Olph's Dwelling. Scout really hadn't been there since the Terrible Day.

"Sure, sure. I know all about the people's kits. Little girls, those was the only kind of kits in my class at Olph's School."

"Girls, is it? Fine, after all, that's half the job," Périgord said upon reflection, impressing Scout greatly. "You shall take me to them immediately."

"Yes, Sir!"

"Where are the boys?" Périgord inquired.

"Dunno, Sir."

Périgord shrugged and tucked away his map. His Bishop had assured him that he would have everything he needed, if he could only employ all the good things they had studied together, which was rather a tall order. He wistfully remembered their tearful goodbye as his beloved Bishop readied for his journey, a prisoner of Dastard Diablo. The Bishop entrusted everything to his wonderful gander, his friend and confidant, Périgord.

The Great Périgord sighed deeply as he and Scout packed up the Book of Good News and the golden seal. As for Scout, she was thrilled to have a new scouting assignment—for a really Great Périgord, no less, despite his looking uncannily like an enormous white goose in need of preening. Ganders are not the size of small people, and Gram-mam never did mention, one way or the other, that he had a big wingspan, like a noble flying bird. It simply had to be. He had the official hat on his head, a miter, he called it, although it sat a bit askew. And his robe, although a bit frayed, was authentic nonetheless. His name was Périgord, just like in Gram-mam's story. He was grand and well-spoken. Surely, this gander-looking Great Périgord was the one, the official new bishop and ruler of the realm, the genuine article, and Scout would be at his side, guiding him onward to his new Cathedral Pond.

38

Ezekiel's Map

St. Mary's-of-the-Future

As they set out in search of Olph's Dwelling-with-the-Bells, Périgord asked, "Who is this Olph you speak of, Scout? And what's her business here?" They hadn't gotten but a few yards when Périgord was overwhelmed by the prospect of their journey.

"Stop," Périgord said, "this won't do at all."

"What's wrong?" Scout asked.

"I must have directions. We can't aimlessly head up this great hill in the mud. This will never do! Never do!" Try as he might to control himself, a squawk or two did escape.

But his secret was safe with Scout. Périgord was large and imposing and spoke with complete authority, that was enough for her. Neither did she look further into his identity, nor question his curious appearance on the shore.

Périgord withdrew the Bishop's worn prayer book again and leafed through its thin pages.

"It's not in the psalms, no, no—" he said, irritated. "If only I could find that passage."

Scout took a seat atop the big Book of Good News while Périgord searched for his instructions. She drummed her tail on the hard surface of its leather cover to the beat of her thoughts. The sound of it drove Périgord to distraction. He suddenly had a thought. Popping up, he swatted Scout like a fly, knocking her on the ground. He rummaged furiously through the pages of the great book, also called the bible.

"Here it is!" he shouted, giving a nod to Scout. "EZEKIEL 45: 3-4."

He stood up tall and stretched his neck, filling his chest with a powerful deep breath. He appeared awesome and in command. Scout trembled in his presence. He began brandishing the golden seal in the air, instructing her to enact the prescribed directives he read aloud from scripture:

'From this sector measure off a strip, 25,000 cubits long and 10,000 wide, within which will be the sanctuary, the Holy of Holies.'

Important point! Use quarter-inch scale," he advised.

"Check!" said Scout. And with the flip of a stick, she ran this way and that way, dragging the stick in the dirt, marking out 25,000 cubits by 10,000 cubits—as it said in Ezekiel—to quarter-inch scale (or thereabouts).

The Great Périgord read on:
'This shall be the sacred part of the land belonging to the priests— etc., etc.—it shall be a place for their homes and pastureland for their cattle.'

He gave Scout a nod of assurance. "This is where we must go, Scouty. The priests are bound to know the whereabouts of my cathedral pond...er...citadel."

Périgord's gusto was met by Scout's enthusiastic, but vacant stare.

"Don't you see?" he snapped. "It's right here in Ezekiel. There exists a territory carved out for the Prince. That would be—uh, me."

He pounded on the verse with the golden seal. "Just as I thought," he said emphatically:

" *'The prince shall have a section bordering on both sides of the combined sacred tract and city property extending westward on the western side and eastward on the easterly side and so on and so forth—' "*

Périgord slammed the big book shut, satisfied. "It shouldn't be too difficult to find, eh, my little friend?"

Scout was electrified by the grand charisma bouncing off Périgord, but these words were far beyond her ability to understand.

"You will lead me to the place I've described to you," he ordered.

"Gee, Your Greatness, Sir, I can't recollect ever seeing cattles in these particular parts. There don't come to mind, not even once, that I seen cattles grazing in the cubits."

"Don't be difficult," he squawked.

Scout knew the sound of displeasure very well, due to years of exasperating Deer. It hurt her feelings and she cowered in the presence of his greatness—making Périgord feel all the more authentic.

"Well, do something!" he commanded.

"How 'bouts another map?" Scout offered sheepishly. Périgord agreed. Then, after sharpening a new stick with her teeth, Scout smoothed the ground with her tail and, utilizing the alphabets and the drawing skills she had learned from the Brown Dress Ladies, she set to work.

The Great Périgord marched back and forth inspecting, as Scout painstakingly placed Olph's Dwelling-with-the-Bells on the Old Road and the red light where the children waited for the crossing guard. Next to Olph's-Dwelling-with-the-Bells she drew the foundation of the Weightless Rock, Pastor's dwelling, and the Realm of the Stone Critters. She placed the riverbank, the Crabby House, Peony Patch with its winding way down to the sea, and the dirt path through the Forest of Solomon's Cedars, the Uppity Bridge, and the bay below it.

Scout stood proudly beside her map. Périgord circled around the drawing. "Perfect, excellent, fine cartography. So, where are we on the map? Where is START"?

"Start?" Scout inquired quizzically.

"You haven't put us on the map. Where are we located? Where is START?" Périgord repeated.

Scout looked at their surroundings. Although she was quite handy at map drawing and had a natural understanding of how to get here and how to get there, it wasn't really in a beaver's perception to reason out such a place as START. Périgord lost all patience, and the crazy goose erupted into a silly outburst. He flapped about spewing complaint after complaint, squawking wildly.

Scout was humiliated. "What kind of a scout doesn't know the way to the cattle in the cubits from START?" She dragged her stick behind her and meekly retired to her seat atop the Book of Good News.

39

The Weightless Rock

Come, let us sing to the Lord and shout with joy to the Rock who saves us. Psalm 95

St. Mary's-of-the-Future

Périgord finally calmed himself and reviewed the situation. He thought about the Bishop's skill in bringing the best abilities out of his flock and matching them up seamlessly with the task at hand. If he could help Scout to use her natural abilities, they could find START.

He leaned against the Weightless Rock, weary from his outburst. The Weightless Rock began to creak. A moment passed, it creaked again. Scout jumped from her resting place and rushed to Périgord. Suddenly, a great knowing dawned on her about START.

"Don't lean on the Rock, Sir! You'll fall into the pit!" Breathlessly, she pushed Périgord into a tizzy and a twirl that sent him skidding away from the Weightless Rock. Périgord was stunned by the spin, but grateful to be saved from such a boiling messy fate.

"The rock, Sir, the rock is where we start. If we can trace the route up the hill where the rock rolled down the hill, we will be next door to Olph's Dwelling-with-the-Bells. That's where Pastor lives. In Gram-mam's story, the soldiers of Jesus Christ come pouring out of Olph's Dwelling after the Great Périgord says these words: *'I sign you with the sign of the cross, and I confirm you with the chrism of salvation.'* Then everyone goes to the picnic grounds for wonderful vittles. All creatures wait for Bishop's Day when the Great Périgord comes to Olph's to speak those words. Believe me, sir, I know about START, and I can guide you straight to Bishop's Day and the kits!"

The Périgord was delighted, but suddenly he found himself caught up in a curiosity, repeating Scout's words over and over. "Prism, isn't it prism? Oh, dear, prism—chrism. I can't recall what's what!"

"It's chrism, sir, my Gram-mam was never wrong."

The gander was shaken by his inability to get things straight. He couldn't be sure about this chrism–prism thing or anything else. It put him on edge.

"Don't worry, sir, if we go up where the rock come down, we'll find Start."

"A satisfactory solution!"

And so, they set out up the hill again.

"The Weightless Rock belongs on top," Scout explained. "So's everyone can see it from far and wide. It would make a mighty fine headquarters for you, Sir Excellent. You can sit up there and see everything. How's about we move the rock back to its foundation?"

"Scouty," Périgord laughed, "you're funny! I must live at the cathedral, not on top of a rock. And how would you aim to budge such a rock anyway?" Scout placed her paws on the Weightless Rock. She lifted it up, squishing her face sideways.

"Here," Scout offered.

"No!" Périgord squawked, scrambling backward out of the way.

"What's the matter?" Scout asked, mystified. "Here," she said again, trying to hand the gigantic rock to the Great Périgord.

But pitiful Périgord dodged every effort. "No, no, don't throw it. Please!"

It was too late. Scout had already thrown the Weightless Rock as if it were a beach ball light as air.

"Catch it!" she cried.

Périgord backed away hiding his eyes with his wings.

With a quick dash, Scout ran from her spot to his spot and caught the rock herself. She tossed it in the air with relief. It was truly weightless.

"Don't be afraid, Your Excellent. This most important rock of the whole world don't weigh noth'."

"Doesn't. Anything. It doesn't weigh anything," Périgord said.

" 'Xactly," Scout agreed. "It sits at the edge of Quicksand Pit, waiting for someone in charge to come along and put it back where it belongs—someone with authority. And that would be you."

She was proud as could be that she could handle the rock skillfully, even though it was not in her authority to take it from its place of captivity. Scout threw it again.

This time the Great Périgord caught it with his bill. And with an impressive bounce, it sprang from his bill to his head, to his back with a one, two, three. He braced it there for the flight uphill. With his robes and his wingspan, his majesty seemed to occupy the entire land. Well, so it seemed to Scout anyway.

The Périgord was poised for takeoff. He waited impatiently for Scout to strap on the big book and the golden seal. Then he began to worry. He became absorbed in a scientific question.

It was just the kind of question the Bishop would ponder, going through endless volumes, reading copious amounts of dry information, formulating his theories, while gander ate his lunch right off his tray.

"Why didn't the Weightless Rock fall into Quicksand Pit?"

"The earth shook it free, but maybe not hard enough," Scout offered.

Périgord surmised that it had to do with its weightlessness.

"But then why did it slide at all? It is scientifically unsound," he knew the Bishop would think so too.

With all of this distinctly un-goosely mental exercise came a new kind of disturbance for the distraught Périgord. A disturbance called doubt. "I don't know about this, Scouty," he worried. "I don't know how to fly anymore. I fell out of the sky once today. I can't risk it again. No, I won't do it. I won't risk my neck for a Weightless Rock important or not."

Scout got back to rigging up straps out of swamp grass to secure the big book. An eerie mass of liquid gathered into a swarm over the swampy pit. Périgord froze. Scout took no notice of Périgord's distress as the swarm came toward him. It circled and buzzed round and round the frightened gander—then splat! He was doused in a frenzied wet attack, soaking his wings and his robe in a fishy-smelling, coating of dead bugs. These ephemeral mayflies were only the opening act for a dank sweating spirit that rose out of the pit.

The threatening specter floated over the swamp grass until it reached the terror-stricken gander. Slowly, slowly, it spun its somber spell around him, finally shattering his nerves in panic and revulsion. He squawked wildly, shouting for Scout.

"Get it off my back. Take it away! Take it away!" He shuddered and shook, and the Weightless Rock rolled gently off his back to the edge of Quicksand Pit. Périgord was caught in a frightening twirl under the powers of the evil thing that had risen out of the pit.

"Your Excellent, stop!" Scout cried as she ran to his aid.

Exhausted, he staggered to a stop. Feara Phalin had arrived.

"What is it, Scouty? What is that troubling thing?"

The silent specter hovered around them still. Black and vaporous, it hung in the air before them.

Scout shooed her off. "Go away Feara, nobody here's 'a-scared of you. Git, git away."

Feara shifted into a mangy she-wolf, bared her teeth, and darted between the trees. Gander collapsed in a faint.

Scout sprinkled some water on him. When he regained his composure, he was still badly shaken. This was not a good first experience for a Great Périgord to have on Scott's official watch.

"That's just Feara," she said apologizing. Feara ain't nobody, Sir, don't give her a second thought. Feara Phalin only gots the powers you give her, none of her own. I shoulda warned you, Excellent, I'm awful sorry." Scout was very contrite.

"Quite all right. Quite all right. What does she want?" Périgord asked, glancing suspiciously at the Weightless Rock, then at the place of Feara's disappearance.

"Noffin', Sir. She wants custody of the Rock. She can't even talk or make no noise; she just creeps around and scares you off so's you never come back."

"I thought you said this was Badad Vice's domain," Périgord said, trying to control his agitation. "The…the one with the boots."

"She works for Badad. He doesn't bother with anyone unless Feara fails, but she never does. Her job is to make sure nobody takes the Weightless Rock and puts it back where it belongs."

"She'd be rather successful, I would think," Périgord said. "Why aren't you afraid of her, Scouty?"

"Me? I'm not important enough to scare away. Feara knows I haven't got no authority to move the Weightless Rock. Only someone like you can. I can see it's easy enough, but I can't move it from this general area. Only a real ruler of the realm could stare down Feara—and then, you'd have to face Badad Vice. Even Bully Bargumo, our Mayor, is afeared of Badad!"

The idea of a little beaver having such capabilities as to move the great Rock back to its rightful place sent Scout into peals of laughter. Gander laughed too, more likely the result of nerves.

Périgord desperately wanted to help his Bishop, but he wasn't interested in another encounter with Feara, and her swarm of stinking mayflies.

Feara's efforts were successful enough, she had paralyzed Périgord's ability to fly. He simply refused. Scout could see it wasn't worth the effort to try and convince him to overcome his apprehension about flying. Périgord was acting like Deer in this way—stubborn. Instead, she found him a good size puddle and encouraged him to wash off the bad smell.

After he refreshed himself for the journey, Scout motioned for him to follow her.

She was proud as could be. Her rig was ready, the book and the golden seal were lashed onto it with reeds. They set off up the hill with a mind to finding the foundation of the Weightless Rock and Olph's Dwelling-with-the-Bells next door.

Scout was anxious to help the children that needed saving and, with any luck, to find Périgord's new home. She even dared to think it might include a place for herself.

40

The Median of the Old Road

*Thorns will overrun her citadels, nettles, and brambles her
strongholds. She will become a haunt for jackals, a home for owls.
Isaiah 34:13*

St. Mary's-of-the-Future

About halfway up the mountain, they reached the Old
Road, the same Old Road, through the mountain pass,
where the beautiful Pink Lady had watched over her
peoples as they went about their comings and goings. Now the
Old Road was an overgrown thicket of pointy briars thanks to the
potent fertilizer the peoples had foolishly mixed with their soil.

It had become the most dangerous of thoroughfares, and no one
crossed it anymore—ever. Because of the poison fertilizer, it
was impossible for Scout to chew through the spiking brambles
that covered the road. Cell Fish meant to control the traffic in and
out of the parish, but in his wildest dreams, he never imagined that
his temper tantrums would have created such an aggressive
poisonous agent as to seduce the peoples of the mountain to do

his work for him. At first, when the peoples mixed the green goo with the soil, it produced ever larger plants, greener grass, shrubbier shrubs, and plumpier produce. They never suspected it to be toxic. Contact with the thorn berries meant certain death. Cell Fish couldn't have been more pleased with the peoples' stupidity.

"Nothing I appreciate more than interactive participation," Cell Fish divulged to Bully Bargumo in a jocular tone. "It's better than watching them dig their own graves."

Bully didn't quite know what to make of it.

From just a few plantings, across the Old Road, a forest of spindly trees had sprung up overtaking the upper half of the mountainside and camouflaging the steeple of Olph's-Dwelling-with-the-Bells. Scout couldn't see any remnant of the trail they were following. From where they stood, there was no end to the miserable obstacles in their way.

They considered traveling north or south to find a better place for crossing, but they feared they would lose the trail left by the Weightless Rock on its tumble down the mountain; they were stuck where they were.

"Persevere," the Great Périgord said, gently patting Scout's head. He had seen the Bishop make this gesture countless times when troubled clerics came to his library for counsel. Scout managed an unconvincing smile. She teetered on the brink of accepting failure, which was extremely un-beaverly.

"Your skills there, Scouty, remember your skills," Périgord instructed. In no time, frustration was poking through in short little squawks. Périgord lost all control. He stomped to and fro, stamping and complaining. By all accounts, Périgord had once been considered the most patient of geese. He had listened to the Bishop rehearse the same old sermons over and over again, yet he was unable to conceal his irritation with Scout.

"Now what, now what? he squawked. "Come on there, hurry uHow will we blaze a trail through this wretched clutter?"

"It's difficult, to be sure, Sir, but I'll find a way," Scout said determinedly.

Périgord was ashamed of himself, but luckily Scout was used

to the nasty tempers that had become the norm in this dark realm, especially with Deer, and after sizing up the situation, she came up with an ingenious idea to overcome the poisonous brush.

"We must crush it, Your Excellent. We must crush it."

"Crush it?" cried the astonished Périgord. "You're mad! How can we crush it—we can't even touch it!"

Scout pointed down the torturous incline they had just scaled. They would have to make their way back to the Weightless Rock.

Scout was sure of her plan. "You shall fly the Rock to this spot in the road," she said.

"Flying! Squawk—No!"

"We didn't nary encounter any treetops too high; it's not too hard a fly."

"No, no, no!"

"You can do it, Sir. I know you can. You can fly over them trees."

Scout looked at the fearsome entanglement of poisoned pointy thorns meshed tightly across the entirety of the Old Road. "It's here where the real trouble starts. If we set down the Weightless Rock at this edge of the briary, we can roll it across Old Road."

Périgord was bombarded by a dreadful attack of anxiety. "I can't, I can't…I haven't had enough practice. My feathers are stuck together. I'm … I'm …"

Scout left him no wiggle room and gave him a hardy push down the slippery gulch.

"SQUAWWWWWWWWWWWWWK!" And down he went, as if on a greasy slide. Scout ran behind him, expertly maneuvering from side to side, shouting out encouragements all the way to the bottom.

"You can do it, Excellent, you can fly!" But he didn't.

At the bottom of the hill, Scout ran for the Weightless Rock, and with a quick two-step, she lifted it onto the wings of the Périgord. He was still seeing stars from his riotous descent down the muddy gulley. He jerked with dizzying shudders of fear and worry. "I can't, I can't. I don't remember how to fly. It's unsafe!"

"I know you can do it, Excellent!"

And with a good whack on his rump, Scout's confidence in him won the day. Périgord skidded into action, with a wild squawk. Scout jumped aboard, holding tightly to the Weightless Rock.

"OOOHHHH!!"

"Off we go!"

And off they went. They flew straight up the mountain to the bramble crossing, where they landed with a thump. Scout eased the rock off the wings of the Great Périgord and dropped it onto the road's thorny cover. Périgord was in a fever of distress. Scout instructed him to assist her as she pushed to get the rock rolling. She had seen the peoples' kits do this, many times, with snow. They would start with a small ball and roll it over the packed snow, lifting it as they went. It was a good idea. Her hope was that the rock would pull up the thorny brambles by their roots.

Scout and Périgord carefully rolled the rock across the road from east to west, and after much effort, they stopped for a halfway rest. They had unearthed the median that once separated the Northbound traffic from the Southbound, and for this, a delightful surprise was revealed to Scout.

"Look, Sir, forsythia! It must be springtime!" Périgord looked around at the depressing landscape.

"Springtime?" He examined the tips of the frail branches. "They're none too beautiful."

"They're a fine sight to see, and flowers just the same," Scout said, refusing to be discouraged by Périgord's pessimism. Scout pushed the rock a bit more, trying to fluff up the bedraggled bushes, but the weight of the clinging earth held them down. Unfortunately, she neglected to consider that the road was by far steeper north to south than east to west. And, so, when they let go of the Weightless Rock on the median of the Old Road— admiring their cleared pathway and newly uncovered forsythia —within a second, of its own momentum, the Weightless Rock began to roll headlong down the median toward the bluff at Peony Patch, overlooking the bay where the three rivers met the sea. It bounced along at a sprightly pace, rolling up the thorns around itself and uncovering the median as it went on its way. The Weightless Rock was out of sight in no time. In its wake, the rock had cleared a path from the spot where Scout and Périgord stood dumbfounded, all the way down the mountainside till it flew clear off the cliff. They were disheartened by their loss as they watched helplessly—jealous the law of gravity stole their idea based on making a snowman.

"Well, Scouty, what do you think of that?" Périgord asked, none too kindly. "You have cleared a very fine path indeed, but we're still not across the road."

Scout looked at him discouraged. She didn't feel it was entirely her fault, but neither did she expect the Great Périgord to own up to any of the blame. Most little critters learned to fight the fights they could win and forget the rest.

"We shouldn't have let go of her, Sir Excellent."

"That is perfectly apparent," Périgord retorted. "Now what?"

Scout's mind raced for another solution to cross the Old Road. She thought it best not to point out to the Great Périgord they had indeed come halfway, which was quite an accomplishment. She gazed wistfully down the mountainside where the Weightless Rock had soared off the bluff into the Gray Bay. And what did she see, but a figure in the distance coming up the cleared pathway.

41

Father Ed Meets St. Rose

St. Mary's-of-the-Future

Father Ed said his goodbyes to Willy and Oz, and unsteadily disembarked from their flatboat on the sandy tarmac of the Coast Road. The two boys of St. A's had dropped him off near the fishing pier, where he was astonished to see the Weightless Rock tucked up against the jetty. He could not understand what it was doing so far from Quicksand Pit, where it had been guarded day and night by Feara Phalin and her disgusting Mayflies. He prepared to skirt around the rock, worried that venturing too close could bring Feara out of hiding, and no one wanted that. Suddenly, he saw a young girl perched upon the top of the Weightless Rock. He cupped his hands and called up to her.

"What are you doing on top of this rock? Don't you know the danger you're in? Please, come down from there before you're hurt."

She was wrapped in a long serge cloak that covered her from head to toe. Her hood fell back to reveal her pretty face and dark hair. She had a radiance about her that seemed otherworldly. On her head was a circlet of roses. She tried to climb down, taking tiny steps, but hesitated afraid to move. "Won't you help me?" she pleaded in the sweetest voice. It occurred to Father Ed that it more resembled a song than a voice. "Of course, I'll help you. What's your name?" he asked gently.

"My given name is Isabel," the girl replied, but everyone calls me Rose."

He surveyed the massive rock, trying to figure a way to help. He determined the slightest pressure might cause the rock to dislodge, and the girl would fall.

"Help me, Father Ed," the girl whimpered. She buried her face in her hands and started to cry.

"Oh, no—now—don't cry, Miss. I'll go for help and be right back."

He looked toward the water. The Boys of St. A's were well across the bay. There might not be another soul coming their way for days, but he didn't want to upset the girl any further with his assessment of the situation, nor did he take notice that she had called him by his given name.

42

Widow Miller and the Mountain Pass

...whether a tree falls toward the south or the north wherever the tree falls, there it lies. Ecclesiastes 11:3

St. Mary's-of-the-Future

It was a woman coming up the Old Road, bent over and huffing along. She wore a calico apron and a good wool skirt, with argyle stockings. Her shoes were leather with thick black heels and one small hole in the toe. A rough wooden walking stick aided her hike up the hill, and in her free hand, she carried a watering can filled to the brim.

A verdant carpet sprang up behind her, as she spilled a splash here and spilled a splash there. Forsythia came to life washed free of the mud that had weighed them down for so long. their yellow branches began to sing of springtime, even in the grey mist. The Old Road now cut a swath of golden yellow down the mountain to the sea, unearthing in Scout's heart that hard-to-remember feeling she longed for—a feeling of nostalgia for the forest, her lodge, her family, and her best friend Deer. She had forgotten the thrill of new life in the earth, which had not been seen along the Murky River since—she didn't know when. The sylvan sash of yellow gold was beautiful in the mist, and if it caused them hardship to see this sign of springtime again, to Scout, it was worth the effort.

"Thanks be to God! Thanks be to God!" the bent old woman called out. Scout and Périgord looked at each other with shrugs of unknowing.

"How did it happen?" she asked, lifting her unseeing eyes to heaven in amazement. Then, intently straining to see Scout and Périgord just inches away, she introduced herself and told her story.

"I'm the Widow Miller," she began. "I'm making my way back to Miller Street, 'tis a pity that this Old Road is overgrown and the sky so dull. The moon shines blood red and casts no light to travel by night. There seems to be no daytime at all anymore. No sun to warm my flowers, nor show me a way up this hill. My sight ain't what it used to be." She wasn't completely blind—just nearly.

She pointed a shaky finger down the mountain. "I went down to the bay a while ago to eat some clams and filled my watering can. I must water my buds down there, or they'll die, but I haven't been able to make my way back. It's too dark and the bramble too thick. Oh, God bless you both. What a wonderful pathway, right up the middle!"

"It was no trouble at all," the Great Périgord said, proud as could be. Scout gave him a quizzical look but kept silent.

" 'Tis a narrow path, but fully blooming now, I'd say," Widow Miller observed.

"Yes, I'd say so, too. Wouldn't you, Scout?"

"Yes, Sir Excellent, full of blooms."

Périgord found the widow most peculiar, as she jerked around nervous as a cat, her water can spilling with every jumpy move.

"I shouldn't have risked it," she said in a whisper.

"Risk? Squawk! What kind of risk?"

She stepped closer, putting her finger to her lips with a wiggle. "God Blessing you, of course! I mean, good bird, if Bully Bargumo were in earshot of us, he would knock us off our pins and send us flying down the mountain right behind that big boulder of yours."

Périgord glared at Scout, recalling his all too recent experience with just such a tumble. Scout was duly contrite.

"I still don't understand what you mean by 'risk'," Périgord said, mustering all the uppityness he could. He hoped to pass over the widow's reference to 'birdness' as a turn of phrase.

Scout knew what she meant by 'risk'. Even the name Bully Bargumo gave her shivers. "Bully Bargummy, Sir Excellent, he's a bad one."

The widow nodded, clenching her teeth against the evildoer. "No bells for Olph's Dwelling no more. He cut them down. Bully says no talk of God allowed. He throws black ink on the windows of our dear Pastor John. Makes life a misery for holy ones who dare speak of heavenly things."

Périgord looked askance.

"He's a certain misery, sir," Scout added, "definully a misery to be sure. He kidnapped my fam and drove his truck over my lodge. But worser of all, Your Excellent, he sent my Deer friend away, full of angry sorrow, and it sads my heart down low."

Widow Miller gave Scout a somber nod. " 'Tis a dark place, this. Sorry for your troubles, pet."

Périgord was alarmed at the plight of his Bishop's new subjects, both peoples and critters alike. The Great Périgord did not want to appear put off by these terrible tales, but he was afraid. Nonetheless, despite his fear, he recalled his allegiance to his Bishop and usurped the conversation. With a good bit of charm and authority, he tried to reassure Widow Miller by changing the subject to something cheerier, just the way the Bishop might have done.

"Ah-hem. Well now, Widow Miller, it is quite lovely to meet you. And rest assured, when we take charge of the realm things will change, you'll see. After all, this mountain is God's domain. We'll put a stop to this nonsense and rule the mountain once again, I promise you."

"We're trying to cross the Old Road to Miller Street too," Scout added, "but our rock rolled away—right under our noses. We can't go no further than right here."

"Well, your misfortune has been a fortunate occurrence for me, I'd say, praise God," Widow Miller gave a cheer, and Scout a jolly pinch on the cheek.

Scout winced, backing away from Widow Miller as politely as she could. "What shall we do now, Your Excellent Périgord?"

"Saints alive! Are you Périgord?" the widow said, surprised.

"*THE* GREAT Périgord!" Scout confirmed with toothy enthusiasm, nursing her pinched cheek.

Périgord was flattered beyond any prior experience. To be acknowledged as so important a figure in his disheveled state gave him the confidence to keep up the charade. "Yes, my good woman, I am the new Périgord of the Midlantic Realm."

The old woman's joy could not be contained. Good news had eluded the sorry realm for so long, she couldn't believe her ears. She pleaded her case again in earnest.

"I need to water my buds. They can't wait. I promised the Sisters—till they return—I'd water the buds every day."

Périgord was moved to heroism. "I am going to walk right over these thorns," he said, addressing Scout. "If we're careful, we can do it!"

"I don't think so sensible, Sir, it's a mighty treacherous stretch," Scout warned.

"I'll paint your blisters red with mercurochrome, and I'll make you tea and cakes, but you must get me back to my garden. I promised the Sisters."

The Widow had a pince-nez on a string around her neck. One might easily have mistaken it for binoculars due to the extreme thickness of the lenses. She put it up to her squinting eyes and came right close to Périgord for better inspection. She examined him carefully from left to right and from top to bottom.

"Am I mistaken—aren't those wings useful at a time like this?" Scout had to agree. "You really can fly, Your Honor, Sir. You just did it. Why not try again?"

"That was different. I can't and I won't. Don't ask me anymore!"

Périgord had no idea why he wouldn't fly. He just wouldn't. It was a product of the lost Gifts, you see, he had lost the spirit of Right Judgment, a handy fellow to have on your side if you happen to be betwixt and between on a big decision. If he had any courage left at all after falling out of the sky, Feara Phalen had robbed him of the last of it. It was like hypochondria of the mind. The Great Périgord simply refused to fly.

Scout could not fathom why one so great as this Périgord, equipped as he was with such equipment, would rather risk the lives of his subjects than save them with his perfectly good wings. But he would not fly, and she would not question his authority. So, there they were—set to cross the Old Road regardless of the pain, or the danger.

The thorns and brambles stretched out before them like barbed wire, riddled with poisonous berries. If they got caught on the thorns, they would be dinner for the ravens—these were the facts made manifest by the appearance of a very big blackbird feasting on a very small woodchuck caught in the thorns. They decided to err on the side of caution.

It was fear of being dinner for the ravens that won the day. Wisdom did not intervene, for Wisdom had gone missing with the rest of the Gifts. But fear is a powerful tool, and angels have been known to utilize it in a pinch. Such was the case when Beneficent Angel sent the raven.

Time passed. Widow Miller, Scout, and Périgord sat helplessly stranded on the median of the Old Road.

"What is your mission here?" the Widow Miller asked Scout and Périgord.

"We must locate Olph's Dwelling-With-the-Bells. We're after finding the foundation of the Weightless Rock, you know, then, we'll go after the rock and put it back," Scout said.

"First things first, Scouty," Périgord interjected with some annoyance. "First things first. We are inquiring after the seat of my realm, my new home."

Widow Miller nodded thoughtfully. "From my garden, I can show you the foundation. It's where the Bambini play. Beyond that, I don't know much outside my neighborhood. Your home could be near; it could be far."

"Not far, I hope," said Périgord. "We'll inquire at Olph's."

"Well, at least that's not far," Widow Miller answered. "Just the other side of this forest."

"Good. I'm simply starving!" said Périgord. "Perhaps they'll have us in for lunch."

Widow Miller patted Périgord around the middle. "You'll have a time of it squeezing through the trees— they're closely spaced."

A magnificent light exploded inside Scout's head. She jumped for joy.

"Trees!" she shouted. "Trees! Of course!" She dashed across the section of the road they had cleared, found a sturdy tall tree, and set to work.

In no time, the sharp snap of the falling tree crackled through the air. She dragged it into position, stood it up, and let it fall across the thorny east-to-west road not yet cleared.

"Timber," Scout called out.

"Timber!" cried Widow Miller with a loud yahoo.

"Timber!" shouted the Great Périgord, all a-squawk.

A triumphant Scout clambered onto the sturdy tree trunk and motioned for the others to jump ahead of her.

Scout gnawed off one branch at a time, passing it forward. They created a bridge to Miller Street laying the network of branches atop the masses of thorns and brambles. They made their way, ever so carefully, across the Old Road.

When they reached the other side, discouragement might have overtaken them, if not for Widow Miller's near blindness. The wise old Miller, aware of his declining health, had the good sense and skill to provide for his wife a nice stone pathway to the church. And knowing her fondness for a walk down to the Crabby House, he etched out a secret trail on Miller Street from the Old Road straight to her front porch.

He didn't imagine she would be contending with thorny brambles and poison berries, but rather, in the event of his death, and her ever-worsening eyesight, he wished only to provide a special means for her to count her steps to and from her favorite places. This is the pathway they would uncover upon reaching the other side.

43

The Sorrowful Bambini

I will never forget you, See, upon the palm of My Hand I have written your name. Isaiah 49:15-16.

St, Mary's-of-the-Future

It had been Bully Bargumo's obsession to keep the peoples of the mountain away from Olph's Dwelling-with-the-Bells. He threatened and barked and imposed fines on everyone, but they still went up to Olph's Dwelling every Sunday for quite some time. It took the forest of bamboo shoots, and scrawny trees sprung from the vile fertilizer created by CellFish's bad temper to finally prevent them. The stockade fence of lifeless, leafless stalks that sprung up along the roadside erased Olph's Dwelling from view, and soon attendance dwindled, and after the priests were evicted, the vibrant parish was forsaken.

As Widow Miller had feared, it proved a difficult effort for Périgord to squeeze between the scrawny trees. Scout had to untangle his robes continually caught in the branches, and un-bunch his wing feathers stuck together with sap. But eventually, once in familiar territory, Widow Miller got her bearings, and they found and followed the Miller's pathway.

She tapped her cane first to the right, then to the left, counting her paces to her porch, and up four steps to the doorway. She waddled through the house jabbering away about the changes in the realm. She lamented the state of affairs under Cell Fish and cheered for their prospects with the arrival of the Great Périgord. Périgord and Scout followed behind.

According to Périgord's observations, the house had the appearance of an old thrift shop. Tchotchkes of every kind displayed in curio cabinets cluttered each room from top to bottom. Scant space remained for the cozy furniture all decked out in crocheted doilies, and antimacassars hiding exposed stuffing oozing from the cushions. All this was somehow pleasantly arranged on a sizable throw rug, homemade and woven from Widow Miller's old stockings. Scout, on the other hand, thought it the most wonderful place she had ever seen (with the exception of Olph's-Dwelling-with-the-Bells).

One, two, three, four, five, six, seven, eight, turn left. They were in the familiar surroundings of her tidy kitchen with its red painted counter-tops and pine cabinets. There were shelves above the stove (an ancient thing) chock full of measuring cups and dishes, and a colorful ceramic cookie jar in the shape of a smiling piglet.

They had a nice cup of tea as they reviewed the day's events with awe, recounting over and over again how Scout felled a tree and chewed through the ornery branches, setting one before the other to make a wobbly bridge across the Old Road. They spoke of how the sweetbriars had grown thick and dangerous, their poison blackberries all the more enticing.

Frankly, the temptation to indulge in the luscious fruit was a powerful nuisance for hungry Périgord, who couldn't recall the last time he had enjoyed a good meal.

Even though the fruit was poison, Périgord's mouth had watered for a taste. Scout and Widow Miller had applauded him at the time for resisting temptation, and the three had praised the Lord for deliverance to the other side.

From the kitchen window, Scout could see a sculpture and, beyond it, the fallen bells of Olph's Dwelling.

"What's that thing?" she asked, pointing to the sculpture.

"The Hand of Isaiah?" the Widow Miller said, looking at the huge human hand, carved out of stone, holding the tiniest baby. "Isaiah 49:15-16." Her tone became dark and serious. "It honors the wee ones who didn't survive."

She stared into her cup as she stirred her tea. "They say it's the worst annihilation in the history of all Peoples. They call it *The Massacre of the Innocents*", she said, shaking her head in shame. She steeped sugar after sugar into her tea, stirring it round and round,in hopes of dissolving the sorrows of the mountain in the sweet brew.

"The Bambini are the survivors," she said, looking up. "Some say they're worse off than the dead. At least the dead are at peace in heaven. Hah! No peace for the living on this mountain. Peace is gone."

"Oh my!" said Périgord. He was shocked having come from the most peacefulplace on earth—well, until it wasn't.

"The Bambini were a pitiful lot when I found them," Widow Miller went on. "They don't grasp the importance of the message. 'Tis useless, I suppose, since Understanding is gone. I try Kindness; I do try to practice its attributes every day, so's I won't forget. I bring them small cakes in a basket to gain their trust, but they yank the sweets right out of my hands and run off to the ruins to play. Those poor children could try a soul."

"Did you say there's no Understanding?" Périgord asked.

"None," she said. "Every so often, the Bambini would complain sorely of an ache in their hearts that won't go away. That kind of yearnin' needs Knowledge of their Creator for the soothing. But Knowledge is gone missing with the others."

"So, the Bambini are left with the awful aches?" Scout asked, sadly.

"It's true." Widow nodded.

"Is there no way to assuage their suffering?" asked Périgord.

"No way, Excellent," Scout said, speaking with the authority of one who has known such an ache.

"Your Excellency!" Widow Miller said, surprised. "You know that only Love can satisfy the heart, but Love is gone too!"

"Where do you think all these fine Gifts have gone?"Périgord inquired.

"Not a livin' soul knows, I'm afraid," Widow Miller said, with a serious shake of her head, "not a livin' soul."

"Where do they live, them Bambini?" asked Scout.

"Those Bambini," Périgord corrected.

"Don't rightly know," said Widow Miller. "All I know is they play on the steps of the church and watch the road. They are certain that, someday, someone will come for them."

The Bambini often played amidst the ruins of desecrated statues of angels and saints, broken to pieces, in the old prayer garden. Sometimes they allowed Widow Miller to tell them stories about the days when the Sisters taught the children of the mountain. They liked the stories about the Sisters but couldn't quite picture them. The memory of the Sisters' wise counsel was only that—a memory. Because the great gift of Counsel was gone, and so were the Sisters—the Bambini had never even seen one.

"No matter how hard I try, eventually the Bambini become distracted. They have little use for stories of such goodness. No use in teachin' them Fear of the Lord," the widow added, "because Piety is gone. And without Princess Piety, it's impossible to comprehend that kind of love where you'd rather do anything than offend the beloved—which just so happens to describe Fear of the Lord. They haven't an ounce of Patience. It's entirely unknown in these parts."

"Oh dear," said Périgord, remembering his bad behavior since he dropped from the sky.

"Everyone has descended into a kind of ignorance, so base that they're easily governed by mischief and wickedness. The mountain has lost its soul," Widow Miller concluded sorrowfully.

It was true. The mountain had become a Godless state. No one could comprehend how it came to be that way. No one could explain it. But Widow Miller had been conscious of the subtle changes from the beginning.

"No one stole this blessed realm from the peoples of the mountain," she said, disgusted. "They gave it away, sure as I'm here to tell."

"Like Esau! He gave his birthright away to Jacob for bread and lentil stew," Périgord recollected.

Widow Miller inclined her head thoughtfully. "My, my, Bishop Périgord, you display a keen grasp of the bible story of Jacob and Esau. But, no, it weren't one impulsive burst like that but slower. No one ever saw it comin'."

Périgord was aghast at the widow's tale, while Scout was rather taken by her fancy flowered china and napery.

Widow Miller leaned in and sipped her tea. "Their eyes grew beady, poor Bambini, from watchin' the waterways through all that fog. Squints yer eyes up. They ain't nothin' like regular children no more. They suffer somethin' fierce from lack of Joy."

Scout understood this sad tale. She wondered if her eyes would hollow out or become beady and cold like the Bambini. She remembered watching the river endlessly in hopes of seeing her family swimming home. She remembered how she and Deer had to learn to fend for themselves, and how they became old before their time, by too much worldly exposure. Yet, they remained childlike and naive in matters of the heart because their hearts ached with an unknowable longing. It became bitterness in the heart of Deer, but it just stayed there unquenched in the heart of Scout, like stagnant water that sits in a gully, neither part of the river, nor part of the land.

"Where did their Mothers go?" Scout asked with a heavy heart.

"Off to fight the War of the Wages," Widow said. "In Big City across the bay. First, it sucked away our Fathers and young men—they had no choice but to go. Cell Fish put demands on them. Lists of must-haves and fierce competitions between neighbors."

Périgord took another sweet cake. He listened carefully as Widow Miller poured more tea. Widow missed the cup and even the saucer by a slight margin. Périgord corrected the flow of things.

"Much obliged," she said squinting at the stain.

"Bleach will work, I think. Yes, I'm sure of it," Périgord encouraged. "Continue."

"To feed the appetite of Cell Fish, it was required the men of Three Rivers work harder and harder. They started dropping dead from exhaustion, many took to drink and strong medications, winding up at St. Anthony's Lost and Found. No one believed that devil, Cell Fish, would send out the mothers next."

Périgord was so stricken by the story that he pushed his cake away. Both Scout and Périgord had tears in their eyes as the Widow Miller described how her vibrant community became a virtual prison. She told how the Peoples filed down to the river, gray morning after gray morning, and boarded trawlers that took them away at dawn and brought them back well after suppertime in the late evening, exhausted.

"They left their children with caretakers, who were not unkind for the most part, but they, too, had left their children in the care of others. It's a terrible yearning going on all the time here. Everyone pining for someone they can't be with. It makes for strange friendships. No one knows if another will ever return."

She took a deep breath and a sip of sweet tea. "Without Patience and Fortitude, it's difficult to hold onto Faithfulness. When Faithfulness disappeared, no one could sort out who belonged to whom, and after that, the peoples became increasingly disagreeable. Cell Fish couldn't be bothered with all that complainin', so he assigned people to children and children to people.

"He said it didn't make any difference, and if kids made folks so crabby, he'd make a new rule—one kid per family, and he'd kill the rest. Or better yet, he would gladly sell them off as slaves.

"When he announced his plan, everyone grabbed some children to ensure their safety, and hoped that someone nice took their children and cared for them."

The widow became silent for a few minutes. "Family life diminished greatly, as you can imagine. I ain't ever seen my son again. Not even once," she sighed in anguish. "I don't rightly think I would recognize him? The happy joy it would be."

"Happy…" Scout said, her ears perking up with the sound of the word.

Périgord's stricken heart raced for an answer. What would his Bishop do about this dreadful tale of woe? What! "And the Bambini?" he asked.

"Ah, them. They were never claimed. They stick together and have made a sort of family of their own. Some was just infants. They're all little girls. Cell Fish sent the unclaimed boys off to work, or to one of his wars. Mayor Bully assigned supervisors to watch over them, but no one bothered much. They do as they please. They can be very naughty and poorly behaved. They ain't never been disciplined. People give them things, then shoo them away like stray cats. That's why you can usually find them here. There's still a kind of peace here—a sweet sense about the place. But maybe it's just my memory of the old parish. Such a place this once was, so full of joy. I do try to be a grandmother to them, like St. Anne were to Baby Jesus. I just don't know. It's something, I guess."

It had become weak and sickly, this shred of Goodness, this spirit of yearning that Widow Miller spoke of—child for mother, mother for child. Beneficent feared it would disappear, like the rest of Goodness, before she could increase its pulse, but the angel remained optimistic. It was still something. It was Hope.

The Great Périgord couldn't accept this dire situation and wished for nothing more than his Bishop's guiding hand back in their library where he wasn't responsible for anything. Then it came to him, suddenly, that 'yearnings' were a byproduct of Love. That seemed right. His Bishop said that Love was the most cherished of all the Fruits of the Spirit. It made sense that threads of it would linger. But how to put it to work?

"I fear their young hearts will turn to stone," Widow Miller concluded. "Ain't no hope for the mountain after that."

"It ca-ca-can't be so!" Périgord uttered, choking out a painful squawk.

"But it is so!" Scout warned. "I knows it's so!"

Widow Miller left the table to clear up the dishes. "Cell Fish has lordship over this place," she said. "Without the missing Gifts and Fruits, we've no ability to break his power. My memory of them, and my vision, are slipping away … a little more every day."

Suddenly, Widow Miller was moved by a moment of intense reverence. She rushed over to Périgord and took a corner of his shredded robe in her gnarled hands and kissed it.

"Thank God you come at last," she proclaimed.

Scout gazed up at Périgord with her toothiest lip-smacking grin. He was disturbed by Widow Miller's bowing, and Scout's faithful admiration. A shudder ran through his feathers. The Great Périgord was crushed under the burden of his charade.

44

The Words of Wisdom Vanish

St. Mary's-of-the-Future

Cell Fish had a master plan, and it was well underway. Three Rivers was just the beginning. He filled 'Mayor' Bully Bargumo's head full of power and orchestrated the changing of local laws to suit himself.

First, it was the theft of their freedoms, then their beloved Gifts and Fruits. With every success, Bully redoubled his efforts. Before anyone even noticed, he and his minions were in control of the town council. Cell Fish couldn't believe it was such a cinch. Bully slipped in ordinances one after another, and by the vehicle of the squeaky wheel, they stirred up trouble squealing and whining until they got their way. The peoples of the mountain barely resisted, not wanting to seem unfriendly, or out of step with the times.

With the sound of a gavel, it had been done. Olph's Dwelling had been condemned as unsafe, and the property was confiscated for the 'Common Good'. Bully Bargumo announced that a community center would replace the church. He banished the

Brown-Dress-Ladies-Tied-in-the-Middle and evicted the priests. He created a bonfire feeding it with holy books. Sweat poured down his back and glistened on his face aglow in the blaze of the mighty spruce he felled and threw on the pyre. Bully and his cronies were exhilarated by the roar of the flames consuming the majestic fir tree. It had stood in the central courtyard of the parish for 100 years, and now, what remained of its charred carcass, was tossed against the side of the church. In its place, Mayor Bully planted a small, dumpy holly tree and changed the name of the parish to Holly Hill.

The Widow Miller continued the sorry history of Three Rivers. "Cell Fish wants to eradicate Christmas. Eradicate! That's what he said. No Christmas cards allowed—only Happy Hollow days."

"Oh, no!" said Scout.

"Strings of colorful lights and sounds of Christmas carols sung by our choir around the great tree are now just memories. Bully's buddies even dug up Pastor's memorial stone commemorating his tireless dedication as if they could erase his memory and all he's done for us. Luckily, some memories aren't so easily dashed."

Périgord was despairing, worn down by every word.

"Next Bully sent out a special order banning Christmas trees of any kind. He even had the holly trees sprayed with something akin to poison ivy. It was a plot to keep the peoples of the mountain from stringin' their Christmas lights.

"How did he manage such a thing?" asked Périgord, perplexed by the logistics of such an unpopular order.

"Well, just as he thought, when folks couldn't find any Christmas trees, they tried to decorate the holly trees, only to discover the vicious things scolded and tore at their skin, causing their hands to itch and swell and not fit in their gloves. Conveniently, this broke one of Bully's favorite new laws:

Anyone found without their gloves at Christmas time will be fined for an environmental violation.

It's too cold to go without your gloves in December," Widow Miller confessed. "We were all fined. And heartsick to boot."

"This is very serious!" Périgord cried.

"But that wasn't enough for Cell Fish," Widow Miller sneered. "He banned all Nativity scenes from sight. No more stables or stars or St. Joseph and Mary, no more Baby Jesus! And we could forget about having shepherds and sheep."

"Is that what happened to Christmas?" Scout asked.

"Yes, that's what happened to Christmas," Widow Miller said.

"I remember, many critters," Scout recalled, "even my friend Deer, they were in the outdoor Christmas pageant every year. It was so much Happy!"

"Imagine stealin' such a lovely thing from the children. Pitiful, 'tis pitiful indeed."

The Great Périgord couldn't believe his ears. "Deliver us from evil!" he called out again," deliver us from evil! Who in the world can help me?" he pondered, sucking in his squawks.

Scout let out a deep sigh. "No one in this world, I don't thinks."

Périgord popped out of his chair with a new determination. "We must go to the church," he announced. "We will take our Big Book of Good News and the important seal and put them where they belong. That will be our first job."

Scout secured the litter with the holy book and the golden seal, and they followed Widow Miller as she counted her paces across Miller Street and up the few steps to the overgrown lawn of Olph's Dwelling.

Scout barely recognized the place. She was dismayed at the sight of Olph's bells, fallen from the bell tower, cracked, and wedged deep in the earth. Slivers of colored glass dangled from the leaded framework of stained-glass windows and sprinkled the unkempt shrubs below.

The lovely statue of Our Lady that had once watched over the comings and goings of travelers along the Old Road lay on the ground. At the base of her brick pedestal, a coverlet of weeds and wildflowers twined over her in the Mother's Day Garden protecting her from further desecration. She, the woman clothed with the sun, that had turned pink in the sunset, now lay like a lovely Queen asleep in the tall grass. She was perfect, but for her hands. They were broken off.

Périgord, Scout, and the Widow Miller came upon a large bold sign stuck in the knee-high grass. The church doors were boarded up and padlocked. The sign read:

Holly Hall on Holly Hill
your
New Community Center

Closed for Renovations

"It's locked, Widdy," Scout said.

Widow Miller sighed, but was still determined to get in."There are other doors."

"Then we shall find them," said Périgord emphatically. And so, they left the book and the seal on the front steps of the church and circled around until they found another entrance.

The door on the south side of the church was chained shut, but vandals had managed to pry it open more than a crack, making it easy enough to squeeze through even for Périgord.

As they entered the nave of the church, Widow Miller held up her glasses to her dim eyes and gasped at the conditions. The reality was even worse than she had suspected. Many of the pews were upended, and trash was strewn about. Statues were broken and smashed. The altar cloth lay on the floor of the sanctuary, with candles dumped on top of it. The tabernacle was empty, the door ajar. The rich upholstery of a large carved chair was slashed, and the stuffing and springs exposed.

Tapping over to the walls with her stick, she laid her hands upon the stucco, moving back and forth, looking closely for some sign of the familiar frescoes. Her companions could see that she was troubled.

"Bully has white-washed every image of the angels and saints from sight. Oh, Heaven forbid. How can this be?"

The Great Périgord excused himself and left the church. He felt defeated and wanted to be alone for a while to wander the grounds. *"Where squawk, is my Bishop?"* he wondered, sadly.

Everything was in such disrepair. This task is too difficult for me, he assessed. He was simply unable to cobble together a plan to take back the mountain. He thought and thought about his Bishop's many instructions before his obsession with his interesting studies. Even in the face of difficulties, Périgord recalled him constantly striving to create a spirit of cooperation and fortitude throughout the realm. But every time Périgord tried to conjure the Bishop's astute directives on strivings and counsels, his thoughts disintegrated into a pile of rubble. Périgord blamed himself, and this caused him great anxiety.

Widow Miller came after him. She approached gently. "Ah, there you are," she said. "I shall be takin' you home for lunch, it's far too disturbin' to stay here any longer."

"I thought I had memorized everything so carefully," Périgord lamented. "Why is it that I cannot retain a drop of benevolent guidance?"

"No one can overcome this ineptitude," Widow Miller advised. "The Realm is crippled without the Gifts and Fruits of the Spirit."

"Perhaps I did not pay close enough attention to my lessons on Goodness and Counsel," Périgord sighed.

"Goodness is gone, and so is Counsel," Widow Miller declared impatiently. "Let's go home now and stop wanderin' around this desolate place. It's too sad for words," she said, giving him a pat and a hug. "You can't be too when it comes to your memorizing', but it ain't easy hangin' on to memories in these parts."

Périgord couldn't share the secrets of his mission. He was trying his best to stand in for his Bishop, but he didn't know what he was doing. He was sure that even this naïve audience of the simple woods critter, Scout, and this nearly blind old lady was sure to evaporate at any moment.

The plan to save his Bishop would be lost, and he would fail to save his dear friend.

Widow Miller and Périgord came around to the front of the church, where Scout was perusing a number of signs and notices plastered across the front doors.

"The town council will name Halloween the greatest Hallowday of the year at the next meeting," Scout read from one of the notices.

"Then the celebration of the birth of Christ will be outlawed," Widow Miller said, woefully.

"That's impossible!" Périgord squawked.

"Not impossible, I don't thinks," Scout said shaking her head vehemently. "It's sure possible for Bully Bargummy."

Scout then concentrated on a large sign piercing the church door with big rusty nails. She sounded out her words carefully.

"Cell Fish say that: when the time comes, the peoples of this mountain'll...umm...be stamped with his mark of service!" Scout was alarmed. "Huh? Oh no, Widdy! That don't sound too good."

"Go on, pet," Widow Miller encouraged.

"And he will enforce his command. Everyone'll bow down to Cell Fish as the rightful Prince—oh boy! That's not right...or suffer the consequences. If anyone refuse—they won't get to buy or sell noth'!"

Scout looked closer, eyes wide, and read the fine print at the bottom.

"Cell Fish can—and will—make fire rain down from heaven! Signed: Your Mayor, Bully Bargumo."

"Peoples won't bow to Cell Fish, not really," Périgord questioned, "will they?"

"Yes, they may," Widow Miller warned. "Cell Fish is very powerful, and everyone's afraid of him."

"Powerful, yes, sir, mighty powerful." Scout's head nodded like a bobble-head doll.

"Enough!" Périgord protested, scared out of his feathers.

Suddenly, an image of his beloved Bishop at full throttle in the pulpit flashed through Périgord's mind, the rafters shaking and the congregation quaking with fear.

"Unstrap the book, Scouty. It's in the big book! Quick, quick," he squawked with excitement.

Scout unleashed the big holy book. Périgord flipped it over on its back, catching Scout's tail underneath. He ignored her struggle to escape and rifled through to the Book of Revelation. "Oh, dear, what was that chapter? Number Eight? No, no, not eight." Feathers flew as he tore through the pages in search of 'the something' that triggered his memory.

"Chapter 13. I remember!" He calmed himself and closed his eyes, then turned solemnly to Widow Miller.

"Here is a description of these dreadful things. I'm sure of it!"

Scout was a captive audience, as the Great Périgord read the verses in a loud voice, starting with verse 13 of Revelation.

> *"He performed great signs, even making fire come down from heavento earth in the sight of everyone... It forced all the people, small and great, rich and poor, free and slave, to be given a stamped image on their right hands or their foreheads, so that no one could buy or sell except one who had the stamped image of the beast's name or the number that stood for its name. Wisdom is needed here: one who understands can calculate the number of the beast………………"*

"Verse 18? The rest of verse 18 has vanished! What happened?" Périgord asked Widow Miller startled.

Widow Miller lost all patience. "Well 'a course it's vanished, you silly goose. Why won't you hear what I am sayin'?"

Périgord gulped at Widow Miller's goosely reference, but he concluded she was only using a figure of speech.

"All of the Gifts are gone, such beautiful spirits," she explained with no little frustration. "If WISDOM is needed—or UNDERSTANDING—nothin' can be written there. 'Cause WISDOM and UNDERSTANDING—ain't here! Why do you refuse to hear me?"

Perigord felt woefully inept. He just couldn't understand why he couldn't understand. He thought about the angels, Beneficent and Marvelous. Perhaps they would come to his aid or maybe not. He would have to figure this out. All he knew for certain was that he loved the Bishop and he was not ready to give up yet.

From Beneficent Angel's point of view, it was interesting to observe, Widow Miller did not suffer the ill effects of the missing Gifts as others did because of her inner sight. Despite her near blindness, she was able to see quite clearly what was right.

Her ability stemmed from a special antenna she used called discernment. It allowed her to weigh all things, sizing them up for the good or the bad. It's how she knew that Bully and Cell Fish were up to no good right from the start. When they insinuated their way into the parish, with vigorous hard work and false promises, they fooled everyone else—but not Widow Miller.

45

The 144th

*...strike the Shepherd, and the sheep of the flock will be
scattered. Matthew 26:31*

St. Mary's-of-the-Future

I don't care what the sign says. I'll bow to no beast!" Widow
Miller snapped. "As my memory serves me, I'll remember the
truth. And I'll be doin' my best to pass it on. I won't be
tricked!"

Périgord shut the Big Book of Good News, much to Scout's
relief, who was still pinned underneath. Widow Miller shook her
finger at the bold sign on the doors. "Imagine! Me worshipping
some slimy fish. Bad manners, that's what he has. I shan't bow
to no beastly fish; I won't do it."

"Me neither!" Scout agreed, stirred by Widow Miller's
conviction.

"My old Miller planted me a vegetable garden in my backyard,
and now that I'm home, thanks to you, I'll eat from my garden
and stay put. Don't need no buyin' and sellin'. And I'll string my
Christmas lights on December 24th just like always."

"Oh-h, careful, Widdy," Scout cautioned. This much defiance was stretching over the top.

"I'll be careful," Widow Miller said. "Even so, I can make vegetable soup with snap peas and tomatoes, potatoes, and leeks. I got what I need right here. Ain't nobody gonna tell me how it is!"

"That soup sounds awfully good," Périgord said. He would have preferred to be back in his pond with Raphael's serenade and the Bishop's stale bread, but lunch at Widow Miller's, on the other hand, could be a welcome respite.

Scout wasn't sure what to make of the frightening story. The Big Book told the truth. And ever since Cell Fish came, everything good slipped away from Three Rivers. Food was scarce, and all creatures, great and small, lived in fear. Survival itself was daunting.

"I don't unnerstand," Scout complained, "this Big Book of Good News don't sound too good to me."

"Yes, yes, well, I see your point, Scouty," Périgord said, mimicking the Bishop perfectly from his crisis management speak.

"The next verse—the one about the Lamb's companions— that one is more uplifting. *'...I looked, and the Lamb was standing on Mt. Zion...'*"

"Is that like our mountain?" Scout asked.

"I think so. Maybe something like that," Périgord said.

"Read on," said Widow Miller.

Périgord gained confidence as he read, imparting the facts to the others with conviction.

"...the Lamb is with His companions. 144,000 who have the name of the Lord written on their forehead."

Périgord looked over his specs with an air of assurance. "They never do bow to the beast, you know."

Scout was greatly encouraged. "Did you hear that, Widdy?"

"I did, indeed," she said with a nod.

"This is a powerful army. We must find the 144th. We shall align ourselves with them," Périgord decided.

Suddenly energized, he felt compelled to make a claim on behalf of his Bishop. "We shall be part of the 144,000. They will help us. I'm sure of it. This is the essence of my destiny, my very purpose."

Scout found the conversation intriguing, if not a bit over her head. She wondered if the 144th were the soldiers of Jesus Christ who got lazy. Or were they reinforcements, an altogether better army. She hoped it to be a superior army because the last one seemed to have lost Three Rivers while nobody was looking.

"These are the Holy Men of God, the 144,000. We must be one with them!" Périgord raised his wing skyward in his best imitation of the Bishop at full throttle.

Suddenly, Scout made an important connection, "Your Excel! Father Brendan and Father John—they're Holy Men of God too!"

"Who are they?" asked Périgord.

"As a manner-a-fact, they're my main job, ever since Bully destroy my lodge. When I'm not scoutin' for you, that is—*The Great Périgord*."

"We should contact them. Where do you suppose we can reach them?" Périgord asked thoughtfully.

"They're in a boat near the swamp grass, last I saw," Scout replied. "Too far aways for speaks."

"Nonsense! It's quite well known that a Holy Man of God can hear a cry for help from a powerful far distance," Widow Miller insisted.

"It's true. I've heard that myself," said Périgord.

And so, based on the widow's strong inclination to believe this notion, Périgord and Scout were convinced that the Holy Men of God would hear their call.

It was determined that Scout would do the calling because it was a proper job for an official scout. She cupped her paws and cried out again, and again, and again after that.

"Father Brendan, Father John…" There was no response.

"Maybe they don't unnerstand critter-speaks," Scout said after a while.

"Nonsense, again," Widow Miller snapped. "Of course, they

do! Holy Men of God always and everywhere understand all language of the heart."

"It's true," said Périgord. "A cry for help is the language of all God's creatures, both of the human variety and also beastly.

"It's an inter-de-nom-intentional-critteristic language, it truly is," said Widow Miller.

"Provided you have a sincere attitude," added Périgord with some caution.

Widow Miller raised an accusing eyebrow at Scout. "This is so. Are you sincere?"

"Well, gee, I think so," Scout gulped, examining her motives.

The three paced about trying to devise a better plan that could hurl their inter-de-nom-intentional-critteristic call into the ethers, to somehow reach the ears of the pastors, Father John and Father Brendan, somewhere out on the Murky River.

Widow Miller finally got an idea. She pointed to the rectory a few yards away. "That there is Father John's house. Let's call out from his porch."

"Splendid, Widow Miller, a very fine plan!" said Périgord.

They all agreed Father John might better hear their cry from his own back porch than just about any place else on earth. They hurried past the empty foundation of the Weightless Rock, crossing the grounds to the old rectory.

Périgord surveyed the ruin around them, broken statues of angels and saints, the grasses had grown taller than Scout. "Just look at this place," he lamented. "Our church is padlocked, the foundation of that Weightless Rock is empty and covered with grime, and the home of the priest is boarded up. What has happened here?"

"And, I might add," Widow Miller offered squinting close to the back door, "it's plastered with another sign from Mayor Bully, no doubt."

"Read it to us Scouty, give it a go," Périgord said pushing Scout front and center.

Scout stepped up to the sign and cleared her throat. She read the sign for all to hear. Its proclamation was very clear:

EVICTION NOTICE
ALL PRIESTS GET OUT!!

For not bowing and scraping to
Prince Cell Fish
Soon to be King Fish
a.k.a.
King Scomberomorus Cavalla

Signed,
Mayor Bully Bargumo

The proclamation ruffled Périgord's feathers. "Strike the shepherd, and the sheep will scatter. That's what this is, a real prophecy come true!"

"This is terrible, just terrible," Widow Miller declared greatly dismayed.

"Unheard of," Périgord went on, "how very bold! Some ruffian has the audacity to assume the role of a bishop, with no authority whatsoever. My dear Widow Miller, this is too much for me. I think I need my lunch!"

"What's Scomberomorus Cavalla mean?" Scout puzzled.

"Some kind of Mackerel monster, would be my guess." Widow Miller concluded.

Périgord perked up. "Mackerel? Delicious!" Is that what we're having for lunch, Widdy?"

"I wish it were so, Your Excellency," Widow Miller said shaking her head. "But catchin' that slimy Cell Fish, and fryin' him up in a pan, that's gonna take some doin'! No Bishop, we're havin' soup."

END OF BOOK I

Scout and Périgord encounter the Sorrowful Bambini as they emerge from the tall grasses tempted by Widow Miller's tea cakes. Beneficent Angel is compelled to search for the Princess Piety and sends Marvelous Angel out with many disguises. The assignment to deliver the warning is suddenly upended when Francie and Lucy devise a dangerous plan of their own, in...

BOOK II

Of

The Sword Lily Parables

A Place to Start

Acknowledgements

My heartfelt thanks to a few of the many angels who helped me along the Old Road. Thanks to Andrew Craft, my teacher, who stuck with me through thick and thin and whose creative advice helped me form a disjointed tale into a real story. Rebecca Stone, Librarian, first to read what I thought to be a completed manuscript, who wisely suggested it was not. Molly O'Donovan, my grand-daughter, Editor-in-Chief for the second draft. Siobhan McGrath, my niece, and champion, who has encouraged me from the very beginning to the very end of this work. Kelli Faherty, my daughter-in-law, thank you for sharing your writing journey.

And a most extra special thanks must go to the great actress Donna Wandrey, who worked with me diligently fighting for every character to have their moment and their just desserts, reading and re-reading them into the fiber of the story. Sincerest thanks to Hannah Conwell, who worked tirelessly on editing, formatting, and leading me through the forest of cover design! And to Elizabeth Stepanovich, the first to help me with production.

Finally, thank you to all my family and friends who have been supportive and enthusiastic in all of my endeavors, first, and forever, my husband, Peter Faherty.

It is finished,
Anita

ABOUT THE AUTHOR

Anita S. Faherty wrote and illustrated *The Sword Lily Parables*. a four-book series beginning with *The Assignment of Angels*. She studied Fine Arts at Marymount College in Arlington, VA and holds a Certificate in Screenwriting from NYU. For the last several years Anita has been teaching religious education at her parish, in the Upper West Side of Manhattan, where she lives with her husband, Peter Faherty.